McGarr and the
Method of Descartes

McGarr and the Method of Descartes

Bartholomew Gill

F
6i1

VIKING

VIKING
Viking Penguin Inc., 40 West 23rd Street,
New York, New York 10010, U.S.A.
Penguin Books Ltd, Harmondsworth,
Middlesex, England
Penguin Books Australia Ltd, Ringwood,
Victoria, Australia
Penguin Books Canada Limited, 2801 John Street,
Markham, Ontario, Canada L3R 1B4
Penguin Books (N.Z.) Ltd, 182–190 Wairau Road,
Auckland 10, New Zealand

First published in 1984 by Viking Penguin Inc.
Published simultaneously in Canada

LIBRARY OF CONGRESS CATALOGING IN PUBLICATION DATA
Gill, Bartholomew, 1943–
McGarr and the method of Descartes.
I. Title.
PS3563.A296M27   1984   813'.54   83-40652
ISBN 0-670-46432-5

Grateful acknowledgment is made to the following for permission to reprint copyrighted material:

Holmes & Meier Publishers, Inc., and Faber & Faber Ltd: Selections from *Northern Ireland in Crisis*, by Simon Winchester. Copyright © 1975 by Simon Winchester. First published in the United States of America by Holmes & Meier Publishers, Inc. Published in Great Britain by Faber & Faber Ltd under the title *In Holy Terror*.

Waltons Musical Instrument Galleries: Lyrics from "The Men Behind the Wire," by Patrick McGuigan. Copyright © 1972 by Patrick McGuigan. Waltons Musical Instrument Galleries, North Frederick Street, Dublin, Ireland.

Printed in the United States of America
Set in Caledonia

For Marty, valued comrade, loved friend
With special thanks to Barbara Spillane
and Fred Mina

"Below me were hundreds upon hundreds of ugly-minded Loyalists, in as mean a mood as one can conjure up on a mild Spring afternoon. The thought struck me vividly at that very moment: all I had to do was to go into the edge of that crowd and put the word around that a young boy—one of their young boys—had been shot by the IRA across the river. The shouting would have turned to rioting within five minutes, the guns would be out before dark, and the [British Army] Highlanders would be hard-pressed to keep Unity Flats intact. . . . All I had to do was pass the word across twenty feet of open air. It was a strange feeling of power—the power of rumour and of instant reporting, and an instant realisation of the effects these two forms of communication would have upon a city and a people who lived daily in such a highly charged atmosphere. . . . I began to have doubts, from that moment on, about the precise role the press—and particularly the broadcasters—were playing in Ireland."

Manchester Guardian reporter Simon Winchester
in *Northern Ireland in Crisis*

McGarr and the
Method of Descartes

Prologue

9 August, it had been. A Monday night or rather early Tuesday morning. Nineteen seventy-one. Belfast.

The day before, Geer had returned from London, where, seven years earlier, he had graduated from the university and begun a career with ITN, the International Television Network. He was now an assistant director, and his mother, who was widowed and alone, had been writing him about the violence: the broken front windows on the Albertbridge Road, where she lived; the gunfire in the streets; the house-to-house searches for arms by the British that had fairly destroyed the interior of their dwelling.

Geer, of course, had seen it himself in the footage that was aired daily in London, but he should have known, the moment he discovered that no taxi would take him to the Short Strand, that conditions had worsened. Still, it had been a shock arriving in the early evening at the verdant highland meadows that surrounded Aldergrove Airport, only to plummet on a rattling, lurching bus into the industrial cut—made all the meaner by the shadows cast by the surrounding hills—that was Belfast Lough and the city itself.

From a smudged window Geer had looked out upon the

narrow streets of low, cramped row houses that wound with epicentric regularity through a trapeze of shipyard cranes, church spires, factory and gas-works stacks, and he had decided that in the gloaming it looked like nothing more than an industrial relic, a hub of discarded cogwheels, toothless where whole blocks had been burnt out, and netted with other junk—the odd, soot-blackened Victorian pile, the spare parts of later attempts at commercial modernity, the eyesores of government projects like the Divis Flats. It had even been aflame that Sunday night in the Catholic ghettos that were surrounded by areas of Protestant dominance—the Market, Unity Flats, the Short Strand where Geer himself had been born and brought up and six thousand Catholics were encircled by sixty thousand Protestants. In other places it was sparking erratically, the street lamps tiny and dim. The weak red beacons of what were either fire, police, or litter brigades everywhere, it seemed.

Later Geer would learn that on Saturday morning a British soldier had fired on a van that was passing through a checkpoint, killing the driver, a Catholic building-trades worker. His mate was pulled from the vehicle and beaten, then beaten further in a Royal Ulster Constabulary (RUC) barracks, and finally released into a milling crowd of Catholics, journalists, and television cameras. What little of the man's face showed through his bandages was a welter of bruises. His eyes were nearly swollen shut, and the sight of him limping from the barracks was too much for Catholic Belfast. Citywide riots broke out.

Even as Geer arrived home a day later, the streets of the Short Strand were in flames. The fires had been set—he would subsequently learn—to dispel the clouds from canisters of CS gas that the British were firing into the Strand. Women and children were rushing buckets of vinegar-soaked rags for the faces, and jars of vaseline for the eyes, of the men and boys who were manning the barricades of hijacked lorries and buses. They had been toppled to seal off the streets from the army and the surrounding Protestant Ballymaccaret and Woodstock neighborhoods. The windows and doors of Geer's own house, which fronted the Woodstock, had been, like the others, boarded up tight; and what had been family furniture before the British search for weapons and was now junk, had been piled up against them.

Trying to get in, Geer was shot at by an army patrol, and then, fleeing toward the dark barricades, by the men there. "For feck's sake, Paddy—couldn't it have waited till mornin'?"

Said another, "Since our wee Paddy took that job in London, he doesn't know he's livin'."

Jealousy, of course, from men who had probably never had one full job of work between them, but waited where? And *it?* After having seen for himself what *it* had come to, Geer had decided that his mother would leave with him to London. He was making good money, and he'd get them a large, airy flat. He was Catholic in background only, his mother having insisted upon *it* when his father, who had been a Protestant and had died fighting for the British in the war, had proposed.

She should have remained in Britain, he had thought, scuttling after his case which had been rent by a bullet, but postwar Britain had offered few opportunities to a young Irish Catholic widowed mother who had completed only her O-levels. Belfast's advantage lay in her mother-in-law's house, which Geer had inherited—the old woman hoping until the day she died that Geer's indifference to Catholicism might mean that he would resume his father's persuasion some day.

Geer had to force the back door with his shoulder, and he found his mother cowering in a darkened corner of the kitchen, which was now obviously where she lived, a broken scissors in her hand. "Ah, Ma—didn't you hear me knocking?" he asked, glancing back at the shivered jamb that would take hours to fix right, and him tired, hungry, and sore from where he had thrown himself to the pavement.

Extending her arms, she moved toward him. "I didn't think it could be you, not with all the trouble that's about. And you were foolish to have come, though your visit will do me, as ever, a great power of good. Give us a kiss, now, and I'll get you your tea."

Geer was shocked at the change in her when she moved into the light—gaunt, her skin slack, her unusual china-blue eyes sunken and glazed as with the onset of death. A small woman with square, bony shoulders and thin, bowed legs, she was usually neat and careful in her dress. But now she was wearing a tattered cardigan, rolled to the elbows, and a gray and spotted house dress below. On her feet were only several pairs of socks, no shoes. Rubber Wellies—which he had never before seen her wear—had been tossed by the door.

Apart from the fridge, the cooker, and the kitchen table, the room now contained an unmade cot, two steamer trunks with broken lids, the family pictures from off the mantel in the front room. Only a strip of the mirror, shaped like a lightning bolt, remained. In it, as he hugged her, all Geer could see was his neck. He had last been home at Christmas.

"Haven't you been eating?" he asked, feeling in her back a near emaciation that the sweater had disguised.

"I've no hunger," she said into his chest, "and, sure, it's not always I can go up street. Bridie Molloy—Barnie's mother—went shopping last month, and when she got back, they'd burnt her out." Geer waited, knowing what was coming. "The Prods. Said she knew it was coming for two whole years now. Said in a way it was a relief to get it over with."

Geer sighed, thinking this a mere elaboration of prejudice. Little could he have known that in three days two thousand Protestants and seven thousand Catholics would find them-

4

selves homeless, many of the latter fleeing across the border into the Republic. Some two hundred dwellings would be torched by their Protestant owners, rather than allow Catholics, as they expected, to take possession.

"Have you had your tea?" She pushed herself away from him and looked up into his face, cocking her head and smiling as she had in years past, though Geer could not help noticing how her once dark, curly hair had grown thin, straight, and white. Her teeth were tea-stained, her lips bloodless. He felt he was holding a carapace, the vitiated husk of a life that was now all but spent. And spent how, in what pursuits? Had hers been a life worth leading? They were questions which he kept himself from asking, then.

"London's still good for you, I can see that. But against your return I've put by some of them rashers you fancy, and the current has been holding since Monday week. They won't have gone off yet. And I've got a cabbage. A spud or two."

After the steaming plate had been placed before him and he had made her sit before her own, Geer said, "We're leaving here, Ma."

She did not raise her eyes from the table, but only nodded slightly, once, as though she had known what he would say. "Back to London?"

"Yes."

Then, "But what about the house and our things?"

He had no idea, but no part of the life that he had just witnessed here in Belfast was worth whatever little value the house might have. And their possessions? They no longer had any, he saw, when by candlelight he poked through the ruins of the other three rooms for a bit of bed to sleep on, his torch having disappeared with the soldiers and his tools. Soldiers had slammed rifle butts through any repairs in plaster, ripped up whole sections of flooring, rent the fabric of the divan and any upholstered chair and pulled the stuffing out by the handful. Anything with a drawer had been smashed open and the contents chucked. A closet door was off, everything in a heap in the corner. No room, nothing had remained untouched. A print of the Annunciation, a gentle thing with the Virgin raising her eyes to a glow on the horizon, had been kicked into a corner and bore the tread of a trooper's boot.

If in Ireland, Geer had some years later realized, history is genealogy, then those troops, in gratuitously defiling what little material history his people possessed, had taken a first but irrevocable step toward their eventual withdrawal from their Ulster. Everything that had been ruined in those rooms had been laden with the history of his family, the paltriness of which made it all the more precious. There lay the shards of the chair in which his mother's brother, who had lived with them all through his early childhood, had smoked his pipe and, in going slowly, word by word, through the papers, had taught Geer how to read. There the smashed ceramic heating elements of the fire grate, in front of which he and his mother and cousins had played cards or laughed and talked at Christmas and Easter. There the frame that had once held the picture of his father on the gangplank of a troop ship, steel pot on his head, knapsack on his back, a rifle in his hands. A mistake, doubtless. But one which it was not impossible to right, Geer would later decide.

No—it was not that, having nothing, they had nothing to lose. It was that the precious little they had had, had been won at great cost, and in it they had placed their enormous, if sometimes maudlin, Celtic pride. Geer had reached down for his button accordion, also a gift from the uncle, and had opened the bellows, which wheezed. In pushing it shut, he made it give off a thin, reedy whine. The ivory keys lay on the floor by his feet, like the chips of so many teeth.

But, for the moment, Geer had been willing to push it all aside. He had his career in London, and opportunities for him there could be duplicated no place else in the world, to say nothing of Belfast. Putting his eye to a crack in the boards which now covered the space that had been the front door, Geer had looked out on the street. It was quiet, except for the murmur of the engines of several Saracen and Saladin armored personnel carriers that were grouped in the shadows of a side street across the road. From the barricades he could hear the voices of men talking, and in the far distance the report of small-arms fire, desultory and weak.

After Geer had repaired the frame of a bed and settled himself by the back door, his mother had asked, "When, Paddy?"

"Tomorrow, Ma. We'll take a plane. First thing."

They never got the chance. At half-four in the morning he was startled awake by a sound he had not heard in eight months. From corners all over the Strand came the frightful clamor of ashbin lids, hundreds of them, being smashed down on sidewalks and up against walls. The din was like none other—a huge noise that engulfed the brick and stone streets and washed in stellar waves down every narrow alley. It was the clattering, barbaric furor that Geer associated with fire by night and the tribal abandon with which men and boys hurled themselves against darkness and armor, only to meet, many of them, the fate of an ugly, low death. It was the bush telegraph of an urban, Catholic ghetto in Northern Ireland, the alarm raised by women and children who, squatting like dervishes in bedclothes, gave the warning that the barricades had been breached and the men should flee.

"No, Paddy—don't you go. There's no need. It's not your fight," his mother whispered to him across the darkness of the room, as he took a few, barefooted steps toward the broken door, which was now partially open.

But it was, he believed, the smell of it that attracted him, and the oily, orange mushroom clouds that he could see flaming up over the row houses in the next street. To him it stank of poverty, burning petrol, indignation, cordite, and fear. Over it lay an obbligato of gunfire, the pop and hiss of CS grenades, and the soft thud of petrol bombs.

"Think of your work, Paddy. Our plan."

But Geer had only placed one hand on the jamb and the other on the door when his wrists were grabbed by two men, who pulled him out into the alley and threw him up against the house.

"Patrick Geer?" an officer demanded.

Suddenly his mother was in the doorway screaming, "No! No! You've got the wrong man. He's from London, he is. His father fought for the King in the war. His father died—" but a trooper, raising a boot to her hip, shoved her roughly back into the darkness, where she shrieked in falling. The door was banged shut.

A small, burly man with bandy legs, Geer tried to spin around, but they had his arms, and something cold and hard was jammed up under his neck, shoving his face into the rough brick of the wall.

"Are you Patrick Geer?"

On the sooty surface, shadows of gun turrets, helmets, and rifle barrels flitted, and from everywhere, it seemed, came the staccato rap of jack boots on pavement, the crack and splinter of doors being kicked open. Shouts, curses, screams. A shot. Loud—like the roar of a cannon. Above the houses, the early-morning sky was a delicate eggshell blue into which— off in the middle of the Strand—black fumes were eating.

"Are you the bloody bastard Patrick Geer?" the voice now screamed.

Geer could not imagine how they had gotten his name or why he was wanted. A mistake? Or perhaps a ploy—given by somebody in the Strand who knew he'd been away and would be released. He nodded.

8

"Say it, you bastard." The point of cold steel was now under the base of his skull, rasping his face against the brick.

"Shoot 'im!" Somebody close by started screaming. "Shoot the fucker!"

"I'm Patrick Geer," he said.

"Louder!"

"Patrick Geer. I'm Patrick Geer," he shouted and was spun around. A rifle butt was slammed into his stomach and then, as he fell, came down on the back of his neck.

"You're a bloody Fenian bastard, Patrick Geer, and you'll not talk to me like that. Put him up with the others."

And Geer, semiconscious, was thrown roughly onto the back of an open truck that was already filled with other partially clad, bruised, and bleeding Catholic men.

The ostensible purpose of "Operation Demetrius" was to capture and intern without trial the leadership of the IRA. But it was as though, Geer sometimes thought, the British actually *wanted* to fail in Ireland, and not cleanly, win or lose, by war, but, rather, painfully, horribly, atrociously, over an agony of time. For internment not only proved the failure of British policy in Ireland, but, more basically, exposed their utter lack of understanding of the Irish people, who over the centuries had shown that they would tolerate enormities—political repression, servitude, a famine that approached genocide—in measure, but gross physical abuse never.

Even tactically the operation was a failure. Of the three hundred men "lifted" by the British, only a dozen had definite IRA connections, though there were suddenly 288 others—to say nothing of the thousands in every Catholic ghetto in the Six Counties—who now wished they had. Though he was not a joiner himself, Geer's experience was a case in point.

From the truck, which was driven on a circuitous route through several Protestant neighborhoods to demonstrate how the army was dealing with the IRA, he and the others with

9

him were transferred to a lorry. There they were made to lie face down on the floor, some on top of one another. They were then covered with blankets and walked on, struck with rifle butts, or kicked, while others rapped their heads with batons and truncheons.

At the Girdwood Park Barracks, where Geer was "processed," he was punched and kicked into a tiny, foul cell with seven other men, many of whom had also been injured. They were given neither food nor water, nor were they allowed to sleep for . . . he could not remember how many days. At night the light was continually switched on and off, the door kicked, and the metal observation slide thrown open and shut. Or the door would open and a gang of troopers would pull out a man and beat him in the hall for no apparent reason.

Geer was beaten twice, and then, when they called him for questioning in some other room, kicked and punched, with a baton slipped between his legs so that he fell on the landing and was thrown most of the way down a long flight of stairs, all the while being abused verbally. He was then made to sit and, when questioned, "Name?," hauled to his feet by his hair.

"Patrick Geer."

He was stuffed down again.

"Address?"

He was hauled—the room swimming before his eyes—back up, only to have an RUC constable lean toward whatever official it was before him and whisper, "This is the one from London. Sean's friend."

Geer tried to speak, his voice lost in the dryness of his aching throat, his understanding of the law rudimentary if—he was later to discover—accurate on the point: "I want"—he had to pause—"I want to know why I'm being held without charge. And why—"

"You *want? You? Want!*" a man in plain clothes roared and,

10

after rushing the width of the room, delivered Geer a blow to the face that drove him into a corner.

A seemingly bored voice then said, "Take him for a good long walk. I can see he's dressed for it," and Geer, with his feet bare, and driven on by a snarling, lunging, snapping team of guard dogs, was made to run as well as he was able through an obstacle course of tree stumps, sharp stones, tacks and broken glass, and a pile of garbage—"Run, you fuckin' bastard. You're garbage yourself"—that they must have been saving for whole months. Three times. Five times. Ten times. The hours passed.

Plans. Was it then that Geer first decided he'd make his own? Perhaps. He'd already been made to understand that he'd been raised too proud and had little tolerance for abuse, physical and otherwise, though he was intelligent enough to understand from his treatment before the official that saying anything—even crying out in pain—would only make matters worse.

More days went by. Two, he thought, but it could have been only one before he was summoned again and beaten and herded out into a yard with some others, for it was then that time became muddled. Of the helicopter journey he could remember only the beating of the rotors, the twilight off to the right and behind them (southeast they were headed, he decided, trying to keep his mind active), and the startling and chilling nightscape of the Maze Prison from the air. It would remain Geer's best recollection of the place.

Set out on the tarmac of the little-used Long Kesh Airport, it was a tight pack of narrow nissen huts with box after box after box of barbed- and razor-wire fences, all swept by klieg lights that were clustered at the corners and too brilliant for Geer to look at directly. From above it was a cube of magnesium burning with an intense and blinding achromatic flame, but of it Geer would see nothing more.

A type of sock, black and rough and utterly opaque, that stung his eyes and stuck to his lips was thrown over his head before they landed, and he was pushed, shoved, beaten, and kicked through several checkpoints and at last into a frigid, all-metal cell. There his hands, which were shackled behind him, were clipped to a hook on the wall. But although he was then suddenly very much alone for what he later learned were six-hour intervals broken only by meals of bread and water, rest proved impossible. The pervasive cold through the metal floor stung the bottoms of his feet, his wrists and arms ached, and the hood that filled his mouth with fuzzy, wet wool whenever his breathing diminished, made him feel as though he'd suffocate if he fell asleep. He had to *think* about breathing, even though he was now finding it difficult to think about anything at all, and the panic that he experienced, believing that if he fell asleep or took his mind from the simple process of respiration he'd choke, was the most terrifying sensation that he had up to then known. Perhaps, he began to suspect, claustrophobia, which had never before affected him, was just another of his weaknesses. But what nagged him most was the *reason* he was there. Could he know that, he believed, the physical abuse would be tolerable.

But there was no reason, he eventually learned, or at least no explanation that made sense even if he had been a member of the IRA. For Geer had been placed in a "black room," which was a preinterrogation technique that the regiment called SAS (Special Air Services) had used in Egypt, Kenya, Cyprus, Malaysia (in all, eleven parts of the world that they considered their colonies) to "soften up" internees. The first step was to so abuse, humiliate, and exhaust a prisoner that he lost his self-respect. The second was to deprive his brain of sensory stimuli, blood sugar, and oxygen and create in his mind a disorientation which, under nonlinear questioning, might be exploited to yield a confession:

"Islington. There's a park there, isn't there, Paddy? Just off the Falls Road."

"London," Geer had responded, puzzled, for Islington was there but the Falls Road was in Belfast.

"Sean likes parks, doesn't he? Did he ever take you there? Lives in one, they say. Now."

But as a means of extracting information, which seemed to be their purpose, the technique was pointless. By the time Geer was questioned in depth—a day, two days, four days perhaps—he could scarcely remember his own Islington address, where he lived only because it was close to his work, much less that of somebody named Sean.

Sean who? Geer had, of course, known several Seans in his life, but none recently that he could remember. And as for confessing to a crime, Geer would not have crossed a street on a caution then, though the desire to exact some sort of retribution, at least from the men who had abused him, had already begun to form in his mind. In his torment he snatched at that. He kept trying to concentrate on and remember the bland, wheedling, upper-class voice of the interrogator and that of the other one—harsh and obscene—who berated and struck him through the head sock in what, even then, before he had researched their methods, he suspected was the "Mutt and Jeff," the hard-cop-and-compassionate-cop, technique.

In the "music room," where they took him next, he was made to climb into a heavy plastic suit, and the head sock was tightened around his neck and another heavy bag placed over it. His feet were then spread, and he was made to lean against a wall.

Pulling back on the bag, they pressed against his back, thrusting his pelvis out until much of his weight rested on his hands, which could barely remain on the wall for the noise in the room. It was an electronic mix, Geer knew, but made to sound like the hubbub made by an air compressor. It was a heavy, regular, pounding beat that hissed, it seemed, in his ears, sucking his eardrums in and out, but fast, as though to make them oscillate.

Louder still were the regular and (he judged) transcribed screams, wails, and shrieking of people who, he imagined, could only have been tortured horribly to have produced such sounds. And then, from time to time, he would hear the bawled orders and the rifle crash—a resonant noise that nearly lifted his hands off the wall—of a firing squad. And finally the real wails of the other prisoners who, he could sense, were in the room with him.

For hours, it seemed, Geer remained in the stance (one James Auld with forty-three hours would hold the record), sweating in the boiler suit, trembling with the wall, fighting for breath and against the noise, the horror of which increased with every throbbing shriek, until at last an elbow buckled and he snapped it back in place, only to have the other collapse. Geer fell heavily into the wall, but was not allowed to remain there long.

With batons and boots they kicked and beat him back into place, only to have him fall again and again, more frequently as his strength waned and his confusion mounted. He thought that anything, even suicide, would be better than the noise, and in falling the next time he tried to bring his head down hard on the concrete, but to no effect, the sock and the bag blunting the fall. When at length—a day and an hour, he later learned—he began screaming with the screams, roaring with the roar of the rifles, he was dragged out and questioned, but his body refused to abandon the tremble of the noise. His head throbbed. His hands and ears were numb but tingled and were hot, as though burning.

When he could not tell them why he had left England on certain dates and flown or driven to Dublin or Belfast, "only to return—a day, two, three, a week later—usually by a dif-

14

ferent route," they first threatened him with the "music room," then dragged him, kicking and screaming, back there. And how in his condition to tell them that after eleven years of virtually commuting to and from London, he took different flights and different connections merely to vary the trip? "Boredom," he said once, though they took it wrong. "To see . . . the countryside," another time, and he was rapped sharply on the ear with something hard.

Again and again he was wrenched from the room, questioned perfunctorily (it later seemed to Geer), and plunged back into the noise. Others, he would learn, were treated even more brutally. In their disoriented condition and with the bags still on their heads, they were herded into helicopters, lifted off the ground, and made to think they were being flown to England. While on the "flight," they were forced to the door of the helicopter and pushed out to discover that they were only a few feet off the ground.

Geer was not among these. During what proved to be his final interrogation, he became aware that somebody else had entered the room and was conferring with his warders, and when he fell from the chair he was allowed to remain on the floor.

He awoke in a sheeted bed in a single, locked room of what proved to be the dispensary of the Crumlin Road Gaol, Belfast. In spite of his questions, he was told no more. After four days to regain his strength and without any explanation, he was given clothes, shoes, and seven new pound notes and released. It was 21 August, a Saturday, 8:15 A.M. The morning was clear, cool for summer, and strangely quiet.

Turning from the gate, Geer walked out into a city that looked as if it had been sacked, for the response of the Irish to internment had been violence on an unprecedented scale. Within hours of the inception of Operation Demetrius, eleven people—three soldiers, seven Ulstermen (a journalistic euphemism for Protestants), one Ulsterwoman—had been killed; after three days, twenty-three had died. By the end of the week over fourteen hundred people had been admitted to hospital with riot-related injuries, and an estimated £10,500,000 of property had been lost, although industrial losses by themselves for the entire year were later pegged at £40,000,000. In the Short Strand alone, a fire storm that raged all day incinerated four mammoth warehouses, a bus depot and fleet.

Only the thick walls that divided row house from row house were still standing along the Albertbridge Road when Geer arrived back in the Short Strand. The roofs, ceilings, front and rear walls of the houses on the perimeter of the tiny ghetto had tumbled in.

Geer stopped before the space that had been his own house. Looking down into rubble, from which wisps of heavy, wet smoke still smoldered, he wondered how it had come to pass that he at age twenty-eight—a university graduate who was respected by his colleagues and peers and who, more to the point, had been born and brought up here—could have known so little about the world that he could have allowed an event such as this to take him unawares. Where was he deficient? Where had his attention flagged? Where had his energies not been applied? And why?

What passed for an answer soon came.

"Is it Paddy?" a voice that he recognized as that of the crone from across the alley now asked, but when he turned to her she could not conceal her fright. "Jesus Lord—save us. What have they done to ye?"

Geer had lost all his front teeth, and his nose and one cheekbone, having been crushed the first night by a rifle butt, had set as they had been broken, making what had been once described as pixyish features grotesque. In a prison mirror Geer had looked at his swollen face, the skin of which was still black, green, and yellow, and decided that he looked like

16

a pug who had continued fighting long past his prime. "The nose can be mended," the surgeon had told him, "and, of course, you can get a bridge for your teeth. But the cheek—"

"Where'd they take you?" the old woman now asked.

Beyond the Girdwood Park Barracks and Crumlin Road, Geer then did not know.

"Did you see Davey Muldowney? He's . . . missing since the swoop, and his mother and missus is beside themselves. One of 'the lads,' it's said, and if—" Again her old eyes searched his face. She shook her head and looked away.

"Where's my mother?" Geer asked.

A small, gnarled fist came up and was grasped in the palm of the other hand. "You mean—they didn't tell you?" Geer waited, watching her head cock resignedly as she scanned the rough pattern of veins on the back of her hand. "Will ya come in for a bap and a fresh cup of tea? I'm only after taking them out of the oven." She meant the sweet rolls that were a Belfast ghetto staple among women of her generation.

But when Geer did not move, she tightened her face into a knot of wrinkles and touched his wrist. "It's fierce the life we're leading here, Paddy, and there's nothing sure no more than that they'll kill us all, one way or another. Like your ma, when yous all were taken away."

"The squaddie who gave her the boot—?" She raised her eyes, which had filled with tears, to his.

Geer blinked.

"She must have slipped or fell over the bed, the one that was there near the door. Broke a rib, said the doctor—Fitzgibbons, you know him yourself—and it pierced her lung, says he. And"—she brushed the tears from her cheek—"that was it.

"When the fires started, the lads busted in and found her there on the floor, blood on her lips, eyes open. Long dead.

"I blame meself, for not lookin' in, ya know. But we had

our own trouble. Liam got lifted, and Francy. And then they broke us up proper. We were after wondering now this fortnight if you'd been released."

"Where is she now?"

The woman sighed and reached for his arm. "Ah, come in now. Come. I'll put on the kettle."

But when Geer pulled her back, she went on. "It's a dozen days gone now, Paddy, and things being what they were, it was best to get all the dead in the ground. You not being here and with everything gone and nobody coming forward—the priest had to do something and, well . . . she was buried by the Council at their expense, and the flowers you'll see on her grave are from all of us here, since we passed the hat."

She waited, then asked, "What's for you, then? Back to London and the job, is it?"

Was it then that Geer decided? In a small way, for the decision to get back his way would take years. But, having had few interests apart from his work and film, Geer had been frugal and saved his money. It came to him there, however, looking down into the wreck of his family's life, that he had no choice but to rebuild the house and begin again, there among his own. Britain's London had become for him an impossibility.

And Sean who? Only months later, after having sat night after night with a pencil and pad, painfully trying to recall the questions he had been asked, carefully trying to reason out their purpose, Geer had decided that they had thought he might have had some contact with or knowledge of Sean MacStiofain, who was then chief of staff of the Provisional IRA. MacStiofain had been brought up in London. He had at one time lived in Islington, a few doors down from Geer's address. And Geer had made the grave mistake of having visited in 1967 a friend who had been imprisoned for belonging to a proscribed organization.

18

It was then that the anger, which had been building in him—at the British, certainly, but at the world that could bring upon him so much pain, and at himself too for having been so naïve as to leave his mother vulnerable and helpless—now provided him with a vague sense of the possibilities open to him. Yes, he would exact retribution for the meagerness of a life that could be brought to a grim, bathetic close on the kick of a trooper's boot. But how?

Beyond suspicioning that the answer lay in the sorry debris of a devastated Belfast, Geer did not know. Then.

I
Focus

1

Fifteen full years after his internment in Long Kesh, Patrick Geer raised a sighting device to his eye. The view through the lens was grainy and polarized. It made the puffs of high white clouds that were raking the bluest of spring skies seem green and cold, like Arctic ice. He thought of the knot of work which lay before them. Loose now, but tighter—please God—as the hour approached. Three months off, it would be, could they get their yes tonight.

Craning his neck, he examined the aperture, then lowered the battered Beaulieu AT-7E that was owned by the International Television Network, for whom he now worked as a Belfast-based cameraman. It had been a demotion from the position he had held in London so many years before, and not really understandable, given his university background. But, as he had heard his section chief say, "The Irish—they're an enigma unto themselves, and if he wants that sorry place, he can have it." Geer had wanted the assignment; he had been filming what he referred to as the Six Counties for over a decade now.

Ballymena, County Antrim. Geer swept his eyes along the square of prim shops, the tidiness making the Scottish and English names above the doors seem redundant. It was the very heart of the colony of freebooters and roundheads who had been planted on the Irish countryside three hundred years before, and for over an hour now he had been watching their progeny reinforce the meaning of that victory. With battered, ancient but gleaming horns, with pipes and lambeg drums that made the cobblestones beneath his feet tremble, the Shankill Young Conquerors had been skirling out such bloody old chestnuts as "The Sash," "The Agahalee Heroes," and "The Green Grassy Banks of the Boyne," while bowler-hatted men in black coats and morning trousers paraded up one side of the square and down the other.

In the full sun of late afternoon the toes of their black leather shoes sparkled on the screen of Geer's viewfinder, as did the gleaming silver handles of their ornamental pikes, swords, and bucklers. From gingerly toted sacks Geer had earlier filmed them removing the laméed and fringed sashes that now draped their torsos, shoulders to hips; had panned in to catch in minute detail the adjustments made to collarettes that identified them as members of several of the regional Orange lodges that the "Big Man," were he so disposed, might have called his own.

For Ballymena was the town in which he had been born and raised, and his appearance here today during a county election campaign was token and unnecessary, except for the purpose that had brought Geer and the others like him to this busy market town. The "Big Fella" was not merely the most gifted politician in all of Ireland, he was, minute for minute, the most riveting footage in the largest colony—a full half province, Geer thought ruefully—of what was left of the British Empire. From London to Lough Neagh heads would turn when the "Good Doctor" (honorary, of divinity; Bob Jones University, Greenville, South Carolina, 1966) and his entourage came on the evening news. A master of media, he well knew on what field the battle for Northern Ireland was being fought, and Ballymena was today only incidental to the struggle. The stage, which had been erected in the middle of the square, was draped with orange bunting.

Geer's hand came up to the focusing peg, and he trained in on a large, hand-painted placard that was being held above the heads of the marchers. Dramatizing an ethos of simplistic, evangelical imperialism, it pictured Queen Victoria bestowing a Bible on a black man who had prostrated himself before her feet. Inscribed in gilt was the legend "The Secret of England's Greatness." The foreground of another rendered a triumphant King Billy disporting himself on a rearing warhorse, while in the background routed Catholic armies fled in bloody disarray along the banks of the Boyne. Yet another offered the anachronism of "Britannia Rules the Waves."

Scattered among the marchers were Loyalist and British flags that spanked in the brisk wind, and in raising the camera to them, Geer passed the lens across the roofline of the buildings across the square. There, with the politician's approach, sentries had begun to appear, rifles in their hands. Later the footage would be edited out but saved by Geer for his personal project, which had even garnered a grant from the National Film Board. It was to be a cinematographic montage documenting a decade of Ulster history—"Warts and all," Geer had written in his original proposal—though the point of the effort was far different. It lay not in a film finished for public viewing, but, rather, in the legitimacy of the quest and a short, part-fiction piece that he would show for the first and only time in Dublin tonight.

Girls. There were few who did not enjoy watching them, Geer included, and, with batons twirling like brilliant pinwheels in the strong sun, a double line of majorettes now joined the paraders as the autocade drew near. Dropping to a knee to angle up the camera, Geer caught the militant bounce of young bosoms and twin waves of cascading orange kilts frothed with pale, juddering thighs. Blondes, they were, or at least redheads, with stark white jumpers and orange tams. The crash of their heels on the cobblestones echoed around the square, syncopating the beat of the lambeg drums, and the crowd coalesced before the stage.

Geer's camera turned to the first car—a black Rover packed with six men that entered the square tentatively, probing—though his eyes, which he eased away from the viewfinder, remained fixed on the men on the roofs. Did they feel comfortable enough here in Ballymena to ignore the windows and rooflines, the alleys and streets opposite their posts? No, they were trained and exacting in their task, Robbie Blount—chief of security—having seen to that. Small and ferrety, he was slouched down in the front seat of the first car, watching them.

Security of that sort was something new for the "Big Lad," who until nineteen months before had employed only a small contingent of retired RUC detectives as bodyguards, saying to all who would listen, "I can go anywhere in Ulster because I lead the people of Ulster," while all knew the truth was somewhat different. There had not been a Catholic mad enough to bear willingly the onus for the slaughter that would inevitably follow his assassination. Without forewarning and a definite plan of defense, the ghettos of Belfast and the other pockets of Catholic population that were scattered throughout the countryside would be overrun. A pogrom would ensue. And thus, whereas other sectarian leaders, like Robert Bradford, Airey Neave, Edgar Graham, and George Armstrong had been murdered with impunity, the more highly visible "Rock of Ravenswood" had remained untouched.

"At the insistence of my friends and followers," he had said, he had hired Blount, but Geer did not believe it. And it was with no little anxiety that Geer wondered if the man, with his now conspicuous success, had simply too much to lose. Or if he had, on the other hand, suffered a loss of will which, perceived as a weakness, would now draw the beads of the many Catholic zealots whom the long strife had generated.

Watching a second and a third gleaming black car poke bonnets into the square, Geer considered the consequences of such a mindless act. History did not often present opportunities which, handled properly, might provide a solution to the thorniest of issues.

Panning in on the long face with its toothy smile that was framed in both a window of the middle car and in his viewfinder, Geer understood perhaps too well that how such an event might come about would ultimately become more important than the result it might produce. It would have to be made to seem like the actions of personalities and the culmination of events which, when looked back upon, could have been foreseen. The men whom Geer would meet with tonight in Dublin possessed that capability. He only hoped they had summoned the necessary resolve.

Ian Richard Kyle Paisley: Member of Parliaments at Westminster and Brussels; Assemblyman at Belfast; founder and leader of the fundamentalist Free Presbyterian Church of Ulster; founder and leader of the ultraconservative Democratic Unionist Party; author of a dozen books (among them such sectarian classics as the *Billy Graham and the Church of Rome*, 1970; *The Massacre of St. Bartholomew*, 1972; *No Pope Here*, 1982); founder and former editor of the *Protestant Telegraph*, a sectarian newspaper; founder of the new Third Force, a paramilitary group about which few knew much but that many feared.

Swinging his long legs from the back seat of the car, Paisley now hoisted his six-foot-four-inch, seventeen-stone frame skyward, his smile rising with him. Immediately he was surrounded by members of the security staff. They had been chosen, Geer knew, because they were not quite as tall as or somewhat less substantial than Paisley, who today, as he had for nearly a decade, was appearing in the palest shade of any in his near presence. No dog collar, no clerical blacks. Not for him any longer. And the shoulders of the brilliant buff-colored slicker, cinched at the waist, seemed broad enough to prop up an entire province, Geer mused, as—dropping down onto a knee—he angled the camera to catch the man's great size, which seemed to dominate the backdrop of storefronts beyond.

Media, religion, and politics. It had taken Paisley more than a dozen years to strike the proper balance, but after a shaky start as the self-proclaimed "moderator" of a church body with a small following, Paisley had gradually abandoned black canonical garb for the white shirt and tie of the politician. To great effect. Blending the dudgeon of Calvinistic righteousness with fierce tribal loyalty and a devotion to that impossibility, empire, he had succeeded in backing the English and Irish governments and his own people into corners from which there could be no acceptable withdrawal.

Within nine years of his first political step, Paisley had filled a new £175,000 Martyrs Memorial Free Presbyterian Church in Belfast to overflowing. Calling it "the largest Protestant church to be built in the United Kingdom since the turn of the century," Paisley now pegged his church membership at over two hundred thousand avid souls. By the early eighties over half of all eligible Protestant voters in Northern Ireland had at one time or another cast ballots either for him or for a candidate of his Democratic Unionist Party, and Paisley had become the single most visible political force in Ulster politics. It was debatable whether, given the need, the other half million of his coreligionists might take him to their hearts. Time and the violence, which Paisley had more than simply encouraged, had only seemed to legitimize his position.

Wheeling the camera down so that its picture banked up, Geer now followed Paisley as he mounted the stage stairs two at a time, the impression of enormous strength and vigor not, Geer knew, an illusion. In the eleven years he had been filming the man, only a bit of gray and a receding hairline testified to the passing of time. Nearly sixty. Paisley turned to the cheering crowd below him and raised his hands. And miraculously, as if on cue, the entire multitude quieted, the hush dramatic. Discipline. An admirable quality in a people, Geer mused, but he wondered how long it would remain once the "Big Fella" was taken from them.

Paisley folded his hands and bowed his head to pray for the divine protection of Ballymena, Ulster, and the British Empire, completing the invocation with "Fret not thyself because of evildoers, neither be thou envious against the workers of iniquity. For they shall soon be cut down like the grass, and wither as the green"—he held the word for a moment only—"herb."

The Biblical citation was a device that Paisley employed often, seldom repeating a reference and never quoting inaccurately. Geer had kept checking until he tired of the exercise. Paisley's application of scripture and his powers of recall were indeed impressive.

"Know that?" the BBC cameraman off to Geer's right asked him in a whisper.

"No."

"Psalm 37 and dead on. Take my word."

If only to continue the byplay, Geer asked, "Why're you being so good to me?"

"Foreign aid. You're a depressed minority. And, then, I wouldn't want the women of Belfast to hunger of a Friday night because of a cleric's quote."

29

Some others nearby began laughing, and Paisley's dark eyes flickered toward them before he launched into his screed for the day. Geer, all believed, was a quiet, patient, pleasant man and a confirmed bachelor, and he had done nothing to dispel the impression. Much admired both for his work with ITN and for the short documentary films that he had done on contemporary Northern Ireland, he had made it a point to be liked by the others, and he now merely maintained his smile and a steady focus on the man in the viewfinder, who had begun his address with a condemnation of the other Loyalist political parties.

As Paisley spoke, Geer scanned his thick, brutal lips, his rough features, the hooded, saurian eyes, the nostrils that flared whenever he referred to "the minority," though in fact it had been the British who had made of the Six Counties a minority statelet when they partitioned the island in 1921. Geer tried not to listen. But there was a kind of perfection even in the way the man spoke which plucked at his attention. Paisley's sing-song, half-Scots accent, with his voice invariably rising up at the end of a sentence, made his words fall in rough-hewn masses, like great chunks of ignorant, immovable stone.

The subject had changed to another hunger strike that had been begun by those who, after torture, had "confessed" and had been summarily tried and convicted of the 1974 bombings in Birmingham. Claiming innocence, they were protesting the manner in which they had been arrested and charged and were being jailed. One had died. Another would soon.

A hand now pointed to Geer. "Where was all this international attention when the victims of those convicted terrorists were being laid to rest? Where were they when all those innocent citizens, who asked nothing more than to be allowed to walk the streets of their city in peace and freedom, had their lives brutally snatched from them. *They* did not ask to be martyrs." Again the hand moved out, this time to a placard that one of his bodyguards was holding up.

It was a photographic enlargement of the Birmingham destruction which showed a corpse that had been ripped apart. An angry murmur swept through the crowd.

"No," Paisley continued, "but"—his voice fell to a hiss— "they were. Martyrs to the holy values of reason, order, and law.

"And what do we ask, good people of Ulster?" he went on quickly with rhetorical ease. "Nothing more than that—reason, order, and law. But—" He waited, his eyes moving through the crowd of rapt, stony faces, reading it, assessing it, reveling in the fact (it seemed to Geer) that he could mold it to his purpose.

First one voice was heard. Then another. Finally Paisley demanded, "Say it! Say it, good people. *We* have nothing to fear."

"*Nothing less!*" the crowd cried as one, and, turning histrionically to the other men on the platform, Paisley smiled.

Together. Their numbers—a rough numerical superiority of two to one within the Six Counties—occurred to Geer, and he again thought of places like the Short Strand. He also considered the several Protestant paramilitary groups, like the Ulster Defense Association, who had armed themselves for any emergency.

As the camera wound on, Geer glanced up at the seagulls that were wheeling in the updrafts high above the square. Off to the north and west, a dark line of clouds was forming. It was late spring, the end of April, but it would storm before sundown. And so much of what had been his life since he had returned to Belfast depended on how he would be received tonight. He checked his watch; half-four. He would have to hurry to turn in his footage, see about Carron, and make Dublin by closing at eleven.

"Yes," Paisley confided in a low tone that made everybody strain to listen, "in spite of the tests that will be put to us in the near future, God is good. And though we have been given little, you and I, we have much to remember and be thankful for.

"Take our flags, for instance. That flag." Yet again he pointed off, this time to a large, white flag, the "Red Hand of Ulster," which of all the flags clustered about the stage was most numerous and conspicuous. "Sometimes it's easy to forget our symbols, the ones our forefathers held dear, the ones that reveal our priceless heritage and remind us of Christ's purpose in putting us here. And though the fable is not Christian, it bears repeating . . ." and as Paisley elaborated the tale, Geer moved slowly to the left and the stairs, so he could include both Paisley and the flag in his frame and be ready for the exit, which was drawing near.

Geer had, of course, heard the story countless times before. It was the myth behind the reality of conquest and confiscation that explained why Paisley and his people, who were originally Northern English and Scots, were in Ireland at all: that two Scottish giants once contested each other's claim to Ulster. Aware that he was losing the race and that the title would fall to whoever touched land first, the progenitor of the crowd clustered about the stage had pulled out his dirk, cut off his right hand, and hurled it over the head of the other giant onto land.

The lesson? In what Geer considered a moment of uncharacteristic candor, Paisley explained, "Sacrifice. We are a staunch people, courageous and steadfast. We began in sacrifice, and we will continue, if need be, to do whatever we must to maintain our birthright. Here!" He plunged down a finger. "In Ballymena. And here." Again. "In Ulster." He then looked directly into the cameras. "And let the world and Margaret *Thatcher*"—he as much as spat the name—"take. Note."

The crowd loved it, as did Geer. From Paisley he could have asked no more than a profession of sacrifice. Yet as he dissolved the focus from the man to the flag, he realized, and not for the first time, how much more the Red Hand of Ulster meant.

The palm erect, the fingers raised on a white background, it was a warning that said "stop." Stop what? Progress? No, not simply progress. Stop change, any and all. History for the people in front of that stage would remain static, if they could help it, stopped at the Battle of the Boyne and with the issues—religious, ethnic, and divisive—that had given rise to that fight. Or at least stopped in the last century, when it had seemed that the traditions of empire, exploitation, and privilege could be sustained, even if by force. It meant that too. The color was scarlet and effulgent, like the most vital blood, straight from the heart.

Geer panned back to catch Paisley as he made his way toward the stairs, then zoomed in tight to show him shaking hands with the assembled dignitaries—but at the bottom of the stage stairs, Paisley stopped suddenly and turned directly to Geer. "Paddy—how's old Red Socks?" It was Paisley's aspersion for the Pope.

Beattie, Paisley's press aide, stepped forward to inform all the others that the remarks were to be considered off-the-record.

"As well as can be expected," said Geer, easing his eyes away from the camera, which he kept running and focused on Paisley, "choking on all that mackerel."

Somebody behind Geer began laughing. It was picked up by people in Paisley's party, and the Big Man himself explained, "It's a paradox, really, that *Paddy* Geer"—his pause making Geer's religious background apparent to the others—"has become my unofficial portraitist. Of all the cameras that are aimed at me, only Paddy's is consistently flattering. Someday I hope to know why.

"Robbie." He turned to Blount, his security chief. "Don't we have a little something for Paddy?"

Blount said nothing, only reached into his slicker, his eyes regarding Geer.

Taking a pencil from Blount, Paisley handed it to Geer: "For your 'Troubles' collection."

On each of the six faces of the hexagonal pencil was printed a different phrase:

"One Bible, One Crown / No Pope in This Town."

"Thank God I'm a Prod—No Surrender."

"IRA = I Ran Away."

The next two were verses from the anthem of the Shankill Defense Association, one of the innumerable Protestant defense groups: "I was born under the Union Jack, / You've never seen a better Taig [Catholic] than with a bullet in his back."

And finally, "Catholics Breed like Rabbits."

Pencils with the first two lines printed on them could still be bought in stationers' and news agents' shops in Protestant areas of Belfast, but Geer had never come across one so much embellished. He imagined it had been presented to Paisley because it was one of a kind.

"Vintage 1968, I'd say," Paisley explained.

Back when, in certain Protestant circles, it had still been fashionable to be snidely sectarian, Geer thought; the bitterness of the ensuing violence had ended that. "I'm overwhelmed," he said. "I don't know what to say."

"A few 'Hail Mary's' will do nicely," said Paisley, clapping the much smaller Geer on the shoulder and turning to his entourage, who with the exception of Blount smiled.

Geer only laughed, as he passed the pencil to the others.

34

"Make sure I get it back. It's priceless, especially the part about the rabbits. Animals have much to teach us, I've always said."

Geer. An unlikely man, thought Blount. There was the matter of his mistaken arrest during the internment swoop, his mother's death through misadventure, the destruction of his house in the Short Strand, which he had then rebuilt. He had subsequently thrown over great opportunity in London to carry a camera after men whom he might easily hate.

It had bothered Blount perhaps as sorely as some of the matters he had handled with the SAS. For the longest time he had considered the artsy-fartsy film projects Geer was pursuing—and his supposed collection of "Troubles Memorabilia"—a mere ruse for some other purpose. But he had slipped into Geer's house and examined the collection when Geer was away, and all seemed to be in place and credible.

True, Geer had taken pains to preserve what he had gathered, labeling every item and cataloguing all in a master file. And other than the traditional music he played on his button accordion, which he took here and there, Geer appeared to have no other outside interests beyond the occasional woman.

Not once had the tail that Blount had put on him come back with anything even remotely suspicious, and Paisley had been shocked to learn that he was being watched. "*Paddy* Geer? He had a dozen years and God knows how many opportunities to do me in, if he wanted, but he's been nothing but helpful." Paisley had gone on to tell how Geer had even opened his personal film library to a company that was doing a promotional film on Paisley's church. "He's the nearest thing we've got to a reconstructed Catholic, and we'd have no problems if they were all like Paddy Geer. He's"—Paisley had paused, searching for a word—"docile, and we're doing him a disservice."

It would not have been Blount's choice of word. Restrained, yes. Perhaps even disciplined. Thus Blount had maintained the surveillance, which was costly in money, manpower, and credibility. Why? Merely to employ Carron, who was an old SAS comrade who needed the work; merely to keep up his numbers of staff and enhance billing possibilities?

Perhaps. It was just a feeling, but he was unwilling to risk the chance that he might be right.

2

$\mathbf{M}$onaghan Town lies forty miles southwest of Belfast and seventy northwest of Dublin. Although part of Celtic Ulster (the English counties of Antrim, Armagh, Cavan, Donegal, Down, Fermanagh, Londonderry, Monaghan, and Tyrone), it is now firmly within the borders of the Republic of Ireland. An ancient city, honored in myth, Monaghan is surrounded by rolling hills and a network of small, pleasant lakes.

By day it is a bustling community, the largest and most active commercial center for forty miles around. But on a cold wet spring night Monaghan can be a chilling place, its tight rows of unpretentious houses and closed-up shops echoing the rumble and thump of a lorry plying a main road, the hiss of tires down a side street, or the staccato clip of a footfall on the stone sidewalks of the town. Blinds are drawn. Interiors seem dim and forbidding. The border with the North is only a few miles distant.

In the front room of one such house sat a no-longer-young man and woman who were watching the compound and intricate eye of an open coal fire dwindle in the hearth. In spite of the heat of the day, the sitting room was little-used and damp. Now and again they could hear the voices of the rest of her family from the kitchen, at the other end of the house, but they were used to such sounds and considered themselves as alone together as they'd ever be, and they were content in that knowledge.

From the shadowed hallway, where from time to time one or another of her little brothers peeked in, only the tops of their heads were visible, silhouetted against the green whorls of the marble-fronted fireplace. His was a tangle of red waves, which inclined slightly to her as she spoke, his voice low, measured, and lacking the usually noticeable local accent. Her hair was lighter—almost blond, nearly red—but brown in the dim light. Having turned to him, her head remained fixed on the nap of the large, deep sofa that was nearly as stiff as the day it had been purchased for her parents' marriage, thirty-nine years before.

Each had a foot on the hassock before them. Only their ankles were touching. Having grown up within a few streets of each other, they were close friends, but perhaps because they had both emigrated to different places—she to London and Canada for eleven years, he to several foreign countries for long periods since his late adolescence—they had never become more than that. It was a relationship not peculiar but perhaps more usual to Ireland, where in country towns and small cities the mere chatting up of a woman had in its day implied an obligation, and several dates a kind of commitment, and all commitments were directed to whatever bonded ease that chance, celibacy, or the Father of the deity pictured above the mantel would allow before the same restricted existence that their parents had pursued became their own. According to those rules, any option was sin. Nearly forty now, both Roisin Johnston and Seamus Rhines had sinned, but not with each other.

Rhines was not a big man. His face was long and thin. His cheekbones, which were set high, devolved to a knobbed chin.

He was not unhandsome, but his skin, blemished in early youth, was weather-reddened and coarse, and, given his unmanageable hair, he had a rough look, as though unfinished. It never seemed to matter what he wore—his usual navvy jacket with the leather shoulder pieces and Wellingtons, or a dress suit—he always appeared poorly turned out.

It was an image which might have seemed devised had it been questioned, but over the last three or four years Seamus Rhines had become a fixture in Monaghan, even though he came and went rather frequently—to earn a bit of money, it was assumed, though when Rhines was asked he never managed to say. Here in Monaghan he had no known occupation, yet he seemed to keep in good order the house which his father, who had been a doctor, had left him, at least from the outside. From the day of the funeral a half dozen years before, it was all anybody had gotten the chance to see.

Yet in the pub few passed his stool without turning in, and Rhines was not like some who over a few jars would say they'd do a thing and then never mention it again. Rhines was as good as his word. He was handy—anything electrical, a "wizard" with wood, some said—and although he was never seen in church, he was a favorite with the pastor, for whom he built stage sets the like of which were seldom seen even in Dublin. There seemed to be no end of effort that he would not lavish on a theatrical production, even at times giving some quiet advice to the actors, which was always well put and well taken. Seamus Rhines was generous of his time, but, of course, he had plenty, all believed.

Contrasts accounted for the attractiveness of Roisin (pronounced "Roe-sheen"). Because of wide shoulders and narrow hips, her figure, which was full, appeared less so and made her seem taller than she was. With thin legs she seemed almost powerfully built, except that in her stride there was a graceful swing. Nor were the features of her round face memorable but for a full and protrusive upper lip and eyes the color of an early-morning sky starry. Her front teeth were spaced. Though not demonstrably pretty, she had a certain appeal, and Rhines wondered if she had had offers.

"You're distracted," she was saying. She had her cheek against the plush of the cushion and the flare of her shoulder turned to him, and when he glanced at her she raised her chin, as though prodding him. "You've been distracted all day. What is it?"

Defensively, perhaps, Rhines reached for her hand. It was the actor in him, he judged, playing to an audience of one, and that a woman. But she responded to his grasp, and the sensation he felt was complex, interesting, but disturbing nonetheless, given what he knew would be his future, no matter the outcome.

He had long since realized that there could be no simple pleasure between a man and a woman, especially between two who had known each other so long and so well. And how to lie to her?

"Is it Canada? You miss it, don't you?"

He tilted his head, always wary of any request for personal revelation.

"Or New York?"

He moved his head to the other side, forcing himself to smile, as if considering the lesser of two evils.

"What did you do there?"

"Where?"

"In Canada. We're having a nice little talk here. Let's begin with Canada."

"*Begin?*" he asked, trying to remove his hand from hers.

"Yes, begin. Holding hands is serious business in Monaghan, you know so yourself."

"Are we *holding* hands?"

"I am yours, and I'll not be toyed with. Not at my age and with my opportunities."

"Which are?"

"Nil, and you know it, which makes me all the more unexploitable. What did you do? What was your work?"

"Where?"

"Canada. Surely you must have had work in Toronto. There're not many who in—how long has it been, twenty years?—become persons of leisure without work of some sort."

"Me?"

"You. And starting with nothing, as we all know you did."

"But me father—" Rhines objected bathetically.

Smiling still, the skin around the corner of her eyes puckered into folds that were now becoming wrinkles, she kept her voice low, the pressure on his hand firm. "Your father was a good doctor, the little he was here, but he was also a Fenian mountebank, God rest his soul. Always on the run or hiding in the house he left you that's now as tarted up as a publican's palace."

"Really? Says who, you? Next time you visit, be sure to knock."

"I will, and sooner than you think. And your garage packed with motorcars and vans."

"It's only an old Humber, for Jesus'—"

"And the Fiat and the Renault. My little brother tells me you've even got an old P&T van secreted away there." She meant Poist agus Telegrapha, the Irish communications authority.

Rhines only looked away.

"And you with the open hand. Dispensing jars to this one and that. Dismissing whole days spent mending some old sot's lost cause, as if you had lifetimes to waste. Either you seek the approbation of multitudes, which is a definite possibility, or you don't give a damn, and I know you do. The only other explanations I can think of are that you're after deciding you'll run for office, or you're a one-man charitable institution. If it's that, we can make a match." She paused, waiting for his eyes to meet hers, and when they did it was with force.

"Give over now, Seamus," she said in softer tones. "You've taken a girl's hand, and she wants the truth."

Rhines glanced up at the mantel clock, which was stopped, and wished he could look at his watch.

"It's half-six," she said, "and I'm counting."

Rhines smirked and eased his head back into the cushion, wanting—again the cowardice—to "give over," as she had said, and reveal to her at least some small part of the truth without in any way jeopardizing the years that had gone into the plan. Like a present, it would be. A gift of truth to somebody who was really quite special to him. And a release to share at least the best part—the theatre—of what had been his life for close to a decade, but he knew the harm that might come to her because of it. "It's not very good, I'm afraid. A small score in the building trades."

"Really, now"—she squeezed his hand—"where?"

He thought of what he had learned on the stage: the enigmatic mien without which there could be no attraction, and, then, he did not want to lie to her in a big way. "It was in Toronto. It's a big, growing place with a housing shortage. I took a chance and put everything I could scrape up into properties there. And now—rents, annuities." It would explain the checks in Canadian dollars, which he had upon occasion cashed at her bank. "Not much over there, mind, but here, with the house and the *old* car and all, I'm the prince of the odd pint, and, having no obligations"—he turned his head to her and smiled—"I wouldn't be after taking any man's money for passing the time of day."

"Where in Toronto?"

"Do y'know T'ron'o?" Rhines asked, appropriating the Toronto pronunciation of the place and moving his head back in a manner that, he judged and too late, gave the lie away.

"A bit." Roisin had served in the operating theatre at St. Joseph's Hospital for three years, but after over a decade she had tired of nursing and enrolled in university. The banking job had then followed. "Had I known you were there, I would have felt under 'obligation' "—again the pressure on his hand—"to have looked you up." She waited.

"Do y'know Bloor Street?"

"Around the university or near 'Little Athens'?"

Rhines smiled. "You *do* know Toronto, don't you? No—I mean West Bloor. Beyond High Park."

"Before the first corner with Dundas or the second?"

The latter street wound round and crossed Bloor twice. "My word," said Rhines, amazed. "You must have been there some time to know that."

She only smiled, and Rhines's eyes strayed to the mound of glowing coal in the fireplace. From in back of them, toward the hall that led to the kitchen, he heard her mother say to her brothers, "Wash up now. Your tea's nearly on the table."

"And to think nobody told you I was there," said Rhines.

She paused; then, "Nobody knew, Seamus, until too late. And isn't that the way you and the people you're with prefer it?"

Rhines felt the tug, as though suddenly he had lost his footing—the start before the fall—but in a way he was glad of it too. She knew or at least he suspicioned she knew, and he hadn't told her a thing. It was a relief; he believed he could trust her. "Obligations—they're sometimes difficult to meet."

"But necessary," she said. "Very necessary, and I hope, for your sake, it's what drives you."

43

Before he could question her, she stood and pulled on his hand. "If you can't stay to tea, you'll have to be going. You know how my father is."

Too well, thought Rhines: tribal chief, guardian, protector, he was Rhines's idea of an ignorant, benighted, biased man, and all on the side of reaction. Johnston had it well here in Monaghan—and the rest of what was and was not the country, the world, and humanity could be damned, for all he cared. What transpired beyond the walls of his house and the lumber-and-brick yard that he owned was of no interest to him, apart from the pounds and pence that it yielded.

But Roisin did not move away from Rhines when he stood, and close, like that, he could feel her warmth and softness. "You be careful, Seamus. There're former exiles among us here as well, and this act of yours hasn't gone unquestioned."

"Act?"

"Act. Wasn't I after seeing you on the stage of the O'Keefe Center. The last night of *Uncle Vanya* it was, and by the time I got past the security and all, 'James Ryan'—what was it the *Globe and Mail* said?—'a supporting actor with the unusual gift of knowing when not to assert the dimensions of the several roles he has played on this stage.' That James Ryan, evidently a *bon vivant*, had already cleared out to the cast party and then on to New York, where the play opened a month later. And not in the phone book, not under Ryan or Rhines. Not in Toronto, not in New York."

In the near darkness, Rhines smiled, blushing slightly, in a way thrilled that she should have seen him. Reaching for her hip, he tried to pull her toward him, but she twisted away.

"It's your reticence, James, that worries me. Along with your traditions, which we both know, and whatever purpose has brought you here to Monaghan to play a fool of sorts."

Rhines began to object, but she pulled him toward the hall. There he glanced up at the deep crack which, even though her father was also a sort of builder, had marred the ceiling since their childhood. But under the globe in the kitchen—a kind of harsh, ersatz moon—Rhines for the first time in his life felt uncomfortable in her parents' presence.

Turning from the set tub, on the board of which he had spread the evening paper, Johnston peered over the top of his reading glasses to find his eldest and favorite daughter holding hands and with the likes of Seamus Rhines. His eyes then met those of his wife, who was knitting by the stove, and an understanding passed between them. It did not matter that Roisin was nearly forty and a bank manager, she was Joseph J. Johnston's daughter first, and while she lived under his roof, there would be no aspect of her life that would pass without his consent, though the latter was often circumvented.

"Off so soon, Seamus?" he asked.

"Yes, sir. Early night tonight."

Johnston girded his bulk and raised the paper, staring down at an article. "Engagements, then? Tomorrow?"

"I suspect so."

"But you don't know."

"Ah, now. Now—" her mother began to say, and Roisin tried to direct Rhines to the door and the entry.

But Rhines's smile only widened, his large features and rough, weathered skin seeming almost handsome. "How'd that job work out, Joe?" He meant a computerized, digital marquee that Johnston had been contracted to install in a complex of cinemas near Dundalk. None of Johnston's usual electricians could complete the job, and after a phone call it had taken Rhines not even a morning to make things right.

Johnston now shifted his feet uncomfortably before the set

tub, and Rhines had second thoughts: it was one thing to do a man a turn but quite another to hold his spinster daughter's hand.

He turned to the mother. "I'll be saying good evening now, Mrs. Johnston. Joe."

Studying the paper as though absorbed, Johnston muttered, "Good night, Seamus." And then, "Take care."

The same message as his daughter, Rhines thought, and in the darkness of the entry Rhines turned to Roisin. "Walk out with me," he said on impulse, which he immediately regretted.

"And where would I tell them I was going?"

"Dublin." It was a mistake, but in his mind he had already arranged how he could make it happen. Perhaps.

"Where in Dublin?"

"Ah"—he looked away—"we'll have some dinner, and then . . . I play with a little group. A piper, a fiddler, a man on the button accordion."

She tilted back her head and her starry blue eyes searched his face. Their thighs met. "And you, Seamus? What do you play?"

"The spoons, if you must know. And I'm warning you—not very well."

"I don't believe it."

"Join me, and I'll regale you with my ineptitude."

Said she, "There's nothing that Seamus Rhines or James Ryan does that he doesn't do well."

Rhines pulled her toward him and brushed his face against her hair; she smelled of some mildly scented shampoo or soap which he could not place, but which seeped through his memory—warm, deep, and familiar. About the same height, their bodies had joined in a way that Rhines did not want to abandon. His hand came up her back and drew her shoulders in to him.

"Hadn't we best see how you feel about this tomorrow?"

Rhines felt the softness of her face against his, the cushion of her chest, and then her lips almost hot on his, fleetingly. A buss. And again, a bit longer. And a longing that was perhaps more a profound regret nearly sickened him. Was it fear? No, he had felt fear before and often, and it was not fear. Then it was . . . ? Rhines did not know.

"But I'm not one for the pubs," she said into his ear, "no matter how well you play. Nor the movies. We'll go to dinner. Dutch treat."

"We'll see about that, then," Rhines scoffed, "but it's a date."

"Is it, now? We'll know that when I hear from you tomorrow, won't we?"

"I'll show up at the bank and stake out your desk."

"Don't you *dare*," she said in a rush, shocked that he might pointedly make the town talk. She had her father and mother to think of.

Stepping carefully through the cobbled pools of silver water in the alley, Rhines passed his tongue over his upper lip, trying to taste of her. And he shivered, suddenly cold to realize how close he had come to making the kind of mistake that would ruin everything and perhaps cost them their lives.

But, then, Saturday would be an impossibility for him, and at the moment he had much to do—the projector, the screen, perhaps a patch cord, some jacks, and, say, a few dozen feet of extension cable. Rhines had it all in the shop that now occupied most of the first floor of his house, and Geer, who would be followed, could bring nothing but the film and a tape recorder, which would also be easy to conceal, and himself.

Five and a half months before they had made the proper contacts, omitting, for reasons of security, the details of the action itself. When they were granted a tentative yes, however, the piper had said, "You're to show us who will do it. How and where. Without that you'll get nothing."

Show. It was an order that had appealed to both of their talents, and then, as Geer had contended, for maximum effect it would of needs be a media event.

Proposal. It was a word that Rhines rather fancied.

3

Carron, George Oswald Henry: six feet, three inches tall, 17.4 stone in weight, with a heavy build which, if anything, had become more muscular in the last decade. Now Carron had achieved a kind of body builder's apotheosis that his age—forty-eight—and the ravages of another preoccupation, which was also seen in his face, rather denied. Carron had a bit of a problem that was archetypically alcoholic; on an information-storage-and-retrieval disc which Patrick Geer kept in a vault box of a Monaghan bank on the Republic side of the Border, he had just about every fact that had ever been assembled concerning the man.

Turning from the small bar in his study on the third floor of his house, Geer stepped to the window and looked down on a wet Albertbridge Road. There Belfast traffic, stalled now at supper time, was passing fitfully, like gleaming beads on a black abacus. With a strong light behind him Geer imagined that the silhouette of him lifting the iced tumbler to his lips was visible from a quarter mile off. But he moved away. After all, Carron was a professional, and it would not do to be too obvious.

Carron's failing, Geer knew, had begun with bravado beer-drinking in his early teens and advanced progressively until, on joining the British Army at age nineteen, he had answered the question "Do you drink? If so, how much?" with "About a dozen pints a day most days." Though not unusual for Belfast dockers, a hard-drinking lot, it was a fair amount by any standard. Yet the examining physician found him in "robust, good health."

Trained first as a Red Cap, Carron distinguished himself as a police trainee and was posted to Kenya to serve under SAS Captain Frank Kitson, who was putting into practice some of the intelligence-gathering techniques that would mark a long and controversial career. And he had followed Kitson to Ireland, where Kitson was moving beyond intelligence gathering to yet another ploy. Calling the campaign "psychological operations" or "psych-ops" for short, Kitson had endeavored to divorce the extremist elements from the population supporting them. To the age-old British practice in Ireland of creating a network of informers, Kitson had added the Belfast equivalent of death squads, which drove through the Catholic sections of the city shooting pedestrians with weapons that had been used by the IRA.

Turning now to the rain-wet window, Geer noted that an anonymous gray Ford Escort that had been parked on the far side of the road was just changing its position, idling down a side street. Geer checked his wristwatch: 6:20. Carron would move the car again at forty-five-minute intervals until Geer departed for Dublin. After all these years, it said something for his training, thought Geer, though Carron's sort made good policemen.

And it probably said something for Carron's essential humanity, Geer mused, that as the levels of SAS violence increased, so too did his intake of drink. Yet in Northern Ireland his qualifications were unduplicable. Not only was he a Kitson-trained careerist; Carron also spoke with the proper accent. Given a chance to change out of uniform, he unfailingly adopted the drab and dowdy mufti preferred by working-class Belfast men of his age and background. He had been gone long enough not to be immediately recognizable on the street or in a bar, but he could, when required, develop sources or make needed inquiries without arousing suspicion.

And Carron's dedication was then such that he questioned no command, no matter how grisly. From the testimony of the survivors of the 1973 McGurk's Bar bombing in Belfast, which killed fifteen and seriously injured thirty-two, an artist had rendered a composite drawing of a man who had entered the premises carrying a satchel and had left shortly before the blast. He closely resembled Carron, who British sources—making a rare admission in denial—said had been at the SAS Hereford Depot at the time.

The statement effectively destroyed Carron's usefulness to his superiors, but they were now finished with him anyhow. His drinking had not bothered them while it had enhanced the ruthlessness with which he pursued their particular pleasures, yet once his cover was exposed, it became a disgusting habit that required a one-word explanation. "Nerves," his record said, though Geer had obtained another report that described Carron as having "violent psychopathic tendencies especially when drunk."

After Carron was deactivated, he managed to stay clean for over two years. Then Robbie Blount, who had been Carron's immediate superior in SAS, and had also retired but to a partnership in Ulster Risks, a Belfast security agency, took pity on him. He was, after all, one of their own and there was no denying his qualifications. Besides, a two-year abstinence had altered his appearance. It was as if with his detoxification Carron had achieved a physical, if not a spiritual, ideal. He was like a gnarl of ancient bog oak, first pickled in tannin, then kiln-dried under pressure. Only his face—ravaged by the habits of his former preoccupation—betrayed his age. It was a deception which, Geer hoped, at least one would soon learn could be fatal.

Formerly an immense man with heavy, rounded features and a dimpled, protrusive chin, Carron now possessed a face that seemed to have collapsed in on itself, leaving only the jaw and eyebrows—like simian, supraorbital tori—and the length of his nose, which like Geer's own had been badly broken, but several times. A brawler, Carron still drank from time to time; only then did he become dangerous. Geer had tried him once before with results that had proved disastrous to the man and his commission.

Turning from the window, Geer switched out the light. Drink was the edge they would need.

With a resignation shared only by the condemned, Carron now followed Geer in his car from pub to pub, dropping down from the North and into the Republic—searching for some place where Geer might pull the accordion off his shoulder and play until closing or drunkenness set in. And he kept asking himself why, from the moment he had seen Geer in the window with a glass in his hand, he had known it was inevitable. The drink and whatever else would follow.

It bothered him that, unlike Geer, he contemplated the prospect without joy. "Off on a toot, Paddy?" he heard a barman call to Geer as he was leaving a pub in Drogheda. "If the 'crack' was half decent here, I'd be tooting with *you*," Geer had said, laughing and, sipping from a flask, had climbed into the battered Fiat wagon that he drove at a snail's pace, weaving, perhaps singing, a hand out the window and the fingers beating time to something on the radio, even though the night was cold and wet.

The "crack," Carron mused, his eyes on the broken lens of the Fiat's right tail lamp. The phrase signified all that he despised about the bandy-legged little bastard, more monkey than man, and his kind: the hilarity, the abandonment of self, the embrace of total strangers, all under the guise of "great fun," a "brilliant evening," and the supposed "cultural superiority" that they flaunted even in the Kesh, when it was nothing more than poor poems and—crossing Kingsbridge near Heuston Station in the heart of Dublin, he slowed the Escort to watch Geer pull his old banger up over a curb and park with impunity on the sidewalk by the quays—monkey music. Gibberish, like their language. Gigs and reels and maudlin, mock-heroic songs that celebrated a childishness that Carron had been taught to detest but he now hated with a fury that he knew would gather in force as the weekend progressed.

By the time he had squeezed himself through the smiling, joking pub crowd, Carron could see from the vantage of his height that Geer had found what he had sought—a seedy clutch in a corner, with a fiddler coaxing a thin refrain from a battered instrument and followed by a tin whistle, some pipes, and a Tinker all red curls with a gold ring in his ear thumping a bodhran.

"Right now, sir?" a barman asked.

But Carron said nothing, keeping his eyes on the image of Geer that he could see in the mirror in back of the bar. Geer had insinuated himself onto half of a low stool that some mot had taken, and was now smiling over at the other "musicians"—Carron thought, tasting the word with bitter pleasure as he would soon a large whiskey—waiting for an invitation to join them, playing his fingers on his thighs and passing compliments on the music to those around him. When a tableman passed, Geer even bought a large round of drinks for all nearby, including the band, and got kissed by the woman. Under the table her hand moved onto his thigh.

But still no invitation to play, though the accordion was in plain sight. Even when the music had stopped, they only raised their glasses to him in thanks, and Geer, nodding, seemed crushed. No more so, however, than Carron, who had decided he *would* drink—as he had on one other occasion while following Geer—only so long as he could hear the accordion playing and no more. And Geer could play the thing too (Carron gave him that), better than what those others had brought along for show.

"Drink, sir?" Carron was again asked, occupying as he did a large space at the bar.

"I would, could I hear a tune," he said, sliding an Irish five-pound note forward but keeping his fingers on the bill.

"They'll be continuing directly. What's your pleasure?"

"The button box, if the truth be known," said Carron, affecting a Southern countryman's speech, as he had so often under cover, North and South. "There's nothing like the accordion to set your feet to singin', now is there?"

"Ah, but we've no dancin' here. No permit. And then—" He indicated the crowd. An older man, like himself, he seemed to welcome the break in the crush of orders, and removed his eyeglasses, reaching behind him for a clean bar rag.

"When I was a lad," Carron continued, " 'twas about all I heard, and now, well . . . seldom."

Fitting the bows back over his ears, the man allowed his eyes to take Carron in. "We'll see what we can do,"

But there was no need. The woman beside Geer had already uncased the accordion and was thrusting it toward him. "The bize won't mind, will yez, bize? Now, give it a go and—come closer while I tell ya—I like it"—she rolled her eyes—"hot."

A laugh went up, and the other musicians swapped doubtful glances, resorting to their glasses until they had heard Geer play. In a blush of either pride at Geer's being, though a Taig, from the North and Belfast, like himself, or the release of knowing he could, he *would* drink, Carron had decided that Geer could make the thing talk, if he wanted.

"There you are, sir," the barman had said, "Whiskey, is it?"

A good judge of custom, Carron had thought. "Aye." The word was a slip and placed him from the North, but not serious. "A large double, and don't rush off."

And what Geer made the accordion say was as familiar as the peat-smoky heat of the malt in his glass, though somewhat less acceptable to Carron—a complicated version, all trills and runs, of "The Men Behind the Wire." A few verses in, Carron found himself following the tune, his hand drumming on the nearly empty glass, his second. After all, Long Kesh had been a part of his own life as well:

> Through the little streets of Belfast
> In the dark of early morn,
> British soldiers came marauding,
> Wrecking little homes with scorn,
> Dragging fathers from their beds,
> Kicking sons while helpless mothers
> Watched the blood pour from their heads.

"You've got a t'irst," the barman said.

"And you've got a bottle," which by closing time had become two, with the liter bottle of Black Bush he bought against the possibility that Geer might leave with the woman. It would ease the length of a cold, lonely night. But Carron only glanced Geer's way once more, when the accordion music stopped briefly. He then saw the little man ease a tape recorder from under his jacket and place it on the table, pushing a button down and giving some excuse to the others, who found it comical.

Carron looked away. Drunk or sober, no matter where he was, the sweet, wee man was always on the make, running something off to his advantage. And not again did Carron turn to him, believing he need only hear the wee monkey fingers on the wee ivory buttons to fulfill his duty. In all, the night was proving itself agreeable: not too much time to get locked but just enough to feel pleasantly . . . blitzed; yes, that was the word. Carron smiled, his whole body glowing.

And then he fell into company with some others. A conversation, it was. Rugby, which he himself had never played, though with his size and fist-battered features he looked the part and followed the game closely in the papers. Finding himself out on the bitter quayside street, which was enveloped in a thick, foul-smelling fog that made the street lamps appear amber, Carron hardly gave Geer a thought. It was not unusual for a publican, by way of thanks, to ask musicians to stay on a bit and play for his pleasure and some free jars, while the staff was cleaning up.

And from across the street, where, in the darkness of the Escort, Carron lovingly twisted free the cork from the bottle of Black Bush and held the spout to his nose to sniff those first, precious vapors, he could hear the music unabated. "A *crack!*" he roared at the windscreen. "A great, an effing *brilliant* evening altogether." And he decided then that in covering Geer, who was a right chap for all his peculiarities, he would have more, Blount be damned. He sang:

Up the long ladder, and down the short rope,
God bless King Billy, and fuck the Pope.

It was a corruption of a Belfast children's song, the other half of which Carron knew but did not sing. It went:

St. Patrick's day will be jolly and gay,
And we'll kick all the Protestants out of the way,
If that won't do, we'll cut them in two,
And send them to Hell with their red, white and blue.

And had Carron been listening closely to the music emanating in dim strains from the pub down the block, he would have again heard Geer playing solo, "The Men Behind the Wire," only to be followed on the final verse by the others. For Geer was no longer in the bar.

As soon as the last patron had left, the publican had dismissed his help—"I'll get the rest meself. Go home now, we've a big day tomorrow"—and Rhines had picked up the tape recorder that Geer had brought with him. After some diddling with a jack, he fitted it to the speaker of the pub's television. Then all five of them—Geer, Rhines, the fiddler, the tin whistler, and the uilleann piper—had repaired to the nearly empty storeroom in the granite basement below the bar.

There all was in readiness, Rhines having seen to the arrangement before Geer arrived, and after the others had taken seats on folding chairs, Geer fitted the reel, which he had concealed in the rounded end of his accordion case, onto the projector.

Given what would happen, if the project became an actuality, the film would have to stand as his finest creation. With the exception of the money he had put into his house and car and the few other necessities he had bought, what was being shown on the screen had consumed, in one way or another, just about every penny he had made in his career. And apart from the footage which Rhines and he had "created," Geer believed that as a documentary of one man and his effect on a troubled province it had few rivals, though its avowed purpose was something different. But he was—he told himself, turning from the projector—a patriot first and an artist only second, and all should be made to serve a revolution which, since 1921 and the partition of the North, had been stalled.

And after focusing the image and adjusting the sound, Geer

did not again turn his face to the screen. Instead he picked up his drink and left the room, climbing the worn wooden stairs to the barroom, where, through the peephole in the pub door, he checked on Carron.

"Well on his way," said the publican, who was standing behind the bar and speaking to the woman. Given a yes from below, she was to be Geer's "date" for the weekend, the cover he would need to lead Carron to what they had planned. "Went off with a bottle of Bushmills, he did, his face redder than his flag and him touting his own. 'I'm not saying I prefer them, remember, but for ruggers it's the North you'd want.' A big fat cigar, a 'Napoleon' "—he pointed to the box in back of the bar—"stuck in his gob."

Geer's own uncle on his mother's side, the publican was polishing pint glasses. "The shagger. And the face on him. A hard man to get on the wrong side of, I'd say. But, you know"— he paused, smiling down at his work, his own Northern accent hardly noticeable now after thirty-two years in Dublin—"a right man to do up proper, given the chance."

Geer had only climbed onto a barstool, unable to keep himself from listening to the muffled sounds of the film that came to them from below.

"You've seen it yourself, then, Paddy?" asked the uncle, who, Geer believed, looked more like he himself would have at sixty-five—almost delicate features, the nose small and up-turned in a round, strong face—had his own not been shat-tered and were he, of course, to live that long, which without any self-pity Geer believed was not likely. The youngest of his mother's brothers, Tom Hanlon was himself a bachelor. He had backed anything that Geer had ever chosen to do, even to sending him for all those years to university in Lon-don. And although the Hanlons were a large family and there were many nieces and nephews, Geer had been informed that the pub itself would become his when Hanlon died.

58

The woman and Geer only traded glances, she knowing the origin of the film but observing the "need to know" precept as she had with the Provisional IRA for nearly two decades. Geer himself did not belong to the organization, though the proposed action could not succeed without its support. One of the men below them in the cellar had been commissioned to grant that, and Anna Flavin, as she was at present called, had been brought in to serve as Geer's cover. "No raving beauty," Rhines, Geer's Provisional contact, had said, "but in the long run credible, if you know what I mean. A solid woman with the proper experience and, more to the point, the proper background." Geer had liked the choice of modifier and what he saw of the woman, but he had been distracted.

Staring down at the drink, which he took little of, he could not keep his mind from following what he knew was the narrative of the film below. He kept trying to weigh its judgments, to measure its effects, until the end was nearing—when, taking the glass in his hand, he headed toward the stairs.

A stunned silence, which was better—he tried to tell himself—than any applause, greeted him as he opened the door. He switched on the lights, leaned back against the cold granite wall, and again waited.

In the discussion that followed, the tin whistler said, "It's right that it be shown like this. It's the bigger audience—not just them in the park—that's crucial if we're to achieve the maximum effect. The whole Six Counties must"—he looked away and scratched his head and in a small voice concluded—"combust."

And later: "It's right as well that we should keep history in mind. When looked back upon, the whole thing has to seem plausible . . . and inevitable.

"And it's bang-on, really—having the three things done by the smaller crime *first* make for the possibility and *then* hide the cause of the larger crime, so the blame falls squarely where it belongs. Or, at least, where people will think it belongs. They'll take the bait, they will, and then, like a jeweler's stroke on a gem—or, rather"—he paused—"a hammer blow to a lump of coal—nothing but the cost."

And still later: "No matter how bloody right this thing turns out, or how bloody wrong, we'll be condemned by those who think they know. They'll say we didn't give a negotiated solution a chance, that we made a thing of the Third Force or the UDA, that we brought on slaughter. But nobody—not a one—will be able to deny the fact that we made the country grasp"—he held out a hand in which was rolled a money belt that contained more hard currency than most men could make in several lifetimes; below it were four passbooks to banks in different countries—"the nettle." He then left to catch his flight back across the Atlantic.

Said the piper, "I've done some bitter things in my time, but none harder than this. I only hope that, after it's done, somebody will see that we believed a big loss with the chance of a permanent solution preferable to the slow death of everything, both sides . . . the economy, the spirit, the mind, the two-thousand-plus who have already given their lives since the sixties.

"And Jay." He turned to Rhines. "I want you to know it's only because it's you who will lead this thing. Anybody else . . ." He glanced at Geer and shook his head. Then, "The vote was close. Everything could backfire and who will be blamed? Us and us alone."

Bending for the case to his pipes, he withdrew a paper pouch. "If"—two fingers fell on Rhines's wrist—"if for any reason you think this file will be compromised, you should destroy it and take whatever steps necessary to contain the loss. It took some doing to get, but beyond yourself it's all that can be traced back to us. Granted, the information may be somewhat dated, but still—these are our people, and the damage that this might cause, were it to fall into the wrong hands . . . And remember, now that we're committed, anything that we can do, we will. Just give us a shout."

At the door, he added, "Apart from ourselves, there're just the two men back in Belfast who know. There'll be the three others, which makes an even ten when all are counted. In the end—seven quiet men, please God. One martyr. Perhaps two. Another who deserved his fate. But, mind you, no more.

"About Duncan? I'm only happy that you've found him a use. He's tried to shop us when we used him before. Doubtless he'll try it again, which is to your purpose. There's always the risk that he could put it together and tell Blaney, but that's a chance we'll have to take."

But Rhines had to press the fiddler. A politician and cautious. He would commit himself to their success alone. "But yourself now?"

A nod only.

"Down the line?"

Another nod.

"You've been deputed to say that?"

"Would I be here were I not?"

"And what about the British?"

His countryman's smile had grown somewhat more complete—canny, wise, a schemer. "Well, I can hardly speak for them, can I now?" He raised a hand. "Beyond telling you that 'down the line' means just that. We're committed, though I'm after thinking that two lads such as yourselves need little more than what you've just gotten from us tonight." He raised his glass. "And a bit of luck."

Not all of it was good.

II
Split Image

4

The rumor of death.

On the blast of a bitter spring evening two days later, it pillaged a quiet neighborhood in Dublin, ransacking semi-detached houses and driving the genteel into the street. Attracted by the police vans, the film crews, the flashes from strobe lights that sprayed the walls of the computer center at the edge of the park, whole families had gathered. Better than anything on the telly, McGarr imagined. Piped direct—*live*—right into their front yards. For all but one.

Chill as the grave, it rocked McGarr, riffling the brim of his hat as he inched forward in the lee of O'Shaughnessy's broad back. At the gate to Herbert Park House, a facility of the Consolidated Irish Bank, a scrum of young flagellants blocked the way: jaws taut, brows furrowed, thick chests blazer-bared in a kind of penance for the death of a former captain. "We're here for *Jock*," one bellowed toward the gate. Said another in an only somewhat more conciliatory tone, "Just one of us. We have to know." The wedge, thought McGarr, and then—? They were the "Libertarians," a rugby club based in the Liberties, an old Dublin section that had grown fashionable of late. McGarr wondered how many of them considered the tactics of their sport an exemplum for life.

Dimples of outrage trained down on McGarr as he pushed past them. He was a short, stocky man who was wearing a dark Chesterfield coat and a bowler hat to cover his baldness. Nearly fifty now, he had a long face and expressive pale-gray eyes. His nose had been broken and curved slightly down to one side, yet his face conveyed the promise of benignity. There were times when McGarr could be the gentlest of men.

"Get out of it. Get out of it now. Have yez no homes to go to?" O'Shaughnessy was saying as he sorted through the last of the crowd. Rainwater from the visor of a uniformed sergeant's cap dripped onto the back of McGarr's hand. He nodded at the ID—"Chief"—and stepped aside to let them through, his eyes remaining on the crowd. "Sorry not to have recognized you bang off, but—"

McGarr now became aware of other sounds that he had been hearing from radios within the crowd—voices that originated no more than thirty feet beyond them, within the ranks of the journalists who were being kept at a distance by other uniformed Guards. They were competing voices—three or four perhaps—speaking over and through one another, explaining to the hidden audience and the actual crowd what they were seeing, fueling what McGarr judged was either ghoulish interest or ersatz desperation.

"McGarr . . ." he heard.

"Chief Superintendent McGarr . . ."

"McGarr from the Murder Squad at Dublin Castle has arrived, which as much as confirms the report . . ."

He then heard shouts from beyond the gate, and the crowd surged forward. And phosphorescent flashes—first two and then two more—blinded McGarr, brilliant bursts that blossomed through the periphery of his vision, making sight impossible.

"Back. Get back or I'll put you out entirely, credentials or no."

"How long—*Jesus*—are we to wait?"

"At least get us under some cover."

"Until I'm told and I tell you and not before."

Nearly stumbling now from his blindness, McGarr felt O'Shaughnessy's hand on his arm, and he wondered how they would appear in the morning newpapers, which had been riding them of late. Two doddering old men superintending too many active cases, to say nothing of the "open" file, a backlog of deaths only a few of which would ever be explained. So much depended on chance, luck, the odd scrap of information which, exploited properly, led to a break that then led . . . usually nowhere.

The majority of cases, however, soon became wearingly similar and attritive in process—a slow grinding away at possibilities which usually did not yield a probability that then, if time and manpower allowed, could be attacked.

Appearances, impressions, "instincts" (as policemen more modern in verbiage than either McGarr or O'Shaughnessy would have it)—how much depended on moment or mood or feeling? Something surely, McGarr decided, as more strobe flashes pursued them: the spectacular arrest, the publicity which silenced critics, and the sort of beatitude which would allow him to forget the enormity of the active file, at least for a time. He could use some of that, he could.

As his sight now cleared, he noticed a squat guardhouse across the drive to one side of the computer center. It was a checkpoint for the car park in back. Inside a security guard sat at a desk, while two others from McGarr's staff questioned him.

McGarr paused under the shelter of a narrow marquee. He reached for a Woodbine, and the bitter wind knifed through his lapels. Hands cupping a lighter appeared. They were wet and shook slightly, reaching the flame toward him. Ward, another of his assistants. Teardrops of ice clung to the black curls at the nape of his neck. A notebook replaced the lighter.

"Name?" O'Shaughnessy asked.

"Duncan, it was. John or Jack or 'Jock,' as he was known."

"The rugby star?" McGarr asked.

Ward's dark eyes met his own. He nodded. "Nine caps," by which he meant that Duncan had played for nine Irish international teams. "Turned down a big contract in Britain. Other offers. He had contacts, social and political. Apart from being a director here, he was also Neil Blaney's secretary." He meant the prominent and independent Donegal T.D., member of the Irish Parliament, who for many years sat in the European Parliament in Brussels. "Had his name splashed all over the papers, year in and year out. A bachelor. Great guns with the women, it's said. A bit of a playboy, could the press be believed."

McGarr drew on the cigarette and turned to peer through the darkness toward the gate. This explained the journalists and the crowd.

"Guard says he surfaced here around two this after'. Unusual, given his position and it being a Sunday and all. Then he was still keen on the rugby.

"Work tours change at six, but no Duncan, not until the guard heard what we've determined were three shots and he went round the back to investigate." Ward turned, as if they should follow him, and McGarr again felt the bitter tooth of the storm.

A wide lawn ran to shrubs and trees and was bounded on the street side by a tall stucco wall. A walkway led to a back gate, which was open.

Said Ward, "Contrary to bank policy, those lights had been switched off at the junction box." He pointed to a cluster of floodlights at the corner of the building. "And the guard, hearing a scuffle and what he calls"—Ward glanced down at the notebook—"a 'horrible, heart-wrenching' scream but from a man, over here by the back gate, he returned to the guard-house for a torch."

A gust staggered them, and icy rain needled McGarr's left ear. He snapped up the collar of his coat.

"By the time he got back, the victim was . . . packed, you'll see, into the wall. Over here." Ward parted glistening leaves of a rhododendron, the branches of which were silhouetted on the glare from braces of achromatic bulbs. Having estab-lished baselines on both sides of the walkway, about a half dozen detectives were now combing the area. Respecting their grid, Ward led O'Shaughnessy and McGarr on a circuit that allowed them to view the body from several angles before they advanced upon it.

A massive man with a broad back and broader shoulders, Duncan had been shoved face up into the crotch formed by the wall and the portal of the gate. His complete torso was bent back at the waist so that, even lifeless, his body rested, like a snapped tree trunk held only by its bark, against a juncture. He was down on one knee, the other leg thrust out behind him, and the large, disc-shaped muscle of his calf—exposed by a tear in the leg of his pants—seemed almost taut.

Ward pointed to the broken shrubs and the several sets of footprints that had been punched into the soft mulch around the plantings. They were now filled with plaster and shrouded by polyethylene film. Ward went on: "As you can see, there was a struggle with two other men, as far as we can now tell. One was nearly the victim's size, the other a little fella. Tiny by the size of his feet." A small man himself, Ward reached a foot toward the print to illustrate.

"Two shell casings have been found. They seem like they'd fit the gun there." Squatting down on his heels, Ward pointed to the shadow between the body and the wall. There, by the knee that was plunged deeply into the mulch, was a large-caliber revolver. It too was covered by a sheet of clear plastic, which with a pencil Ward now lifted to reveal the gleam of high-polish chrome and a grip carved in ivory: a bull's head with a sweeping rack of horn, the nostrils flared, the eyes brooding and truculent.

"A Ruger, .357 magnum," said Ward. "Three shots gone. Not a mark on him, though, apart from the abrasions on his face and whatever"—Ward cocked his head, one dark eyebrow arching—"happened to his back.

"But somebody got hit, and well. There was blood beginning here"—taking a torch from his pocket, Ward directed the beam into a chrome-colored puddle, brown at the edges— "and running out along the sidewalk to the curb. Gone now with the rain.

"And then there's this." Ward walked back to the wall and indicated a round object that was being shielded from the rain by the body of the victim and yet another square of polyethylene. He had to edge his back close to the stucco to play the beam on it, and he then handed the torch to McGarr.

It was a large reel of what appeared to be magnetic recording tape contained in a pouch, which was again plastic but seemingly devised for the object. There was a pressure seal at one end. Near the reel was a sodden and dirt-spattered cardboard envelope, padded like a mailer.

"What's that on the plastic itself?" McGarr asked. It was a dull dark-gray object, nearly the size and shape of the reel within.

"After pouring the casts, McAnulty went in there." He meant the chief superintendent of the Technical Bureau. "Says it's stuck to it. A magnet itself. Fixed like that, it probably destroyed whatever was recorded."

McGarr finished the cigarette and stubbed it out against the wet wall, placing the butt in his coat pocket. The wind had increased, the sound changing in pitch from a soft roar,

as from a distant crowd, to a frenzied keening. Like shooting
stars, snowflakes were now passing through the lights and
across the top of the wall. It had been a long, bitter winter,
which even now refused to end. McGarr redirected his gaze
to the tape, the empty packet, and Duncan. The victim.

Observed O'Shaughnessy, "Whoever they were, they came
equipped." He meant the magnet.

"And finally," Ward said, "there's this." Playing the beam
of his torch behind the iron grating of the open gate, Ward
picked out a further, milky-white object. "Like the rest, Chief—
we left it where it was found."

Within a Technical Bureau wrapper was a soft hat, light
green in color, with a small spray of iridescent feathers in the
band. Alpine in style, and purchased at MacGonigall's, Belfast. New by the look of it. Certainly nothing that Duncan
would have been wearing.

Said Ward, "Size ten. Immense, and a match, perhaps, for
the larger of the two footprints."

Pointing to the ground near the victim, McGarr glanced at
Ward, who nodded. McGarr approached the man who, even
down on a knee like that, was nearly his height.

Six five, McGarr mused, or six six. Like a farewell salute
or a gesture of defiance raised to the heavens, the right forearm had been thrust over the head and now rested against
the wall. It was thick and covered with curly blond hair through
which the rain was now tracking. The fist was partially curled,
the knuckles abraded. He—Duncan, the rugby international—had turned his face to his left side, if only (McGarr
imagined) to avoid striking the stucco with his forehead, nose,
and mouth. His large, regular features were contorted in what
could only have been pain. And if the appearance of great
vigor and strength were beauty, then Duncan had been handsome. His mouth was open, his teeth were clenched, even

his nostrils were still dilated from the struggle or whatever agony had been brought to bear on the seventeen stone of his broad, muscular frame.

He was wearing, appropriately, a rugby shirt—green with a single black-banded gray stripe—gray slacks, and coarse-grained brogues. Into the eye that McGarr could see, rain-water, which had collected on the eyebrow above, was dripping. It was hazel in color, as shallow as wet marble, and seemed to be focused on the snowflakes that were flitting, like quarks, through the light above them.

But it was the position of the body with its curious contrary bend that held McGarr's attention. In all, a kind of giant of a man—a great physical brute who, McGarr could remember, was capable of bulling a whole group of other men down a field—had here been felled, and McGarr could not even guess at the weapon or the method or the force that had been required to bring him down.

Reaching toward what appeared to be the point of the break—the waist itself—McGarr began tugging up the rugby shirt, which, strangely, was still neat and in place. However, he only got a glimpse of the skin, which was smooth, unabraded, but bore beneath the surface a curious bluing, either from the pallor of death or from the trouble deep within the trunk, before Ward said, "Watch it, Chief." McGarr only just stepped back. Like a sculpture from a poorly balanced pedestal, Duncan's corpse lost forever the verticality to which it had been clinging and toppled at McGarr's feet. The arm remained raised, the head twisted, the back bent. There were scrapes and bruises on the side of the face that had been rammed up into the corner of the wall.

McGarr felt a hand on his arm. O'Shaughnessy. Stepping around the body, they moved through the back gate, out into a side street, which had been blocked off. Bright nylon line hung from stanchions, tracing what had been a path of blood to the curb. On both sides of the street, police were noting car registrations and tax numbers. Others were knocking on doors or interviewing residents who had ventured out on their doorsteps or to the edge of their lawns.

"Where's McAnulty?" McGarr asked.

They found him inside the building, in a metal-and-frosted-glass cubicle tagged with a plastic nameplate that read, "J. W. W. Duncan, Director HPH." McAnulty was standing back from the desk, regarding it. His left hand was cupped, and after each pass of a cigarette to his mouth, he flicked the ashes into the palm of the other hand, which was then slipped into the pocket of his jacket. It was a steady process, like the swinging of a pick, and seemed to pace the transit of the man's thoughts.

As McGarr stepped into the cubicle, McAnulty's head turned to him, his dark, close-set eyes falling to McGarr's hands to see if he was smoking too. A small, taciturn man whose usual dishevelment contrasted sharply with the care he lavished on the most minute detail of his commission, McAnulty was a man who defined himself almost exclusively through his work. His head was a weal of unkempt hair; his collar was nearly black. He had needed a shave yesterday, and McGarr wondered when he had last been home.

And having had to deal with the man for nearly a decade, McGarr merely waited. An explanation would come. In many ways mulish, McAnulty would now view even a cough as an affront. He was thinking, for him an activity practiced with resolution. And like a dutiful child at a piano, McAnulty would eventually get the tune right, but with little panache. Etudes, McGarr thought.

From the work area outside the cubicle, he could hear a woman crying and from time to time O'Shaughnessy's deep voice, trying to calm her.

Finally McAnulty muttered something that McGarr could not catch. "How's that?"

"I said, it's hot, it is."

"What's hot?"

McAnulty's eyes, suddenly critical, rose to McGarr's. "The desk, of course."

McGarr let that pass, and when no further explanation came, he checked the clock on the wall behind the desk—11:37 and a Sunday at that. The morning would come soon. "*Why?*"

McAnulty nodded once, as though having been waiting for McGarr's insistence. "A good question, that, and I've got a man coming"—his own eyes darted to the wall—"Jesus, where the feck is he? He'll deliver us of all this"—with the cigarette he circumscribed the set of tables that ran off the desk at an L; on them were whole series of machines: a video display terminal, a computer keyboard, what appeared to McGarr to be storage cabinets and two printers—"lot." McAnulty shook his head disapprovingly and again resumed his silence.

And it was only when McGarr's hand fell to his own jacket pocket for a cigarette and McAnulty's eyes devolved upon the packet that an explanation, prefaced by a sigh, was given:

"I suspect, goddamn it to hell, that more school is in order. Been putting it off, ya see, telling myself I'm no longer young, the revolution's just begun, and—mother of Christ—I could get by, you know, until . . . retirement." The mere word was a scourge in his mouth; with distaste he considered the gluey end of the cigarette. "Says I, I'll hire somebody in. That class of thing. Not easy in itself, though, never knowing just who you'll get.

"But now? Come here and listen to this and—mind"—his eyes widened warningly—"you're not to touch a thing." The cigarette, burning end and all, now disappeared with a hand into the rumpled brown suit, where it would smolder until it was remembered or extinguished itself.

Advancing cautiously upon the desk, McAnulty pointed to the telephone, the receiver of which had been removed. His finger then followed the cord down to a lower drawer of the desk that two wires—the other leading to the table that contained the computer terminal—had kept from closing completely. After opening the drawer with an end of a pencil, McAnulty pointed into the darkness, where yet another machine, announced by a single red, glowing bulb, had been placed. In its yoke sat the telephone receiver.

McAnulty explained, "That there is a modem, so I'm told. It's a device for transcribing messages into sounds. In that way they can be passed over the wire to other phones and modems and computers. A common enough device, but not here." He glanced to make sure McGarr had understood. "Not allowed, not by computer operators, not by the director. T'eft, it is, or was, but listen—"

By the stiffened end of the cord, he lifted the receiver from the yoke and reached it toward McGarr. Even before it touched his ear, McGarr heard a high-pitch mechanical bleeping.

"Jammed. My guess is he never got the stuff out."

Before McGarr could inquire further, Ward appeared in the doorway. "Out in the street, Chief, we've found something you should see."

"What is it?" McAnulty demanded.

"A P&T hutch that was put up sometime last night. A neighbor who works for P&T himself thought it curious that just one van and driver would be looking into any problem here at the bank, but he didn't think to inquire, and it slipped his mind. Until now."

Passing through the work area, McGarr heard the woman saying to O'Shaughnessy, "I don't know who else would have known of it, but he told me it was just something to do with the rugby pools, and where was the harm in that? The machines themselves are never switched off, and he only ever accessed his tape when they were idle. Sundays, like now. An odd holiday, and not often."

"How often?" O'Shaughnessy asked.

With what McGarr interpreted as an admirable hopelessness she had struggled to shore up impending collapse. Her hair was the color and texture of iron filings—an unnatural, wavy black with silver highlights, and, he imagined, hard to the touch—and her makeup had caked wrinkles into sags. She was wearing just a bit too much rouge and a wavy line of too much lipstick, and through the hot-plastic and ozone stench of the computer center her perfume was precipitating, like alum through a turbid flux.

She was leaning against the edge of a table, and McGarr could see that her girdle was too tight, so that it flattened everything but her hips; her brassiere too firm, so that it raised her breasts toward her shoulders; and the line of her legs, one of which was cocked stylishly, too definite. The calf had grown too big, the ankle too narrow, and yet there was a beguiling appeal in the nearly formal attire—a clingy turquoise-colored dress—that she was wearing. More for a Saturday night than for, as she had said, Sundays, like now.

"Five times." She looked down and considered her hands, which were bare of rings. "Six, counting today."

"Where are the others?" O'Shaughnessy now asked, as though having read McGarr's mind. He looked out across the many empty desks. McGarr and he had worked together now for a decade, but with the tall, severe Galwegian McGarr also shared a point of view.

"Others?"

"The crew. Surely you don't run this place yourself."

She looked away. She blinked. Suddenly her eyes again filled with tears. "Off at six."

Raising his collar to the blast that was now laden with fat flakes of heavy, wet snow, McGarr stared down through a manhole into a communications culvert. It was packed with thick woven bands of electrical cables, circuit boards, and switches. Standing among them was McAnulty's electronics expert, a remarkably young man—nineteen, twenty, tops— with a milk-white, boyish face and the fine but wavy hair that the woman in the computer center had hoped to imitate.

"This is—" he began, his hand moving confidently toward a small metal box, when McAnulty shouted.

"*Don't.*"

Shocked, the boy jerked up his head and touched a hand to his chest. Color came to his face. After a pause, he continued. "*This,*" he nearly shouted, "is a radio transceiver. Home-made, I believe, but without a doubt adequate to the purpose. It takes skill to place anything with decent power, broad-casting from a hole, into a parcel like—"

"Jesus, I said *don't.*"

"—*into a parcel* like this. But you can tell what it is from the aerial." He paused. "Can you see the aerial *here*, Chief?"

"Where?"

"Here—I've got me hand on it, so I have. The wire is piped right up to the traffic standard you're leaning against yourself."

McAnulty swore and the others looked away.

"What we have here is the source of the noise that you heard on the telephone, Chief."

Asked McGarr, "What would have prevented whoever it was who was trying to send"—he glanced back toward the gate and the pathologist's van, which was just heading off— "out information, from using another line?" He could remember having seen several buttons on the phone in Duncan's office.

Said the boy, "Well—as you can see here, an entire circuit

is wired, covering all lines leading out. The ideal setup at the other end of these devices would process the radio signal through a computer programmed to switch on the jamming device."

"How would that work?" McGarr asked.

"With sophisticated software developed over what I should imagine would be some time, the program might include the recognition of individual speaking voices or even certain words said by those voices, but what would be the point of that, since those voices could as easily say those words over some other phone system at some other time. And I take it this apparatus wasn't placed here by the bank itself.

"But, say—" The young man glanced up, to be sure that they were still with him.

Said McAnulty, "Go on, Colm—we haven't all night."

"—say the signal were transmitting computer language from a disc or—"

"A magnetic tape." McAnulty's lips popped as he drew on his cigarette, the head of which glowed as bright as a poker.

"Yes, a magnetic tape. Then the program on that tape or disc could have had written into it a safeguard—a bit dropped here and there throughout the complete program, so that it would be nearly impossible to search out and eliminate all. In that way, even if any other programmed safeguards were defeated, the computer monitoring all calls at the other end would only have to 'hear' that bit to activate the jammer. If the sender tried to switch lines, the next bit would knock it out and so on and so forth, until"—he gestured with his hands at the cable into which a maze of wires had been patched— "there wasn't a call that could be made from Herbert Park House."

"But"—McAnulty's head twisted in a manner that appeared quite involuntary—"*why?*" He looked up the dark street, which was beginning to fill with snow.

"For security."

"Security? But the bank—like the money, it's *their* business to keep *their* information in house, not whoever put that there."

"What if it wasn't their information?" the boy asked.

McAnulty did not want to admit that he did not understand. The cigarette glowed.

Said the boy, "What if it was only the bank's computer and not the bank's information that was being used?" He waited a moment, then concluded, "And whoever placed these devices here did not have personal access to a computer of its size and type, but did not trust whoever it was who did?"

McAnulty turned to McGarr. "The rugby pools, like the woman was saying."

McGarr only shrugged. It was far too early for conclusions, and he had one more stop before his night would be through. Flicking the snow from a shoulder, he turned toward the cars.

With a pipe in his mouth and a book in his hand, Neil Blaney, T.D., answered the door to his Dublin flat. He was in his early sixties now, and the features of his somber, saturnine face seemed to have become more definite since McGarr had first become aware of his presence on the Dublin political scene, years before—lined, creased, puckered so that, standing there, regarding them from under a dark shelf of eyebrow, he seemed owlish and forbidding.

"Mr. Blaney. It's good of you to see us at this late hour."

"Nonsense, I was only reading. What's it about, gentlemen?"

O'Shaughnessy explained why they had come. Blaney only averted his dark eyes, as though listening for some sound in the hallway beyond. He then stepped back into the flat and the sitting room that they had seen at the end of the hall.

"Come in. Come in, of course. And excuse things. Bachelor digs now, and I . . ."

In the hearth a coal fire was burning with a yellow flame. Blaney slid a mark into the book and placed it, along with the pipe, on the mantel. Indicating other seats, he resumed his own by a reading lamp. He lowered his head, looked down into his palms.

His father—a Fianna Fail stalwart—had preceded Blaney to the Dail from their Donegal constituency, but the son had gone on to hold a variety of important Cabinet-level posts, three of which McGarr and O'Shaughnessy, having discussed the man on their way over in the car, could remember: Posts and Telegraphs for a short while, Minister for Local Government for nearly a decade, and then Minister for Agriculture and Fisheries from 1966 to 1970. In the second post Blaney proved himself extremely influential, drafting most of the legislation that provided the infrastructure—planning, housing, and roads—for Ireland's recent growth.

But it was in his final Fianna Fail ministry that Blaney achieved his greatest notoriety. When in 1969 the Lynch government failed to send Irish troops into the North to contain the slaughter there, he and two other Fianna Fail Cabinet ministers—Charles Haughey and Kevin Boland—decided that something should be done to protect the Catholic minority against the Protestant militias and the British troops. Thus they began a high-level effort to acquire and ship arms into the North. They were discovered and sacked by Lynch, and then tried but acquitted in a court of law.

Had Blaney, like Haughey, who went on to govern the country as Taoiseach, remained in Fianna Fail, he most certainly would have resumed some Cabinet-level position in succeeding governments, but he declared himself unwilling to truck with a party that refused to recognize that "they are our people up there, and that is part of our country. It was taken from us and is being maintained by force against our will. There is no way that situation should be allowed to continue." Instead he stood for election as an independent and became a constant reminder to those in all other parties of what they were not doing about the North, though he continued to vote with Fianna Fail on most other matters.

It was O'Shaughnessy who had remembered Blaney's words. When Blaney stood for the European Parliament, the respect in which he was held was such that O'Shaughnessy and eighty-two thousand other Irishmen sent him to Brussels, where for the betterment of the island entire he attempted (not always with success) to forge an alliance with Northern Irish politicians. In a close election a decade later, he lost the seat.

"How did it happen?" he now asked.

It was again O'Shaughnessy who explained, and as he spoke, McGarr watched the firm mold of Blaney's features crumble with pity for his fallen secretary. The features were rough, the beard heavy, the skin somewhat coarse, and it was not in his appearance alone that Blaney reminded McGarr of the form of the men who inhabited the wind-swept, treeless hills of Blaney's native Donegal. There had always been a directness about Blaney that was admirable, if—McGarr imagined—difficult to maintain.

"I heard the phone ringing," he now said, "and if, you know, a politician were to jump for every phone . . . but"—his dark eyes flashed up at them—"you know that, given your own profession.

"His *back?*" he asked.

"Lower back," said McGarr, "snapped."

"*Jock?* Jesus . . . who?"

McGarr went on: "We found a revolver beside him. Three shots gone, and blood, not his. There were at least two other men. We also found a spool of magnetic tape that one of his colleagues seems to think had something to do with rugby pools. And a hat. Alpine in shape, green in color. From a shop called MacGonigall's, Belfast.

"Did he wear hats and would you happen to know . . . ?"

Blaney was shaking his head. He then stood and reached for the pipe. "Jock Duncan. A good fella certainly and a man of many—perhaps too many—talents, but if Jock had a failing it was that he was a bit greedy. He wanted too much—rugby star, mathematician, businessman, computer expert, socialite, politician without a political base, lover of beautiful women without any love of his own, sports cars, to be known in London and Paris as well as in Dublin. And now rugby pools.

"There's just not enough time in any one life, I once told him, to do all of that well. At some point you've got to pick and choose, though I never had cause to complain of what he did for me."

Turning in front of the fire, packing the pipe, Blaney shook his head. "I don't know how I can help you gentlemen, as much as I wish I could. There was the difference in our ages, our involvements—like I said—and though we came from the same part of the world, it wasn't just the border that separated us. I'm a simple and—can I use the term?—a *specialized* man."

"How did he come to be your secretary?" McGarr asked.

Blaney struck a match into the pipe, some dark tobacco that gave off a deep-blue smoke. The backs of his hands were covered with a fine black hair that seemed to reach his knuckles. "Applied for it, he did. My family's gone now, and, well, being alone and getting along in years, I found the correspondence and the crush of daily affairs a bit much. I let it be known among my friends that I could use some help, and wasn't I amazed when Jock Duncan showed up. Like you, I was always after reading about him in the papers."

Said O'Shaughnessy, "When did you see him last?"

"Friday for lunch. The Shelbourne." It was a hotel across from St. Stephen's Green.

"And he seemed—?"

"Himself entirely. Great form, as usual."

"His duties for you were—?"

Blaney frowned and looked into the bowl of the pipe. " 'Public relations' is a term I despise, but when I was engaged, it was a treat for the people who were trying to see me to meet and speak to Jock instead. Especially those from our—I mean, of course, *my* constituency. Jock had"—with the pipe Blaney reached out, and McGarr noticed that his eyes had glazed—"magnetism. And the physical man was, well . . ." Again he shook his head. " 'Commanding' does not do him justice. It's hard to believe." Blaney was wearing an old cardigan, slacks, and house slippers. Somewhere off in another room a canary had begun to sing.

McGarr debated how, given Blaney's involvement in the arms trial, to word the question. He said, "Please accept this query as one that we must ask, as a matter of form. Could it be that Duncan was a member of an unlawful organization?"

"*Jock?*" Blaney removed the pipe from his mouth and smiled down at the stem. "Please, gentlemen—Jock was too smart for that."

McGarr inquired if, perchance, Duncan had kept a desk or maintained files to which Blaney might have access.

"A desk, yes. Files, no. As I suggested, his duties for me were largely ceremonial. 'Secretary' is a term which in one direction is infinitely expansible, but in the other . . . suffice it to say that it allowed him to take the proper sort of leave from Consolidated Irish."

"Full pay," O'Shaughnessy suggested.

"The same."

"Surely there wasn't any need?" McGarr said.

83

"Isn't there always? And, sure, the bank could spare it for a little influence with a one-man political party."

At the door, he added, "I'm beginning a long holiday in Portugal tomorrow, but I'd like to be there to go through that desk with you. He was, after all, my *private* secretary. But I'm afraid all we'll find are clippings. For all his notoriety, he was a vain man, Jock Duncan."

And Neil Blaney a careful man, thought McGarr. There would not be a scrap of paper that had not been scrutinized front and back by the time a Murder Squad staffer arrived in the morning. But, then, who could blame him, given the trouble he'd had?

5

Roisin Johnston pulled the key from the lock of her parents' front door and turned back into the wintry blast, directing her steps toward the house two blocks distant. She was beside herself with what she viewed as her own foolishness, and she would not simply give over, not without some resolution of the matter.

She had made herself, she believed, into a spectacle who was all the more pitiable because of her age: sitting for two nights, waiting for Seamus Rhines in the lounge among all the other "available" cows, glancing in toward the bar hopefully after a man who might yield her a spare thought or allow her to accompany him for an hour or two after closing, were he capable or even present. She had had to fend off men her father's age—a butcher, the tailor, an old flame who had married her best friend and now called his wife—who had given him six children, mind—a "bloody bitch," while crying in his cups like a spoiled child. Her seventh and doubtless most troublesome.

Trying to cheer herself and tightening the collar of her fur coat—a gift from a doctor lover who had begged her to marry him, though he should have known better than to beg with her—Roisin decided that all men could and perhaps should be divided into two parts: the little boys that were searching for a surrogate mammy to take care of them and who could be hated properly, and the others, the former hunter/warriors. Each of that class had sorted out the world according to a greater or a lesser plan, of which he and he alone was the center.

Listening to her heels, which beat on the stones of the walkway like an especially harsh clock, she reckoned that she had squandered her time and the several opportunities that had come her way, trying to find somebody different, when it had been only a lack of mental rigor that had led her astray. She should have cleaved to the decision she had made when she quit nursing and returned from Canada to attend university and go on to the bank: there was and could be no Mr. Right, no man who would truly share life on an equal basis. Here in Monaghan she had resigned herself to the prospect of growing old among her brothers and sisters and whatever offspring they might create.

"*Seamus Rhines?*" she said aloud, her voice echoing up a dark, wet alley. The very idea of him and becoming any part of what he was about. "What could I have been thinking of?" she asked herself, though she well knew. She had been thinking that, since after all the years they had again found themselves here, they might—could he free himself from his involvements—live out the rest of their lives together. And she had had the picture in her mind of him on the stage of the O'Keefe Center in Toronto—transformed from the young boy she had known, masterly in the role of a character cultures distant from Monaghan and Ireland, and so incandescent in the persona that only moments after having thrilled to identify him, she was made to forget who he was and believe in the character he had become.

But here, now, he had been playing some curious, years-long, greater role about which she could not begin to guess, and, like his house, which appeared momentarily through the now driving snow, Roisin Johnston's future loomed like a dark, inscrutable monolith. She thought of a cairn, a dolman, the keystone of a passage grave, and she paused before raising a hand to the bell, trying to calm herself. He had, after all, only given her a kiss and made no greater promise than that they might kiss again. Dinner, which had meant bed, and she had accepted the idea. An adventure. She was needy, she realized, but not by how much.

She heard sounds from round back—a scrape, a muffled rumble, the creak of a car door being opened—and she followed them down the dark alley, feeling the rough dashing of the wall until it cornered with a fence. The back gate was closed but unlocked. Her eyes had by then accustomed themselves to the dark, and, opening the gate door, she saw before her the large, rounded shape of a bread van, the "K.C. Confectionery Ltd." vaguely discernible on the door.

She passed down its length and was nearly at the rear of the truck when the back door of the house opened, showing in a thin and momentary flash, which she only saw because of her position there by the yard wall, Rhines silhouetted on lights which were blazing within. The door as quickly shut, but suddenly, miraculously, Rhines was outside. Lugging something, straining under its weight, he passed close by her and set the object roughly onto the bed of the van.

She thought, at that point, she should say something, but she did not want to startle him, and then she heard the door open again, though she saw nothing until it was just about closed and then only a thin glow, a diffusion through the blowing snow.

Disoriented because of the door, curious now, and still desirous of satisfying in some way the temptation that Rhines represented, she felt for and found the handle and pulled it open, only to discover the interior of the house dead black.

87

There was a pause and then Rhines called out, "Paddy?" She was about to answer when she heard a click from behind her, and the lights blazed on. Cupping her hands to her eyes, she dropped her purse and, looking up from it, saw Rhines in the doorway with a gun pointed at her head. The fingers of his other hand rested on a small plastic box that was attached to his belt.

He cocked his head and seemed to sigh, but as quickly— as though deciding in an instant—he turned the gun to examine it there at arm's length himself, saying, "Strange what a hand can catch in the dark. And while"—he glanced over at her, the red and coarse features of what otherwise was his handsome face assuming a histrionic composure—"so much more was being offered."

The house had been changed since she was last in it as a girl, the kitchen shortened so that, almost like a stage set, it appeared as deep and complete from her perspective, or, say, from a window or a door, as it had been, whereas actually it had been adumbrated to less than half its original size. And Roisin could not keep her eyes from straying into the room in back of Rhines, which seemed like a shop or a work area, packed with machines and equipment. "Paddy who?" she asked.

Rhines glanced at his wristwatch as he lowered his hand and tossed the weapon, as though it were a thing of no apparent worth, on the kitchen table. "A friend."

Everything was new or at least recently constructed, neat, orderly, with the tang of fresh paint and turpentine and newly worked wood in the air. It was the ambience of her early childhood when her father's concern had spread—warm and secure and total—throughout the house. Gentle talents, his. And Rhines's—quiet—even to the acting "A comrade, you mean?"

Staring down at the gun, hands on his hips, Rhines nodded resignedly. "A comrade, Roisin." But, glancing up suddenly, he smiled the smile she had seen at the O'Keefe Center, the one that pierced the footlights, the darkness of the theatre, and that could—she now realized for the first time—disarm and win hearts on cue. "And what are you?"

She felt her head move back and her proud smile, the one that challenged, form bold knobs on her cheeks. "Me?" Why, I'm the woman who came here to love you, she wanted to say, but she could see now that he had been carrying things out, as though to leave. "A friend, of course. A *good* friend," she added.

But they heard a noise from the back, and they were again plunged into darkness. Roisin heard Rhines snatch up the gun from the table, while his other hand moved her behind him, into the other room.

"Seamus?" a low, labored voice asked quietly.

"Paddy," said Rhines, and as suddenly the lights were back on to reveal a small, dark man who was propping against the kitchen wall another, larger man. The second man's mouth was open, his breathing a troubled sigh, his eyes flickering white discs of sclerae as he kept pushing out with what appeared to be his only good arm, rocking the smaller man, grasping at—it seemed—the little consciousness that remained. The other arm lay limp by his side. As a knee buckled, he jerked it back up and blood gushed from the eyelets of his right blucher.

"The alter ego?" Rhines asked.

The smaller man's eyes—an unusual light china blue—moved beyond Rhines to Roisin, who recognized him as a customer from the North who maintained a safety deposit box at the bank. "Leave it to your man to pull the gun."

"Jock!" the other now said in his delirium. "Jock *Duncan.*"

"Give us a hand, now. He must weigh twenty stone, and me own—" Geer glanced down at his own shoulder, which only now Roisin saw was bloody as well. As she had in the eleven years she had spent as a nurse, she moved forward, but Rhines's arm stayed her.

"This isn't for you."

"And why not?"

"Because"—he paused, as though torn—"it's not, that's all. If it were just—"

"Ah, Jesus—give us a hand, Seamus. I'm fadin' now."

And in two steps Roisin had slid a shoulder under the larger man's good arm. As Rhines took the other, the man cried out in pain, and with their hands around his waist they directed him through the workroom, across the front hall, and into another room and onto a table there.

"First we'll get this off him," said Roisin, pulling off her fur coat and reaching for the man's greatcoat. "I'll cut the rest."

Again he cried out, but she eased his shoulders back onto the table, holding his large head. When she lifted his sodden legs, a dark stream of old blood splatted on the floor by her feet. She looked around.

The room was furnished like a surgery, right down to the table, lamps, sinks, and cabinets full of medical equipment and supplies. But everything seemed new or at least newer in style than what had been available during the period in which Rhines's father had done his doctoring. And then—if Roisin could remember rightly—the surgery had been in another room, farther down the hall. "I don't suppose a doctor comes with all of this?"

Rhines glanced at Geer, who was holding his arm and had eased himself onto a chair. His head was sagging; he would have to be back at his work in Belfast by morning, although for Carron there could be an excuse. "The tape, Paddy?"

Geer's curiously colored eyes opened once more. They were glazed and his speech was thick. "Destroyed it. The shots brought a guard. And then—"

"And the list?"

Geer's hand tried to slip inside his jacket but fell into his lap. His eyes closed, and he eased his head back against the wall.

"How many names?"

"Six, I believe," said Geer. "I really didn't have time . . ."

"That's good. It'll give us a bit of a choice."

To Roisin, Rhines then said, "No doctor, I'm afraid. Not until tomorrow. And not if—" we are to continue with the maximum potential for security and therefore success, he wanted to say, but Geer anticipated the thought.

"It's just a nick. Pop on a patch. I'll be right enough for the morning, and back in Belfast I can get somebody to give it a look."

Bravado? Rhines thought not. A strange little man was Geer, with his film collection and his history, but committed and resilient, Rhines judged. And if as J. Rheiner—the name by which Rhines was best known among his comrades—he had allowed every minor disruption to foil his plans, he would have accomplished nothing in his career. And this the capstone.

He glanced up at Roisin, who turned back to the wound. It seemed simple enough to her. Nothing broken, no major artery breached. A drain and some antibiotics and bed rest. "I'm no surgeon, I'll have you know, and it's been years, but—" In the operating theatres of several hospitals she had been left to close up many more serious injuries, and this appeared rather routine.

Geer slept, and only the sound of the scissors cutting his shirt from his shoulder—a regular clicking, like the wiper blades against the windscreen of his battered Fiat—brought it all back: Friday and the proposal and the showing of his film. They had gotten their yes and near dawn he had left with the woman—Anna, doubtless an alias—feigning because of the hour and the plan a near drunkenness that caused Carron to pull the Escort in close. Paternal in his regard. Shepherding them.

Woman. In her Clontarf flat, which looked out over a storm-tossed Dublin Bay, Geer had submitted to her as well and with little enthusiasm. "Come now, Paddy—give us a touch. I've been through this before, and it'll take your mind off things. And sure—who knows when we'll next have the chance? You or I."

Carron was across the street in the car park of a strand-side hotel, and Geer's job, which was as essential as Rhines's, required much less application. At clocked two-hour intervals the man grappled his bulk from the confinement of the Escort and sought a boozy solace in the bar.

But though she offered Geer the pliant angularity that in a woman he preferred, he could achieve no release and remained wakeful the night long, imagining every class of disaster until by Sunday, when he was to receive Rhines's call, his nerves were frayed. In Sach's Hotel on the Morehampton Road, they were, not far from Herbert Park House, having coffee and chat while Carron, perhaps beyond caring that he might be seen, lurched into that bar.

"Paddy Geer. Mister Paddy Geer of Belfast. You have a phone call."

Geer had searched through the sullen pub crowd who were trying to nurse truant spring from the bottom of a glass.

"We're on," said Rhines. "We called him right. It began at 8:47. Tried four other lines, he did. All to his home phone. All negated."

Turning to glance at the corner of the bar where Carron was brooding over his drink, playing the mirror game again, Geer felt at once relief and a profound regret over the many lives—his own, Rhines's, even that of the man Duncan, who was no better than a thief and a traitor—which would be transformed on the word of a phone call. Then there was Carron, who in spite of his brutal past had as much as befriended Geer or, at least, realized that the sinecure he had been given would have to be drawn out.

But more the lives of the others, who were utterly innocent of what they were intending. It was that loss, which would be inescapable, that now weighed on Geer most.

"And you're to take care, now," Rhines had continued over the phone. "Duncan'll know only too well what this means."

A kneecapping at best, thought Geer. A bullet in the back of the head, were it put to a vote.

"He'll be frightened and angry, you'll see." Along with the list this was, of course, what they had sought.

And yet Geer said nothing, momentarily confounded, his courage drowning in the murmur of the pub crowd, knowing how once it all began there could be no letup for him.

"Paddy?" Rhines asked.

Turning so he might be heard in Carron's corner of the bar, Geer called in to Anna in a lounge, "There's a bit of a bash on over by Herbert Park, wherever that is."

Several heads turned to him.

"Where by Herbert Park?"

"And how am I to know?"

Reaching for the phone, she shook her hair once to fit the receiver over her ear, her smile a gauntlet challenging any and all to match her acceptance of the moment and him, and Geer had wished fervently that he had allowed himself the pleasure of her easy grace. "Yes?" She listened. "Brilliant! Now—what's the address?"

But all had begun, and Geer, now mouthing "Gents," pointed to the men's room and headed off, neither turning in there nor looking back, knowing Carron's eyes—drunk as he was— would be on him.

Nor did Geer pause in the hotel lobby. As he had on one

other occasion, a year earlier in Donegal, he shoved open the front door and stepped out into the storm. Carron, the British-trained professional, former sergeant major SAS, would soon be on his heels. It was a gambit—the woman, the shill phone call, the announcement of another intention—to be expected, the guilt and paranoia of the drink in a way making Carron all the more vigilant and, Geer hoped, exploitable.

But he had overestimated the one and underestimated the other. And, more, he had not in reality understood the strength and the weakness of what they were intending. For with a gruff assertiveness that Geer should have pitied, knowing the man was doomed, Duncan was already waiting at the back gate of Herbert Park House.

"*Money,*" he demanded, the great dimpled arc of his jaw firming predatorially as he glared down on Geer, who was less than half his size, weight, or strength.

"Money *what?*" Geer asked, toying with him, turning to peer into the darkness behind him. Fear.

"You've *got* the money?"

"Oh—aye, Ah doo," said Geer, insisting upon their difference and wondering at his own anger. Were things predetermined? he asked himself. Had he been meant all along to be the man's judge, jury, and—in a way—executioner? "If you've got the list and our tape, Mr. Duncan."

"Money first." A hand came out, the other clutching under an arm the paper pouch he had been given earlier, as he had so many rugby balls on the playing field.

"Yehr fahncy, surr," replied Geer, reaching for the £1,600 that would have bought a squad of Duncans in Belfast. Duncan, he thought, formerly of the linen mill but having sold out for life here in the South. Duncan, with his political pretensions and his sports and his sports car and his sporting life style, outlined as gaiety and high times in the social columns of *Dublin* papers. That he, of all people, should, first, be the

94

beneficiary of such largesse and, second, prove himself false, seeped into Geer's world-weary consciousness, like acid on lead. "Though you should know we wouldna' shopped *you*."

The open palm shot out and snatched up Geer's lapels, lifting him off his feet, smacking the back of his head into the pebbly dash of the portal.

Geer's wallet dropped from his hands and Duncan kicked it through the open gate into the darkness of the shrubbery. "You guttersnipe. You wee Belfast bowsie—you'll not bait Jock Duncan. That tape I was playing home had nothing to do with you. You'll get this back"—he shook the pouch—"when I speak to your man, Rhciner, and not before."

In a tone that was low, tight, and curiously calm, Geer said, "Then you're a liar as well as a thief, Jock Duncan."

It was then that a revolver came up to pin Geer's head against the wall and another force struck them from the side, rasping Geer's face over the wall and knocking Duncan away. The gun went off—a roar that deafened him. It burnt his shoulder and the inside of his nose. It made the chambers of his head feel as if they'd been scorched and were charred. Then the pain set in and Geer felt himself falling.

Somebody—Carron, he hoped—was screaming, "Mooger. Yer a deid mahn mooger. De-id."

Yes, Carron. He was on top of Duncan, who threw him off, and as the gleaming barrel of the gun swung round through the driving rain, Geer kicked at Duncan's forearm. The flash blinded him, and he heard Carron cry out in pain.

He could remember next only the soft and repeated thumps and groans—kicks, they were—and when his vision cleared he saw Duncan crouching over Carron, who was down on his hands and knees struggling to get up. Every time Carron's legs tensed to pick himself up, the great ham of Duncan's thigh flexed and the top of his foot thumped up into Carron's ribs. It was a complex, hollow, but muffled sound, like a mattress being struck by a bat and followed by a wheezing cough. Yet Geer could now recall that Carron's eyes had been watchful even then, it being a scenario that he well knew.

Carron, who had been given the surveillance of Geer as a reward for atrocity. Carron, who in the three years they had been "together" had even grown somewhat familiar with him— knowing Geer knew, but also realizing that some distance, some semblance of pursued and pursuer, actor and witness, would have to be maintained. Yet Carron had twice sent a mechanic back for Geer when the old Fiat had broken down on the highway, and Geer had reciprocated by choosing, when he could, accommodations that might also free Carron from the cramp of the car. And only once before had he played upon the man's weakness, as a prelude. A test.

"Old man—you're one of them, aren't you?" Duncan was saying. "But you've not got it in you, so. Only two of you here"—his eyes flicked to Geer, who was struggling but could not feel his right arm to raise himself—"not three or four with half an army of weapons and a bomb or two."

And it was as if the suggestion that they were in fact united galvanized both of them. When the thigh flexed once more, the foot aimed at the face, Carron's good hand leapt out for Duncan's ankle, and Geer found himself on his feet. Head down, Geer drove the full weight of his short, compact body past the wrist with the revolver, which he grasped, and into Duncan's stomach.

Yet again the gun sounded, the force of the blast just enough to knock them both off their feet. They fell back into the shadows and the shrubs beyond the gate, the weapon jarring out of Duncan's hand, Geer's head again coming up against something hard.

When he turned back to the struggle, it was Carron who had Duncan's arm jacked up behind his back, riding him, driving him into the corner, where the wall formed a column for the gate. They struck the stuccoed brick with the full force of both of their bodies, a side of Duncan's face foremost. And then behind him Carron—seen from Geer's perspective below—seemed to disappear, as though the force that he now applied to Duncan's back required every atom of his being.

"Gud mahn wi' yer feet, aye now, lad," he heard Carron roar. "Pu'in' in the boot on an old—say it—*old*. Say it!"

"Old!" Duncan's large voice made his shriek all the more terrible, and something was pressing in on his body, making it jounce and bow inward, as if it would break on Geer, who now began to gather himself to try to crawl from under them.

"But ye're a moog, ya're. Saft soap. Any *mahn*—" Duncan's belt buckle grazed Geer's forehead, and the whine that the big man now uttered was despairing and pitiable, sounding suddenly like that of a despairing and defenseless child. Its message? That Duncan was made to appreciate the special terror of knowing that his life was over before it actually was, though he did not have to endure the torture long.

"Any *mahn*—" Carron thrust down and Geer heard the heartwood crack, like that of a noble, green tree snapping before it fell. And yet Duncan did not fall. Trunk broken, he jerked once, and a knee, buckling, nearly pinned Geer beneath him.

It was then that Carron—still holding Duncan's arms, a knee still firmly in Duncan's back—leaned past the other man's shoulder until he was eyeball to eyeball with the dead man. "Any *mahn* cood a' kicked me ta puddin', but you—? Na' you, lad. Na' fer all your size."

Hatless, both their large heads were running with the bitter rain, and it was as if the water now cleared Carron's vision, just as he weakened from his exertion and the loss of blood.

He blinked and moved his head away from Duncan's, as though to improve his focus. "Jock?" he asked in gentle surprise. "Is it Jock?" A pause, then an agonized "Ah—*noo*. It's no' Jock Duncan now, is it?"

But they both heard somebody shout at them now from near the building, and Geer dragged himself from under Duncan. And it was not what to do—for he well understood in detail what that was—but what to do first that threw Geer into a panic. His inexperience. He believed he would make further payments for it now.

The tape, it was foremost, and from the packet, which had fallen from Duncan's grasp nearly in front of him, he pulled the spool. A printout slid out and dropped back into the wetness. Geer snatched it up—six full names and histories? yes— and forced its stiff folds into a pocket of his jacket.

What next? The tape itself, which—thinking of extricating Carron, who had again fallen, and of the continuing project and Blount, Carron's master—Geer judged too cumbersome. Digging his fingers into the mud, he snatched up the tape, while the other hand pulled from inside his jacket the magnet, which he clapped onto its side and dropped. Would it suffice? He had been told so—by Rhines, which was recommendation enough.

His wallet. Jesus! Where had he been? There by the gate, of course—not having as yet been invited in, he thought wryly—and Duncan had kicked it. . . . Down on all fours, heedless of the pain that was now flaying his shoulder, Geer crabbed after it, his hands probing the bushes blindly, frantically, until he finally chanced on the rain-slick leather and stuffed it under his belt.

The torch light was getting closer, its beam boring a beige cone in the storm. He again heard a shout, ". . . out" or ". . . lout," and Carron, now drunk or delirious, saying, "Jock

Duncan. Killed him, I did. Jock. Played together . . ." though, given the difference in their ages, there had never been a chance of that.

The gun? Why? Duncan had brought that, but who else had touched it? He himself, he realized—briefly, enough to knock it loose—and Carron? Probably, he decided, his mind winding through the event furiously as he searched, but to no avail.

Carron himself. It was time now; the light was halfway down the walk and being played into the shadows. "Whoever yez are, yez got no business on these grounds. Get out of it, now. I've phoned the Guards. Hear me? The Guards is on their way."

Said Geer, bending to Carron, "George—we've got to get shut of this place. Listen, they're coming now. We've got to get out."

Carron's daze seemed to clear, and he looked up at Geer. "Because of you, I've killed Jock Duncan."

"Aye, George, but *you* killed him, and now I'll get you out of here. You're hurt. You need help."

Allowing Geer to take his arm, Carron staggered to his feet and then away from the corpse, which remained oddly upright, effigial and stalwart. They blundered through the shrubs and out the gate.

And it was only after Geer had gotten Carron into his battered Fiat and was across Dublin on the Malahide Road that he remembered Carron's hat. And his car, though that would have been hired and, given Carron's professionalism, under an alias. Prints? Aplenty, Geer feared: in the car, on the hat and the revolver and the magnet, but the words "down the line" came to him as they trekked slowly toward Monaghan, taking back roads to avoid sobriety patrols or the odd security check. And they would need but a few months.

Only once did Carron speak. Turning to Geer, he asked, "*George?* How do y'knoo mah name?"

It was the key question, but one to be answered in time.

Geer now opened his eyes. The woman, the nurse friend of Rhines, had returned to Carron, whose wound, Geer knew, was more serious. "What do you think?" he asked Rhines, a man whom Geer had sought out. It had had to be him, nobody else.

"That you were lucky. It's an omen."

"You believe in omens?"

Rhines smiled and shook his head. "There's no such thing as luck, only planning."

"But Carron?"

"We're covered. It'll just mean an extra step, and we'll only bind him the tighter for it. You just carry on." He paused, his quick brown eyes—as glossy and bright as paint; a man of moderate habits—assessing Geer, then fixing his gaze. "You'll make your work tomorrow?"

Geer questioned his body, which was riddled with pain. "I'll try."

Rhines nodded once. "You're the"—his smile was sudden, a burst of delight—"jaunty survivor. A bash, it was. Ballinamore, County Leitrim. Carron's details can then be put in place, and it'll explain the scrape. Remember, Anna will have taken the number plates and the tax stamp, and wiped down the car. It'll give us the lead we'll require." Standing above Geer, Rhines reached down and touched a finger to Geer's cheek. "What about the camera?"

"I'm right-shouldered, right-eyed. Planned it that way."

Said Rhines, "You're a rare, brave man, Paddy Geer, and you're to keep yourself whole."

Thought Geer, For in a few weeks I'll be in bits.

Hearing a noise four hours later from below them in the kitchen, Roisin Johnston raised her head from the crook of Rhines's shoulder, where she was feeling a greater general sense of well-being than she had in years. "It's Paddy," said Rhines. "Today of all days, they'd miss him most."

They listened while Geer stopped at the note Rhines had left him with the circular tin of film he had found on the bloody floor of the Fiat. It said, "I thought we needed this for 'insurance'?" It was the film that had been shown in the cellar of the pub, their "proposal," as it were.

Geer was exhausted, his body a universe of dull, throbbing pain. Just getting himself out of the bed and down to the kitchen had made him break into a foul, sick sweat. Tucking the film under his good arm, he wondered when again, if ever, he would complete a work of its length or . . . quality. Yes, he affirmed, it had more than done its job. It *was* good. But the reality at which it pointed seemed impossible to him as he passed down the length of the bread van and opened the tall gates of Rhines's back garden.

A barrage of wind-driven snow, whipping down the alley, staggered him. It needled the scrape on his face and turned the sweat to a frigid chill. But on the front seat of the Fiat Geer found a large Thermos of hot, sweet coffee and a foil-wrapped sandwich crammed full of rashers, his favorite.

Details. Could they know too much? Biting into the sandwich, Geer thought not. And, then, in a thorough understanding of the possibilities of every variable lay options and the cover with which all could be concealed and thereby justified.

6

McGarr awoke at first light, which was all the day would see of the sun. It was spread in a blaze of scarlet to the east, like a reward for the wakeful that slowly winked out. He watched as a juggernaut of cloud, cold as steel shot, wheeled inexorably across the horizon. A wintry gloom then fell over the island, and the thin rain again turned to snow.

One eye was fully open now and, having pulled off the covers, he waited for the cold air from the two open windows to chill his body so that he would be forced to seek the glow from the Aga solid-fuel range in the kitchen. There he slid back the draft, put on the kettle, and looked out into his garden. For whole minutes he stood there in his dressing gown, shifting from bare foot to bare foot, staring wide-eyed and unblinking out the window and thinking no thoughts.

It was a procedure that McGarr observed most days of the week and that pleased him greatly. Why? He did not care to know, and once in a while at his office, when a break in the rush of detail permitted him the liberty, he tried to recapture the ——— of those moments, but it was never the same.

Only gradually did he become aware of the fact that his wife, Noreen, had joined him whole minutes earlier, glancing from the window, to him, to the teapot, which had begun to moan and ping before initiating its low whistle.

Placing a hand under her copper-colored curls, which she tossed back, she asked, "Is it this that you do down here every morning?" She was a trim, well-formed woman with bottle-green eyes that in the pale light now assumed the smoky, obdurate aspect of dark jade. The light also made her features, which were regular nearly to a fault, seem severe and assessing.

Twenty years McGarr's junior, she had since their marriage nine years before been moved to observe and question him closely at just at those moments when he was being most unself-consciously himself. It was as though she feared that then he became somebody she either did not or could not know, and the possibility, far from relieving her of the burden of further thought, as it did McGarr, rather frightened her. Apart from the intrusion, however, her concern pleased him. At the times when she appealed to him most, he thought of her as rosy and diminutive but strong, like somebody from a better, more finely made race.

"What—?" Her movements quick and birdlike, she darted her chin toward the window and then back at him. "What do you see out there?" When McGarr's eyes—a stormier gray than the leaden sky—only wheeled slowly toward her and then back to the window, she continued, "Is it the garden? Are you worried about that?" It was another aspect of his life that he believed she resented though she had never said so: the hours he lavished on its care, summer and winter; the magazines and books that he read on compost and mulch and tilling. Soon now, whenever the weather broke, the garden would absorb all his free time, and she would feel both compelled to, and guilty that she did not, help him more. Already the cellar was filled with the heady funk of flower and vegetable shoots growing under hothouse lights.

"Or is it the weather?" she now demanded. "Certainly it can't be the weather." She cocked her head jauntily, now realizing she was running on. "If you let the weather bother you here"—she meant Dublin and Ireland—"why, Janie, you'd fly off your knob."

The pot had begun to howl, and she turned to it. But McGarr had already reached back with his right hand and placed it on a trivet. He then took one of her hands in his and pulled her to his side, and together they looked out at ——— until she said, "Me feet, Peter—they're freezin', and I've got more to do than commune with a blasted back garden." Noreen managed her family's picture gallery in Dawson Street.

He released her hand, and though the spell was broken he remained there until he noticed that the lights were on in the kitchen of the house next door. There the Rabbi Viner's children would be breakfasting for their long bus ride out to their school in Belfield.

School. The first organizational ritual, with regular hours, lessons, and evaluations. And then grades, promotions, distinctions, or dismissals. Even from afar, McGarr's Dublin Castle office, with its old brick walls, cobblestone courtyards, and tall windows—appearing like an array of white, crossed flags through the gloom—resembled the Victorian piles that had been the schools of his childhood. With the difference (thought McGarr later, as he climbed the Castle stairs) that here either he was master or the masters had conveniently absented themselves to Phoenix Park, the site of Garda Siochana headquarters, or to Leinster House and the Dail Eireann.

The state. Passing down a worn aisle knobbed with battered desks toward his cubicle, which was cramped into a corner with a dim window, McGarr considered the futility of serving a construct so imperfect that the only liberty it allowed was that of error on every level. Stooping to pick up a photocopy of a journal entry from an investigation that was—he squinted down at the caption—nearly two years old, he despaired of ever fulfilling the expectations of his post. "At about 1:15 A.M. on the night of 21 November in Henry Street . . ." the report began, and, given the lapse of time and the variables—in the evidence, the statements of the witnesses, the observations of some two dozen investigators and the opinions of a like number of legal officials, to say nothing of a jury and the jackals of the press—were anything more than approximations possible? And how to pose such doubt (almost always now compounded by the accused himself: "Ach—at the time he was not himself at all, Your Worship. I have here affidavits from three psychiatrists stating that . . .") against the certainty in fact that the person in the dock either did or did not commit the crime? Why, with the massive structure of the police and their bureaucracy and the courts and their show of due process, fairness, and legality, of course.

Was McGarr, then, merely another but a more duplicit sort of charlatan? There were those who thought so, he realized, as he slid the document back on the desk from which, he guessed, it had fallen. And there he was himself, front page and center on a newspaper there: his eyes closed, his face a hardly discernible, overexposed oval capped by the snow-laced brim of his bowler. "JOCK SLAIN," the headline said. Some further scurrility sketched his presence at Herbert Park House. Feeling as bleak as the day, McGarr clutched his bowler under his arm and passed through the office into his cubicle.

"Bad form today?" he heard somebody ask.

In a stagy voice that was overloud, McKeon, the desk sergeant, replied, "Not a bit of it. That's his bald, chubby-cheeked Buddha-like stare. Late night, is all. He's giving us a dose of *elan*—the mistake of litership."

Somebody began chuckling. Another laughed.

In McGarr's cubicle O'Shaughnessy was seated by the side of the desk, a newspaper spread over his lap. Tall and broad-shouldered, he was today wearing a trilby, and although McGarr could not see his eyes, he knew O'Shaughnessy did not look up.

Ritual. Could McGarr's real commission—pursuit, arrest, trial when lucky; or simply pursuit—be no more than that? A process, an ineluctable manipulation, a *trottier* that wound back on itself?

Sitting at the desk, he plunged his hands in his trouser pockets and ignored the work schedule and assignment sheets on the blotter. Five seconds. Ten. He'd give her a minute before he got up himself, and then—?

A veritable tent of blue uniform suddenly filled the doorway. Tacked with silver buttons and cinched with a tie, the mass bent slightly so that the shoulder—which led to the arm, in the fist of which a mug of coffee was obscured—might negotiate the jamb, and then a face ringed with bright red hair appeared. It was a pretty face in silhouette, but as it turned to McGarr it revealed a jaw more like a mandible, a forehead wide as a thigh, two patches bright as roses on the knobs of each cheek, and—alas—two small, suspicious dark eyes that narrowed down on him appraisingly.

"Your caffee, sorrh," said Ban Gharda Bresnahan, who was the most recent addition to McGarr's staff and had objected to fetching him coffee as a sexist task. Even after it had been explained that perhaps as many as half of the men on the staff had gone for coffee in their time, Bresnahan had performed the service reluctantly until she realized the access it gave her to McGarr and his several moods. By them, expectations—for the day's duties; for the progress of an investigation—could sometimes be gauged, and her mystagogic status in that regard was now well established.

She set the cup in front of McGarr and stepped back.

McGarr's eyes cleared and he focused on the vapors rising from the brim—Bewley's Blend, steam-brewed, no milk, no sugar. No additions, *yet*.

She was waiting for the hand to fall to the lowest drawer, left side, of the desk, so that, when the question was asked "Did he go for it?" she might nod knowingly. "Bad?" the questioning would continue. Canting the great red riot of her head, the hair of which was thicker and more unmanageable than electrical wire, she might say, "Oi've seen him whorris, so I have," or, "Shockin'. *Desperate*, the mood that he's in. He's like a bear with a sore head," which was not so vile a mood as that which caused her only to take her place at her desk and fold her hands under the globes of her breasts, as though praying. At such times office conversation was muted and intermittent, and paperwork became a refuge for the wise. McGarr's more sanguine moments concerned her less; in her native Kerry she had early been made to appreciate the tooth of the saw concerning bad news.

"Bresnahan?" McGarr now asked without looking up from the cup.

"Ah, nuttin', sir—I was just t'inkin', foin day."

Only McGarr's eyes moved to the window, which was a scrub of charcoal streaked with snow. They returned to the coffee.

"I mean, fine day for winter." The floor groaned uncomfortably under her weight. In the palm of one hand she was kneading the mighty fist of the other. It was supposed to be spring.

"A Monday," she blundered on.

O'Shaughnessy shook out a crease in his paper. He sighed and turned a page.

Out in the office two phones began ringing at once. In mere minutes McGarr's cubicle would be filled with the key members of his staff, and only moments later—it would seem—

the morning would be gone. Monday was the busiest day of their week.

"Well," she said, "I'll be going now." When McGarr's pale-gray eyes drifted up to hers, she added hurriedly, "I mean, out to me desk. You know—the job." Her mouth was unfortunately small, her lips rosebud and definite. Scanning McGarr's expressionless face, she pursed them and, lowering her head, strode purposefully toward the door. But there she stopped and glanced back.

With a smack O'Shaughnessy's paper came down on his thighs. A long arm reached behind him and opened the bottom left drawer of McGarr's desk. It removed a liter bottle of Hogan's Own, from which the cork sang like a drone. Holding the bottle to the lip of the coffee cup, he glanced at McGarr.

McGarr blinked.

O'Shaughnessy poured a dollop, glanced up again, and poured some more. He paused, then filled the cup to its brim, and turned to Bresnahan as though to say, Satisfied now? When she had left, he added some to his own teacup and replaced the cork and the bottle in the drawer.

Shortly afterward, the men filed in, six of them from the staff, seven counting Colm Walsh, the boy who had been used by the Technical Bureau in the Duncan case. As the most recent investigation, it would be dealt with first; eleven others would be discussed. McGarr reached for the coffee.

Ward, who would supervise the Duncan investigation, began speaking, leaning against one of the walls and looking down at his notes. The others had taken up what were standard positions—resting on cabinets, against the edge of the table, and so forth—depending on rank and seniority. At the broad window sill, McKeon moved over to make room for O'Shaughnessy, who had offered the boy, their guest, his chair.

"John Wesley Walter Duncan. Born 22 July 1943. Derry. Son of the son of a linen manufacturer. When Duncan was still in his teens, the father sold out what was left of the business and invested heavily in the Ulster Trust Bank."

McGarr blinked. It was one of the banks that had combined to form the consortium now known as the Consolidated Irish Bank.

"Green Tory," Ward went on, meaning conservative but Irish Nationalist in political perspective. "The father." Although small and dark, with the finely chiseled features and the glossy black hair of the Spanish-Irish, Ward had in many ways modeled himself on his fellow Galwegian O'Shaughnessy. His suit, which was black wool pinstriped a delicate blue, had been cut in Italy. The older man looked on approvingly. "Not so the son, at least at university.

"UCD." Ward meant University College, Dublin, which for many years had been the Dublin-area Catholic university, most Protestants attending Trinity. "Joined NICRA"—he pronounced the acronym for the Northern Ireland Civil Rights Association as though it were a word—"at its inception, back in '64. Got t'umped in the forward lines of that movement, as well as in the scrum for Northern Ireland. Began playing for Ireland in '67. It was then that the father sold out and the Duncans removed themselves here to Dublin. Howth. One of the ultramodern houses on the cliff face near Gaskin's Leap.

"Could have been something of a student in mat's." It was the Irish contraction for mathematics. "But there was the sports and"—Ward lowered his head, as if to consult his notes—"women, it seems."

"Familiar turf here," McKeon whispered to O'Shaughnessy, winking; Ward's own interest in the opposite sex was more than simply passing. "Though he needn't go any further, our young Lothario."

Ward had stopped speaking, though he did not look up from his notes. It was yet another ritual—McKeon the office shut-in, who in his own life had experienced several tragedies, venting his spleen. After a while, Greaves said, "All right, Bernie—who done it?"

"Why, Lady Ballinasloe, of course," he said, pronouncing the name of the Galway town slowly. "The grip on her! Thigh-balled him to death, she did, after he 'shot' her with his gun."

"Bit of a punter yourself, Hughie, I gather."

There were chuckles, but no laughs, and McGarr reached for his cup. The hot potion scorched down his throat, then diffused its warmth to his chest. He gently swirled his neck on his shoulders. He was feeling somewhat better now. He remembered to blink.

Said Ward, "The bank was a natural for him—the father, the mat's. Computers were just being introduced, and IBM flew him out to the States to acquaint him with their larger machines. Took to it, he did. And with the sports that continued, and him in all the papers. Well"—Ward paused and glanced at McGarr, as though to speak to him alone—"on a social level he could not have asked for more."

Sang McKeon, "Come back, Jocko Duncan, to Ballyjames-duff, / The women out here they all give out the—"

O'Shaughnessy shifted his feet and fixed McKeon with a baleful gaze.

"—*guff*, for Jesus' sake. What did *you* think I was going to say—'fluff'?"

But they were down to business, and Ward continued. "Town-house apartment. Ultramodern. Milltown. Eight thousand, five hundred quid per annum all found. Lotus sports car found in the company car park behind Herbert Park House. Rumors of an illegitimate daughter, affairs, betrothals, trysts, jealousies, hatreds—all the *stuff*"—Ward glanced at Mc-

Keon—"that's pumped up in a certain class of paper. But nothing definite, except that the company that Jock Duncan kept was often international and pricey, and even on a salary of forty-two thousand he must have been hard pressed to maintain good form with the ladies of Nice/Cannes"—pronounced "nice cans"—"France." Ward did not smile.

"Then, two years ago, Duncan became Neil Blaney's secretary. Thick with certain of them, he was. Played on the 'Libertarians' with the Taoiseach's son and with Minister for Justice Suilly himself.

"Consolidated jumped at the chance of having yet another Dail connection." Ward then mentioned several other Consolidated "employees" who were either T.D.s or serving the Dail in other capacities. "And the salary, of course, continued." Consolidated was the largest bank in the country, and Suilly's position with the "Libertarians"—McGarr seemed to recall—was, like Duncan's with Blaney, honorary alone. Scrum half. Third string.

"The weapon, the revolver, is his. Part of a pair, holsters and all, that were given him on one of his American jaunts. A cowboy hat. Boots." Ward touched a finger to a dark eyebrow, which had arched, as though trying to ease it down. "Though two other people touched it. The gun. The Technical Bureau is still working on them, and the others on the magnet that was wedded to the side of the magnetic tape. Same with the P&T van, though whoever drove it there and set up the two devices in the culvert wore gloves.

"No report of a gunshot wound having been treated within the Twenty-six Counties," by which Ward meant the Republic.

"Then"—he flipped a page in his notebook—"all cars in the area have been matched with their owners but three, two of them rentals. One is from a Dublin agency—and we

111

should have the name of the person who rented it by noon—
and the other from Belfast. Again we've put in a request. Nothing yet.

"But it's the third car that's ours, I believe. An '84 Escort,
gray. High-performance engine. No number plates, no tax
stamp. Wiped down, and thoroughly, by somebody who knew
how. Dome-light lens hood and bulb found in the glove box
and also clean. Seat back as far as it can go. It was only this
morning that we found it parked behind the Sachs hotel. The
thought was that it was a demo or had just been purchased
by one of Sachs staff or had been left there by some of the
nearby sales agencies that had run out of room. But there's
nineteen-hundred-plus miles on the odometer, and no agency
in the country seems to know where it might have come from.
It's not on the stolen list, not here at least. In addition to
querying Ford, we've wired it north as well. The hat, as we
know, was purchased in Belfast."

Somebody swore. Relations with the RUC were not at their
best, and any noncompliance would effectively eliminate that
aspect of the investigation. As well, the Northern involvement
suggested the possibility that an unlawful organization might
be involved, which was the jurisdiction of Special Branch.

"Here"—Ward's hand touched a small stack of documents
on the table, against which he was leaning—"are statements
from the Herbert Park security guard, Duncan's female assistant, the woman we found at his Milltown address, and
from a brother, next of kin. Whatever he was doing on that
computer, which—I think we can assume—led to his death,
he kept to himself.

"Which brings us to the tape"—Ward pointed to the tagged,
clear plastic bag on McGarr's desk—"and Mr. Walsh here,
who has some thoughts on the matter and the two gadgets in
the culvert."

112

McGarr's eyes moved up from the rim of the coffee cup and considered the boy, who now blushed—his clear skin and baby face that had yet to feel the scrape of a razor; the worn woolen jacket; the scarf with his college colors. Walsh was uncomfortable seated there, and McGarr, who had a budget to consider, wondered how useful he would be if they required more from him. What the prosecutors in the Central Criminal Court required was the proper sort of expert witness, and Walsh was obviously too young to convince.

Said McGarr, "Before we begin—let's not trouble Mr. Walsh unduly. He was kind enough to come here this morning, but we all know this might go on for weeks."

Some looked away. Weeks? It might go on for years.

"Who do we have who knows something about computers?"

Feet were rearranged. Computers aided their investigations daily, but in spite of free instruction, incentives, and an increased chance of advancement, not one of them knew why.

McGarr waited, hating the implied accusation and the moments wasted.

Finally McKeon spoke up. "Well—apart from Rut'ie, Chief—"

"Who?" McGarr asked.

"Bresnahan," several of the others said in a low, dismissive chorus. It was not just that she was their only woman and seldom wrong, but that she was *such* a woman—not pretty, not chic, not chirpy, and sometimes (like themselves) not even pleasant. Then, her youth, her reserves of energy, her rude country ambition, and her commanding physical presence rather intimidated most of them. And when she was right, she made them feel it, though she said nothing.

"Then it's Bresnahan," said McGarr. "Would somebody please bring her in?"

When she filled the doorway her eyes were wary, her expression suspicious. She had never before been asked to join McGarr's inner circle. "Chief?"

McGarr reached for his cup and stood. Indicating his seat, he said, "The Duncan case. The computer tape?"

Always current, she nodded.

"I'd like you to hear this." Turning, McGarr stepped toward the window ledge, which McKeon now abandoned for elbow room on the file cabinet. Delaney then moved to a spot along the wall, displacing another, who assumed a lesser position, until the bumping procedure was completed and Ward, the least senior after Bresnahan, found himself standing near the door.

There Bresnahan had not moved.

"Well, sit down, Rut'ie, we're waiting," said McKeon, her immediate superior. Intimidated by her personally, he always treated her gruffly when with others.

She glanced around the cubicle at the standing men, the seated boy, and the desk and its empty chair, which was obviously too small for her.

Said McGarr, realizing that it was wrong even before it was uttered, "Something wrong with the chair, Bresnahan?"

It was a painful moment. Blood rushed to her face. Her step faltered as she moved forward through a palpably studied silence. "No indeed, sorrh, there is not." As though having braced for her, the seat itself first accepted her hunkering bulk, only to yield an unlovely, disquieting creak when she settled herself fully. She raised the broad blue hams of her forearms. Her elbows came down on the blotter. She twined her fingers and lowered her head, ostensibly to listen, though the position looked more like prayer.

Said Walsh, "You asked me for an opinion, and I'll give it, since anything else would require long lab work with the tape and a pass at an IBM-360, either in Herbert Park House or

114

some place else. But I'm after thinking that a key element within the tape itself is similar to what we found in the external devices in the culvert—security."

Walsh removed a small notebook from an interior pocket of his jacket and flipped it open. "With Chief Super Mc-Anulty"—he paused slightly—"I examined the tape roughly from two A.M. to half-six or so"—his eyes met McGarr's—"this morning.

"We discovered first that the tape is exotic. By that I mean it's foreign to the Consolidated Irish operation at Herbert Park House. An imported product and American made, the reel *and* the recording tape. Consolidated's own tapes are discount items, Hong Kong mock-ups of the IBM product. It was a Duncan innovation to cut costs. I work there myself from time to time, as a consultant."

Standing at the window, McGarr had turned his back to the gathering. He raised the cup to his lips, tasting only as much as would agreeably and effectively get him through the long, detail-laden morning. Duncan—he wondered what Walsh's opinion had been of the man professionally.

"This tape, then, came from outside."

"The country?" Ward asked.

"Perhaps. Perhaps not. The point I'm making is that Mr. Duncan must have been given the tape for processing. As I said, I know the operation out there, and Sunday evening would have been perfect—the bulk of the previous week's work is by then completed, there's hardly anybody about, and Mr. Duncan had, as you saw, a terminal in his office. At one time he looked after things there, and who was to know? Even if they did, who was to say anything and to who? And with the rugby"—Walsh paused, reached for a word—"*ruse?* Well—I know for a fact that Consolidated Irish contributes to several rugby teams. And had it been discovered that the director of computer operations was spending a few hours each week assessing his team's chances during slack time, I don't believe much would have been said.

"But"—Walsh's brow knitted and he looked up from his notes—"to what purpose? To be better able to lay down a few bob on a test match? I doubt it. The racecourse punters have tried computers with limited success. Too many variables—say, a dozen horses and a dozen riders on varying tracks in varying conditions. But rugby? There are thirty different human beings on the pitch with thirty different sets of physical characteristics, in varying degrees of physical conditioning, moods, hormonal cycles, astrological signs—it could go on and on. And, then, each group of fifteen must work together as a unit, and how would one gauge the relative effectiveness of such an integration? In my opinion, Duncan's personal assessment of a team's chances would have been more valuable than any computer projection.

"By processing"—Walsh's eyes rose to Bresnahan's, only to move away quickly, dismissively—"I mean that whoever delivered the tape to Mr. Duncan had a specific problem that they wanted solved. But they were so concerned about the security of the information on the tape and so sophisticated in the"—Walsh spread his hands and twisted his head, admiringly—"creation and application of the electronics equipment that we saw in the culvert, that even for the relatively short period of time that Duncan was to have the tape, he was not trusted with it. Conclusions? Several:

"First—that person or persons did not possess an IBM-360, which is an enormously expensive and therefore not common machine. Banks, governments, building societies can afford such equipment, but few smaller groups or individuals. Why, then, store information on such a system? Again, security. All organizations, businesses, research groups, and so forth require records. Show me one that doesn't and I'll show you one not complex enough to survive in a modern society. Customers, billing, profits and losses, the names of employees—everything that formerly went down on paper is better stored, retrieved, sorted, and arranged by a computer. The cheapest and easiest method of computer storage and retrieval is the computer disc, but it's universal. There must be two dozen brands and literally thousands of computers using them right here in Dublin alone.

"I'm going to wing it here, but say, for instance, you had some information that was most private and which you found yourself referring to only seldom. Since there are few IBM-360s, putting your files on a tape that could be loaded only on a 360 would alone afford you some measure of security protection. If the tape were lost or stolen, it would be good only to somebody who had the use of a similar machine.

"Again"—Walsh paused and ran his hand through the waves of his deep-brown hair—"I'm convinced that what was found in the culvert would have been merely the final link in the security net that was devised for the use—Duncan's use—of that tape. I don't know what the tape contained. I don't even want to guess, but I would be willing to bet my"—Walsh looked around—"my jacket"—he grasped the lapels of his tattered coat—"that whoever programmed that tape wrote in a number of traps—codes—to prevent its being copied. Those codes would have been complex and multiform. Not a line or two or ten, but, rather, a security screen that pervaded and subtly protected parts of the program. If a copy were attempted without 'debugging'—locating and changing the codes—the tape would effectively destroy itself by having had programmed into it a safeguard which would write meaningless patterns of numbers over its information."

His jacket indeed. In a corner of the window, which with the storm outside had become a mirror, McGarr watched Walsh's head cant, as though signaling his uncertainty of what he was about to say. And McGarr considered the impossibility

117

of attracting into the Garda the young, incisive minds that could keep abreast of the breaking technological revolution and meet whatever challenges policing that new world might pose. Somehow, he feared, the zeal of the Bresnahans of the country would just not be enough, but he could not blame Walsh. In not a few years Walsh's lapels would be worth McGarr's monthly salary, and his was a knowledge the Garda could not afford.

"One could, of course, crack the code, examine the instruction lines, override and bypass the safeguards, but that would take time and patience. And care. In debugging a code, you're actually changing it—deleting the line of code you don't want and depositing other instructions in its place, just to load it and take a copy. And, then, a truly sophisticated screen would include a counter that would record the number of times it had been 'booted' or loaded onto the computer. If more than, say, once, it too could be made to activate a process that would destroy the information on the tape, but it would destroy the tape as well.

"And finally—as I believe happened here—if Mr. Duncan believed he was being watched or followed and could not take an actual physical copy out of the building, he might have tried to employ a modem to relay the information to some other, more accessible computer that would copy the tape for future reference. I believe such a system was found in Mr. Duncan's apartment?"

Ward nodded.

Said Walsh, "The ideal counter-ploy would be to have had a signal—bits scattered here and there throughout the tape—which would alert yet another computer, operated by the owner of the tape, monitoring lines in and out of Herbert Park House while the tape was in use. Any voice conversation other tape or disc relay would go through unpre-empted, but once the defensive computer 'heard' the tape's security code, it would activate the jammer and negate the information being forwarded over the phone. In this case all lines in and out of Herbert Park House were covered. They were taking no chances."

"But where, then, was the 'defensive' computer?" Ward asked.

"Wherever the radio signal was being sent." Walsh glanced down at his notes. "North, northwest. Range about eighty miles at the outside, unless whoever it was—is—has a large and visible antenna, which is, of course, against the law." Turning his head to the wall, Walsh allowed himself a slight smile before flipping a page of his notebook. He then said, "Mr. Duncan devoted nine Sundays in the last year and a half to the 'Rugby Project.' That's according to the Consolidated Irish computer log. What other time he might have spent on it, what other safeguards were built into the tape, and what it might have taken him to eliminate them—and obviously he was not successful—"

McGarr looked for a second smile but was pleased not to see one.

"—I can only guess. And why? What the tape might have contained?" He closed the notepad. "I don't know. I don't think anybody ever will. The magnet that was placed against it was strong, some alloy that is super-ferromagnetic, and meant to destroy it."

"But"—said Bresnahan, her usually purposeful voice coming out as a hoarse whisper—"but"—she managed in a more audible tone—"isn't that usually done by running the tape past an electromagnetic head?"

Walsh nodded. "Indeed. But it appears that the murderer had neither the time nor the means."

The silence was deafening; some of the men traded glances. Color again rose to Bresnahan's cheeks, and her fingers, which were still twined, grew white.

Said McGarr to the window—below him in Dame Street lighted buses, ferrying commuters into the city, were passing in convoys, like liners through fog on an uncharted sea—"But the magnet—it destroyed the tape?"

"I don't know," said Walsh. "I assume so. It seems to have been designed to that purpose by those who would know. Something might remain, but, of course, the 'language' would have to be determined, and the many checks, which Mr. Duncan obviously did not find, overcome. And now, with a garbled tape? It would be almost impossible."

"Which means some might remain?" McGarr pressed.

"I don't know without checking. And—" It was plain Walsh himself was not interested in such a task, and Bresnahan could not decide if by requiring her presence in the office McGarr was asking her to give the tape a go.

Buddha-like—it was McKeon's observation about McGarr and said in jest, but the aptness of the remark now struck her: him with his banter that sometimes was not play, the whiskey in the morning, the long stares—gray-eyed and glacial—looking through you or out the window. Whole days, he spent. Like now.

It was over, the discussion of the Duncan affair, and as McKeon checked his short list and began speaking of what they had new on the Phoenix Park slaying, Bresnahan ventured to rise from the desk, wondering if anything would be said.

Nothing. He was still standing there: back to them, hands in his pockets, his face turned toward the glass, which was as dark as slate. She began to reach for the plastic sack that contained the computer tape, thought better of it, and again glanced toward McGarr, who nodded once. Only then did she see that he was watching her reflection in the pane.

In a way thrilled that he would trust her with it—and in the Duncan murder, which had made and would continue

120

to make the front pages of papers the country over—she picked it up and walked as softly as she could out of the cubicle, the blasted old boards squealing under her feet. What had that little gurrier Walsh said, "almost impossible"? She—Ruth Brigid Honora Ann Bresnahan—would see, so she would.

The hours passed, and McGarr, sipping patiently at his coffee, endured the litany of crime only partially revealed. A Tinker (now known as a Traveler) child dropped for the winter in Dublin to live by her wits to "harden her," or so said the man claiming to be her father, though McGarr had his doubts. Age ten. A pretty thing by the facial photograph—wild, unlikely blue eyes, and curls the color of sun-dried hay. There were dozens of them the city over, wrapped like aborigines in filthy blankets, greatcoats quilted with newspapers, begging on street corners, sleeping over steam pipes in alleys, relieving tourists of their billfolds, and—McGarr did not doubt—satisfying the untoward desires of any citydweller with the money and courage to brave their dirt and lice and the others like them who predictably fell on the mark when he was least vigilant. This one, however—McGarr lifted his cup—had been gored, garroted, trussed in a burlap bag, and tossed, like a dead kitten, into a canal. No leads, other than the list of the "bent" that the staff had assiduously developed over the years.

Computers again—they'd match the victim's age, sex, physical characteristics to the "preferences" of the *citizens* in the file. Pity, he thought, the machine could not conduct interrogations.

Then came the murder of a dowager in Sligo; a Belgian businessman in Wexford; a young fellow whose bones were exhumed beneath a ton of lime on a farm in West Cork. Throughout it all McGarr merely maintained his vigil at the window, his contempt for the written record such that he had compartmentalized each crime in his mind. As new information was brought forward, he added the details to those funds of knowledge, which, in some cases, were more than simply extensive. Every so often he might ask a question or make a suggestion, but he had been known to say little or nothing about certain matters for whole weeks.

In such a way—after all the others save O'Shaughnessy had left the office—he returned to the first and most recently initiated investigation. Duncan: autopsy not in, of course, but the break in the lower spine, the way he had been shoved up into the wall. A big man. Huge. Powerful. It troubled McGarr— how *that* had been accomplished. One man? Two? In what way, by what sort of manipulation?

Duncan's acquaintances would have to be questioned, along with the personnel at the bank. Ward. The computer tape. Bresnahan. The equipment in the culvert. McAnulty's people would still be going over that, but there was an intimation that had occurred to McGarr twice and was again nagging him: when Ward was speaking and from Walsh.

Walsh. McGarr remembered him down in the culvert, the bright beams of the Technical Bureau lamps making his shock of rich brown hair iridescent. Why, of all the details, was he remembering that now?

The stanchion. The aerial: north, northwest. Range, eighty miles.

McGarr turned to the desk, beside which O'Shaughnessy was again sitting, reading yet another newspaper. Ritual. McGarr sat, reached for the bottom left drawer and the bottle, filled both cups, then removed a slim, worn notebook from the center drawer. After spreading it on the blotter, he lifted the telephone. One forty-four P. M. It was nearly three o'clock before McGarr had worked through his list of inspectors, barracks sergeants, and the several uniformed superintendents

within the eighty-mile radius on a north-by-northwest axis.
An electronics expert. The P&T van.

Said O'Shaughnessy, "Try Art Dromgoole in Monaghan.
Retired now, but if ever a man had an ear to the ground it
was—*is*—he."

Ah, yes, thought McGarr. Dromgoole. Retired for at least
a decade but on last report still sound. Some of McGarr's own
people—his uncle Mick and now his cousin Terence and Terence's wife, Maire—lived on a farm a few miles to the west.
It would mean some chat, of course, but worth the effort,
pensioners being left with little but gossip.

Dromgoole was out; this was O'Shaughnessy's sole contri-
bution to the day's proceedings.

7

$\mathbf{R}$hines passed the morning and much of the noon hour before the screen of the VDT in the workroom of his house in Monaghan, checking over and over again the details of what they intended.

Any decent plan of this sort, he believed, required at least three layers: what ostensibly happened; what "really" happened; and what, in fact, had been made to happen, how and by whom. Like a pearl, Rhines would permit the first layer to be peeled back slowly to reveal a more luminous truth below. The hope was that those whose duty it would become to know and explain the event would be satisfied with that, but it was Rhines's concern to make certain that any glint of a deeper truth remained in the nebulous realm of conjecture and surmise; rumors, scurrilous reports, banner headlines in the least responsible journals of the tabloid press. That and no more.

He thought of the tragedy in Dallas so many years before, and how, like a house of cards, the elements in that event had been made to implode in such a way that the third layer now would never be known.

But it was the first layer (or, rather, the second skin of the first layer; the thought made Rhines smile) that concerned

him now. Combining the six names that Duncan had extracted
from the tape at Herbert Park House with other information,
which Geer had painstakingly assembled over (Rhines could
only guess) a dozen years, he had devised a program that
would, he hoped, help him make his choice: physical attri-
butes, background, history of service, but most especially
their needs.

Hearing the click of precise heels approaching the door,
Rhines tapped a command that darkened the screen and
another that raised the level of the indirect lighting in the
room.

A rap. Once. Twice.

Rhines paused, if only to reinforce the idea that he was
never to be disturbed abruptly. "Yes, Roisin?"

"Seamus—he's much improved. I can tell, though he's still
said nothing. He's—"

He heard her hand fall to the knob.

"May I come in?"

"Of course."

The door opened slightly, and her face—eyes searching the
nearly empty room—appeared from behind the door. On seeing
him, she smiled. "Perhaps it's time to speak to him. I must
get back, I'm already late. The bank."

Good cover, Rhines thought. The best. If, later, things went
awry and it all came out, she could claim coincidence: Rhines,
the old friend and (he tilted his own head and returned her
smile) lover, and Geer, the customer.

He nodded assuredly. Histrionics. How he hated resorting
to that with her, but the less she knew the better. It was
plain, however, that she would have to be told more, if—

"Roisin—I've been meaning to have a word with you."

Seconds went by. Finally she said, "Yes, Seamus?"

"Perhaps I'm assuming too much, but I wanted to say,
here"—he could not seem to help himself and he swirled his

hand dramatically, as though to include the room, which, like all the rooms of the house, he soon would not see ever again— "and not—"

She blinked; in bed was the conclusion.

"—that I—" Another pause frazzled the silence. Both knew what was required to be said. Some explanation, some assurance was called for, and he did not want to resort to any obfuscation apart from what was necessary to protect her. Time—they had wasted enough of that as it was. "—that I very much enjoy having you with me but, you know, once begun, a thing like this continues."

After a few more moments of silence, she stepped into the room, closing the door behind her though she kept both hands on the knob. And her eyes—blue and starburst, the flecks silvery and luminescent and deep—scanned his rough features for any telling sign. A man who necessarily more than others was not given to personal revelation—she imagined how hard it must be for him. Yet it was precisely in that difficulty that she believed she could seek reassurance.

Returning to her family's house to change for work Monday morning week, she had had a flaming row with her father because she had been out all night and without an acceptable excuse, which at thirty-seven years of age she would not give. And it was as if the night of selfhood and release had shattered whatever comfort she had felt living there as a continuing part of her parents' lives. It made her realize just how much she had let slip by; and regardless of Seamus's involvements, she could tell from little things that he wanted her very much, and that alone was nearly enough. Then, there was no denying that in his own quiet way he was an accomplished man, and without any prompting he had assured her that whatever he was up to now would be his final act for whoever it was—and she feared the worst—he was with.

And there was the passbook, which he had shown her before she had even considered the question of how they would get on. Both had their talents, she had thought, and she, as she had supposed he, had saved a bit of money. Then, he had his house, which certainly was worth something, even if they decided to live some place else. But the figure—laid out across the page with no interest yet recorded—had at first seemed to her an elaboration. Argentine pesos. She had dismissed the amount, thinking it most probably inflated, until later in the morning, at the bank, she had worked it out. The total had frightened her. What in the name of God could be worth that much money? What single act? What process? What commission? And, more, what was she getting herself involved with?

Days later it had occurred to her that, with that money, they could live anywhere else in the world. Was it then that she had first begun to think in the plural? No—it was earlier; and she had slid into it without conscious thought, though she wanted to preserve the illusion of having made a decision. Roisin Johnston knew herself not to be mercenary or grasping, but the lot of a prison widow rather frightened her, as did the gun which he had shown her, concealed in a refabricated section of the radiator in the sitting room. "Which means?" she now asked.

Rhines smiled, finding it curious to realize that he, who had summoned the courage to meet events that would make other men cringe, now tried but failed to hold the level of her gaze, widened in a sincerity that was genuine. It was as though she were saying, You're an actor, Seamus Rhines, and you've lied to others, often and before, but, please, not to me now.

He forced his eyes back. "That if you're willing I'd like to make this definite. I'd like you to come with me."

It was not so much where or why but what exactly he had in mind that troubled her, though she now decided it was best not to ask. "When?"

Rhines noted the rake of her shoulders, the way her body narrowed to hips that were perhaps somewhat too small. The slight bow to her legs. Her feet, which were small. But mostly the way her eyes had suddenly clouded. A commitment and firm.

"Soon. They could be on to us, because of him." He pointed to the small stack of newspapers near the door that detailed the Duncan death and the continuing investigation. "He's to see them now."

She nodded. "The lot?"

"Of course—if he's to contemplate his offense in all its enormity." But Rhines's stagy cynicism rang hollow, and his eyes again surveyed the room appraisingly. Then, "It's a good old place that's served well, and I was never happier here, Roisin, than in the last few weeks. I'll miss Monaghan," but then we'll have our life together, he wanted to say, though he could not summon the words, nor did he think he needed to.

"Yah," she affirmed softly with her slight, feline, and gently possessive smile and a nod of her head. Just once, was all. Rhines could have asked for no more.

"I'll take them in?"

"If you will."

Having picked up the bundle, she looked down on the first paper and the bleached-out picture of the policeman in the bowler hat. "When, though, Seamus—if you can tell me?"

"Tonight. I'll be in touch."

It was not the *when* that she had in mind, though she let it pass.

"And him?" Roisin meant Carron.

"He should be off too, as soon as he's able. By Friday at

128

the latest, but I'll speak to him about that directly. Remember, now—there's the room to be wiped down."

"Shall I tell him you'll be in, so?" she asked, wanting most just to continue speaking to him: on the surface all had seemed too simple—a partial statement; a nod and an avowal—when both knew that the currents of life were complex, various, and turbulent, and all the more so now that they were conjoined. "Ah, Seamus"—she blurted out suddenly—"could we but have known earlier."

To Rhines it was a speculation without point. "There was nothing that could have been known," he replied, without adding, Then or now, which from his long experience he realized was the only way to approach a violent future.

She appeared at the door again, the woman with the nurse's manner but without the nurse's smock. A nun, perhaps, in civvies—older, pretty, not drawn from child-bearing. A nun was more likely here.

Where? The South, to judge from her voice and the little Carron could recollect—Dublin he'd been to after Geer, though the purpose with which she now placed the stack of newspapers beside the bed made him fearful and wary. Ill. Still weak. She could snuff him out with a pillow, were she of a mind. "Any wee thing I might get you, Mr. Carron?"

His name. Alarm flooded through him. Regarding the stack, he nearly said, "A drink," though he profoundly did not want one. Why? Of what beyond the pain (a bullet; he had felt the sear of lead before in Kenya, Cyprus, and Magherafelt) was he struggling not to become aware?

"Then I'll be leaving you now. And locking the door," she added, turning. "For your own protection, so you'll see."

No, Carron nearly shouted, but hot and soft and nauseatingly sweet, like waves of warm blood, it came back to him: the great vague guilt that had begun—he could now remember clearly—as a sense of resignation. With it he had followed Geer from pub to pub, as they dropped down into the South, until the kip on the quays in Dublin where Geer had pulled out his button box and played with the others he'd run into there.

And Carron *had* drunk and smoked—a fat, acrid cigar, he thought he could still taste it in the back of his throat—and in the inevitable conversation, which was what he hated most about himself when drunk (the revelations, the lies), he had spoken of . . . ? His head now swung to the stack of newspapers, the headlines of which were, fortunately (why fortunately?), turned away from him.

Later, much later—"Bize, stay a bit and play for me, while I clean oop. Let me get yous something for yer t'roats"—Geer had rolled out of the pub, the mot wedged under his shoulder, like a crutch. Carron had followed and not at a distance, fearing the odd chancer, a smash-and-grab gang, or somebody out for whatever the woman might offer, though she soon had Geer in the car and herself behind the wheel.

Clontarf by the sea. A bedsitter, no doubt, but well placed, with the hotel across the street on an angle. And of the rest of the weekend, only a few impressions remained for Carron: his need on Sunday, when the hotel bar failed to open at noon sharp, and he—quaking, sick, having to dodge fantasies packing out of every shadow—had for the first time in his life abandoned a surveillance to search for an open pub. He could also remember that evening, when, after having heard Geer announce that he would do one thing, he saw him do another and pass right by the gents' and out into the lobby. A mistake? A whim? No—the phone call, the woman. To Carron it was like a red flag.

And when he got outside it was cold—he could now remember at least that much—and slippery under foot. The shot? A mugger, huge, and the bastard had a gun. Like a clean blow from a hated enemy, like the thumping he then took to his ribs, it was an agony that he had felt before and that was therefore tolerable.

Not so the eye that did not blink. The eye into which the sleet was lashing, gray-blue, like his own apart from the eyebrow that was blond and young. And the oppressive, smothering guilt—a hangover indeed from his Presbyterian past—that now lay upon Carron's mind, like the counterweight of a ship's derrick. It called forth a tangle of emotions in Carron—impressions, experiences, images: the sorry, narrow dockside streets of his Belfast childhood (clean, though, where those he had once called *his* people lived) and how, come what may, any man with pride stuck to form—chapel of a Sunday, work and on time with no excuses. The pub, aye, but only for the man who could pay, and not just in money alone.

Not a religious man, Carron—how could he have been, given what had been asked of him and what he had done?—but a . . . traditional man. Aye. It was that which galled. The form, which he knew he had now broken. How? Once again he chanced a look at the papers. Run amok, he suspicioned. It had happened before, but never, not ever, while on duty. A traditional *man?*

No *man,* that. And, struggling to keep his eyes on the papers, finding in his weakness his focus blurred, Carron realized how impossible were the horns of his dilemma, and he succumbed to self-pity: duty and drink. In spite of all he had done, the first had come to nothing but the pittance of his pension, which now dwindled with what little the pound would purchase, and the ignominy of having been given wee Geer. And the drink? It had been his sole solace, the reward at the end of the day, for Carron had only ever had a soldier's use for women and that now had all but passed. But the drink, what had it brought him to now?

He was about to reach for his reading glasses on the night

stand by the bed—how had they gotten those and his wallet, his pen, even the chain with the key to his flat?—when he heard the lock on the door slide back and a man stepped in: the Tinker from the bar on the quays. Friday. The one who had played the bodhran. The rough, pitted face and red curls, but no ring in his ear today, only a white jacket and pants, like a doctor, or— No. Carron could make out the "K. C. Confectionery Ltd." on the pocket. A *baker?*

"Mr. Carron, sir—how are you feeling today? Better, I'm told."

Carron opened his mouth and was about to ask a spate of questions when the man, raising a hand and with a frank, friendly smile, stopped him. "No need for thanks. Have you seen the papers? No? Well—in due time. Let me say this, though." Moving toward the night stand, he reached into his back pocket and pulled out his wallet. "It seems that you're involved now, at least peripherally, and I can tell you one of us is certainly thankful. But consider *our* position, when you get a chance. If we are to continue, then, well—we're hoping that you'll understand.

"At the same time, there's no end of help we might offer you in this matter." The man nodded toward the papers, then drew from the wallet a bank note so large that he had to turn back its folds, which he snapped out. One thousand bloody pounds sterling, which, like a get-well card, he propped against the water glass. "To get home with," he explained, his eyes meeting Carron's briefly, and then the smile.

"The key, which you'll find on your chain there, matches the locks of an Escort similar in nearly every way to the one you rented in Belfast. As long as it's returned in the near future, there'll be few questions. Number plates and the tax stamp are in place, the odometer corrected, and, figuring you'll have some difficulty reaching for a while, we took the liberty of removing the bulb from the interior light. That and the lens hood you'll find in the glove box, according to the form that you prefer.

"Now then, here"—stepping to the closet, the red-headed man opened the door—"are clothes which are duplicates in every way except wear to those that you had on last weekend, right down to your hat." From the top shelf the man removed a plastic-wrapped Tyrolean. "Size ten, MacGonigall's?" he asked. "I'll leave it here." He hooked it over the knob of a nearby chair, then bent once again. "Bluchers." He placed the shoes on the seat of the chair. "Socks, underwear, your tie, and so forth you'll find on the hangers here. Don't worry if you feel a bit stiff and make a mess." The man touched his own left shoulder. "We understand. Nor about any prints. All will be rubbed down, and this lot"—he meant the bed covers and such—"taken away.

"Now, then"—visibly drawing in a breath, the man seemed to regard the room with no little satisfaction, the affable smile remaining—"you're probably as anxious as we are to leave, but don't think you must. Your meals will be provided until you choose to depart. But the sooner you report to Mr. Blount, the better, don't you think? You'll find your wallet, your pipe and tobacco pouch, all your personal effects in the left side pocket of the coat.

"There too is a card of a Belfast surgeon who will change your dressing without question or expense. Along with it is a receipt from a Ballinamore, County Leitrim, guesthouse, covering the weekend, and two others from Killashandra and Newtown-Gore for this week that you've spent 'recuperating.' The names of several pubs, where owners will swear in a court of law, if necessary, you drank in their premises, are included. That list you should study and destroy."

He then moved toward the door, which he pushed back against the wall. Pausing there, he said, "You came to our aid, Mr. Carron, when we needed it, and we thank you. You're an unlikely ally, highly skilled and courageous, and there're those who might value your talents and for once in your career be willing to pay you what they are worth. You can fault me for being presumptuous, but I'll hazard a guess. Your £2,330 annuity, that flat of yours on the Shankill Road, the £847 pounds you have in the bank aren't worth a fraction of what you've put in. And for whom? I know you've asked yourself that."

Rhines then turned and walked down the hall, leaving Carron to the newspapers, which he would now read, to whatever else he could recollect of his experience, and to the thousand-pound note. Gingerly, Carron lifted it off the night stand and began rubbing his fingers over the vellum.

Glancing up from it, looking toward the open closet and the chair and the hat, Carron wondered what in the three years he had covered Geer had he missed? Something, surely. This money. Duncan. The Consolidated Irish Bank? Could that have been . . . could it be what the "sweet, wee man" had been plotting all along with the film, the library, the little museum, the job that was less than his ability but allowed him to come and go? A heist? Consolidated had a Belfast branch. One great, glorious hit and then a long, soft exile?

No, Carron (who had himself once stuck up a bank but on orders) decided—crinkling the bank note into his palm—but whatever it was, it was real. And when, he asked himself, had the British Army last stood up for him and been counted? McGurk's? Not a bit of it. He'd been cashiered, plain and simple, and the drink was just an excuse.

The drink. When he opened the cabinet doors that formed the bottom of the night stand, he found a bottle there, as he suspected he would. But Carron forbore, at least until he was dressed.

Then, sitting on the edge of the bed, trying to gather himself and his thoughts, he poured himself three fingers and reached for his pipe and tobacco pouch, in which he found a small box of waxed matches. Yes, he had killed before, but never in anger. Yes, he had murdered, but only by command. And Jock Duncan, who was—in spite of his politics—one of his own, whose career he had followed scrupulously in the papers even to having felt a kind of bitterness and sorrow the year that Duncan was passed over for the national side and announced he would pack it in? Why him of all men?

Staring down at the box, yet again trying to avoid the papers, which now were scattered about the bed, Carron read, "Place of the Oaks Inn, Usher's Quay, Dublin." Complimentary with the cigar, the mere thought of which now nearly made him nauseous. Below the name in brackets was "Derreigh"—Irish for the name of the inn and the city that Carron knew as Londonderry. Another coincidence, Geer having been attracted to a pub with a Northern name?

Circles, Carron thought, and none too good. Funny how his own life and Geer's and—he suspected, his hand reaching out in a kind of reflex for the glass—the lives of others kept winding back on themselves. Passing a finger over the raised letters of the snaky Gaelic script, he wondered what, if anything, it meant.

He stood suddenly and felt the floor begin to rise up at him, but he forced it back.

Strength, another illusion. It was something—he told himself, slipping the bottle into the pocket of his "new" overcoat—that he had never lacked. And self-pity, the first sign of a sot.

He then left, and none too soon.

III
Subject

8

From afar at sunset the low, rolling hills surrounding Monaghan appeared to McGarr as from a dream relived. How many times had he trekked north, like this, to help his uncles with the first turning: the ground under foot still cold but the air—coming to him through the open window of the speeding Rover—almost hot on his face? Dozens, it seemed. And now the plaintive bellow of cows waiting to be led through the shadows of mist-laden fields, the lighted barns that appeared to him, like small cities on a darkling plain, the town through which he clipped, splashing the walls, the stopped traffic, the clutches of homing school-children with chalky blue light, seemed a kind of Dantean reward.

Was he destined, year in and year out, to relive this journey back up into the Ulster countryside? Had his life for all its . . . diversity been that good? Surely, it was a pleasant prospect, but—slamming the car into third to send it hurtling past a lorry—McGarr doubted its cogency. Had he forsaken that life for other . . . *pleasures?* It was a word he believed he now regarded only in the breach. He thought of his garden, most of which now, with the change in the weather, he had planted.

139

By late afternoon the day had become burdened by detail. A Friday, but special. He had spent most of it at Garda Siochana headquarters, where an assistant commissioner had summoned him to review the Murder Squad's active file. It was an extraordinary event, which only occurred when some question—administrative, legal, or ethical—had been raised at the highest level about the functioning of a Garda department. But, having inquired about the cause, McGarr had received only an evasive "Just touching base," though an eyebrow had been raised at the number of open cases, the notoriety which several—the little Traveler girl; the Belgian businessman; but most especially the Jock Duncan case, which was now over a month old—had received, and the all too obvious fact that little, if any, headway was being made on even one.

In the Duncan case: for the car, the Escort that had been found stripped of its number plates and tax stamp in the lot of Sach's Hotel and wiped clean of prints, they could find no registered automobile of its type missing in the Republic. Requests for an inquiry by the RUC were—it was assumed— going forward according to procedure, though no acknowledgment had been received. Same with the hat, and the prints— two sets complete enough to be identifiable and one partial— that had been found on the magnet used to destroy the computer tape or on the weapon itself. Those too had seen sent north for a comparison with prints in RUC files, but again, nothing yet. Not even word of receipt of the request, which was in itself curious.

Back at his desk McGarr had glanced at his calendar and wondered if a bank holiday or some other holiday in the U.K. might explain the lag or if, perchance, there had been a sudden deterioration in political relations between North and South. Political himself only insofar as politics controlled the emphasis of police activities (the Minister for Justice oversaw the activities of the Garda Siochana, the commissioner of which was appointed by the regnant political party), McGarr forced himself to keep at least current with the major happenings of the day, but he could think of none disturbing an atmosphere of steadily improving relations between Britain and Ireland. Some political analysts believed that the Thatcher government might even be willing to seek some accommodation with Ireland on the North. In six weeks talks would begin.

Succumbing to his impatience, McGarr had finally picked up the phone and called his opposite number in the RUC to learn if there might be some way the man might expedite or himself handle the requests. And although McGarr had gladly done the same for the man in the past, he was told, and curtly, that he would have to go through channels. Undaunted, McGarr had phoned RUC Records, only to be told his call would be returned. It had not been. Finally he had tried to phone MacGonigall's in Belfast; a stilted British voice told him that the number was no longer in service.

So, what had they? The car, which had been scoured. Why and by whom? How many had been involved in the crime? From the foot- and fingerprints, at least two had fractured Duncan's spine, the mere thought of which made McGarr's eyes shy from the page. But one of them had been wounded, and the other either had had to help him away or else had not had time—because of the security guard—to carry off the tape. The hat. Why else would they have left it behind?

The uninjured of the two would probably then have had to search out some medical attention for the other, though nothing like that had been reported. Would he then have returned to wipe down the car and make its ownership—which eventually would come to light—more difficult to trace? Or would this require some third person? Why not simply drive the car out of the area to some haven? No key, no skill or means to take it away otherwise?

McGarr worked through the list of overnight guests at Sach's Hotel without hoping to learn much. Of a Sunday afternoon, its several lounge bars were usually packed with unattached young professionals. A jazz band, of all things, was featured there.

Four people, McGarr decided, counting whoever had been up to eighty miles north-northwest of Dublin to interpret the message received by their monitor. With five the culvert cover could have been replaced and the P&T stanchion and van removed. With the fifth member and some time, the phone taps could have been disconnected and the devices removed.

Conclusion? There had been four of them who had expected to have more time to clean up the details of their—? The gun, its three reports, and the wounding of one of them had spoiled the completion of the operation. But why had Duncan, of all people, believed he should arm himself, and so . . . explosively? A .357 magnum was a small cannon. Because he knew there would be two of them who—? Because he knew and was *frightened* of their . . . connections?

The words of Colm Walsh the young computer specialist occurred to McGarr. "What if it was only the bank's computer and not the bank's information that was being used? And whoever placed those devices here did not have personal access to a computer of its size and type, but did not trust whoever it was who did?" Duncan, who was not trusted and did not trust.

McGarr remembered the man's involvement in NICRA, the civil-rights movement, but that was nearly two decades before. Still, one made friends, and McGarr knew that many of those people now thought of themselves as a coterie of the brave, having borne the brunt of RUC baton charges and British Army rifle fire on the several days of death of which Bloody Sunday was the most infamous. But how close to the front had Jock Duncan been? Had he marched and how often?

Could the disillusionment that followed those days have led to some more militant approach to the problem of the North? McGarr sorted through the file, but could find no reference to that part of the victim's history. He penciled another note in the margin that they should find out, and he thought of Neil Blaney, the independent politician who, it seemed, still believed that arming the Catholics in the North was necessary.

Money? As he turned the pages that listed the accouterments of Duncan's apartment and life, it was plain that Duncan had been a man who had enjoyed what money could buy, though his bank balance with Consolidated hardly totaled £2,000.

Of women—another expensive item—there had been many, but none for long. Scanning the statement of his most recent companions and considering what the woman in the computer center had said, McGarr judged that Jock Duncan had been a hard and unpleasant, if sometimes an appealing, man. "A man's man, I'd say. No niceties. Came right out with it. 'No rings, no engagements, nothing long-term,' he told me after . . . (pause). 'I'll give you a call sometime. If you want to continue, well—that's your decision. If not, so be it.'

"And weekends? I felt like Cinderella. He was just a prince until half-eleven of a Sunday night, when he'd chuck me out. 'I'm sorry,' he said the first time. 'I live here and nobody else. If you need somebody to hold your hand, get married.'

"But, you know, when Jock was on, he was gas. Rugby parties especially. All night and day, two, three days running, and him having to play—and *well*, mind you—in the afternoons. And when he finally slept (is that thing switched on?), he was like a bear hibernating."

And later, "No care for expense. We'd party for days. We once flew to Paris for breakfast, Rome for dinner."

What information, then, might be important enough to kill for? Bank information? No—McGarr leafed through a state-

143

ment from Duncan's superior, the corporate director of Consolidated Irish Bank: the lists of bank depositors, bank investments, bank profits and losses, while considered private and not for public dissemination, could not have compromised the institution. An audit had just been completed a week before and no irregularities discovered. Given the circumstances of Duncan's death, however, another check was being carried forward. And, then, Walsh believed that the tape, which had been found with the deleting magnet attached, had been brought in to Duncan for some type of processing.

Why? What had they required of him?

McGarr could not begin to guess, but, whatever it was, they had had money to lavish. Duncan would not have come cheap, nor the equipment that they had left behind. And their concern for security? It had been primary in some aspects— the tape, the Escort—but seemingly inessential in others. The P&T van, the prints that had been left, the hat. It was as if they had decided what had to be retained and what could be yielded, given the need. Or what *should* be yielded? No. Why?

All of which—McGarr had looked up from his desk—spoke of planning in depth and experience, but (again) to what purpose?

Information about . . . arms, arms purchases, arms shipments, or contributors, their names and addresses, the dates and amounts given? In an Irish setting it was always a possibility. And then the . . . elaborateness of the equipment in the culvert, the radio signal directed north, the hat from MacGonigall's, Belfast, and the absence of a report concerning a gunshot wound's having been treated all pointed to it. McGarr preferred not to consider the possibility, though the involvement of an unlawful organization would remove the investigation to Special Branch and provide a modicum of relief.

And, then—McGarr had reached for a Woodbine—he

thought of the newspapers again. Sport pages were featuring retrospectives of Duncan's rugby career, while obituaries in journals as august as the *Times* waxed elegiac in praise of the "unlikely public and patriotic man." Letters to the editor complained of the lack of police protection in residential areas, of which Herbert Park was one, and a general disdain for the security needs of the "ordinary and law-abiding resident of the urban areas of the country." Of which, McGarr mused, the gun-toting Duncan had been one? Then an *ad hoc* committee of captains of rugby teams had complained of the "torpor" of the police, of the seeming unconcern of the Murder Squad over the death of "a national hero," and finally of McGarr's "inaccessibility." They had sent an emissary to quiz McGarr, and he had been met by Bresnahan.

Turning a page, McGarr had glanced down at a thick, stapled report from the Technical Bureau concerning the devices that had been found in the culvert: McAnulty, compensating for his guilt of knowing little or nothing about electronics, had ordered some poor sod to type up a sheaf of polysyllabic drivel. Across the facing page, Bresnahan had written, "Nothing new here."

Good girl, McGarr had thought, seeing her fill the doorway of the cubicle. In some ways she was worth two of any of the men on the staff, though, to be fair, there was not one without some special talent. And Bresnahan's was . . . ? Application, McGarr decided; hers was a passionate devotion to the most minute particular of her job. Her energy could only be admired.

She now placed two sheets of paper, wedded by a clip, on his desk and began to leave. The top sheet read, "Art Dromgoole. Line 2."

"Who?"

"*Page* two, sorrh."

McGarr had flipped the page and found a computer printout

of Superintendent (retired) Arthur F. X. Dromgoole's Garda Siochana record, ranging from his service during the Revolution with Michael Collins to his last post prior to his retirement: Monaghan Town, in which he had been born and raised and now resided. Pensioner. Octogenarian.

Dromgoole met the Rover at a corner a block distant from the house that he believed McGarr might be interested in. He was a dark man whose features with age had seemed to recede, leaving only a broad cone of nose and deep creases. Wearing a heavy coat and a cloth cap, he was indistinguishable from any number of retirees in towns the country over, and McGarr wondered at the effectiveness of a network of such people. Gossip, the word behind the hand, the seemingly studied indifference with which he and the others like him observed the smallest events of their few remaining days: together they constituted a system that no computer would ever rival, could communication links be established. It had taken an entire month for the message, left on a pad by a neighbor's phone, to reach him, and another four days for Dromgoole himself to remember to call back.

Too much time, McGarr feared, reaching across the now empty front seat to take Dromgoole's hand as the five others who had accompanied McGarr north to Monaghan left the car to assume positions around the house. Easing the old man into the Rover, McGarr asked him to close the door.

"Ran onto your uncle Mick a fortnight past," Dromgoole said, his voice a soft, pleasant lilt. "Shameful the state he was in."

"Locked?" McGarr asked, depressing the clutch so the car could roll.

"Jarred."

In a lightless hush they drifted down a slight hill until at an alley McGarr turned in, blocking at least that exit from the house in front. "Vapors off the taps?" McGarr's uncle, who had retired from his farm a decade earlier, did not drink.

"The same. Says I, 'You could spend your time more profitably in the church, Mick, for all the pleasure you get off this place.' "

McGarr smiled and thought of all the "chat" he had been hearing the day long.

"Says he, 'I'm having a grand time, and I'm nearer my God here than in any church. His is an evil presence, which resides at the bottom of your glass. Would you take another and depart in style? We won't be seeing each other for a good while where you're headed.' "

McGarr laughed and, checking the clip of the Walther, followed Dromgoole up the alley. It was lit only by the arced fang of a crescent moon, though the rough dashing of the stucco wall carried the heat of the day. Fifty or so paces in, Dromgoole stopped before a bank of dark garage. The house across the alley was lightless.

"Isn't this a bit much?" Dromgoole meant the precautions McGarr had taken. Across the alley Delaney was standing in deep shadow, a snub-nosed automatic carbine at the ready.

"You did say Seamus Rhines?"

"I did." And, like that of a man being visited by a revelation, Dromgoole's cloth-capped head rose to the moon as he listened while McGarr explained how, having entered the name on the Records computer, they had been informed of the possibility that Seamus Rhines might be the alias of one James Ryan, who was also known as J. (or Jay) Rheiner to his own.

"The Provisional?" Dromgoole asked. "The one from the barracks?" He meant a bombing that had occurred in a British Army barracks in Strabane when a man, posing as a colonel, arrived on a scheduled round of inspection. Since he was recognized and greeted by the commanding officer, his Land-

Rover was allowed within the compound. Soon afterward, however, he and his driver disappeared. In the explosion which followed, seven soldiers (nine, counting the actual colonel and his driver, who had been garroted) were killed outright, three lingered horribly and later died, three were maimed, and fifteen others seriously injured.

Although the British immediately tightened security, a checkpoint in Armagh was decimated, a customs house in Larne, a patrol boat in Carlingford Lough, another barracks in Newtownards—all, it was rumored, sent up by a man now heralded as the "Barracks Bomber" in both song and verse.

"Sure," said Dromgoole pensively, "now that you mention it . . ." and while he began detailing Rhines's comings and goings, his several talents (mechanical and electrical), his love of the stage, McGarr ran a hand up the surface of the door, feeling where windows had been replaced with neatly fitted tongue-and-groove paneling to match the lower half. His hand then fell to a padlock, a Validus by the shape of it. Swiss and expensive and difficult to pick, though he judged he should.

A tout's tip and doubtless a fabrication. A name mnemonically close. Something to buy time with. Minutes passed. Out in the street a heavily laden lorry whined through a stage of gears, only to groan to a stop a few blocks distant. McGarr could smell the sweet chemical stink of auto lacquer, freshly applied.

After stepping in and closing the door behind Dromgoole, McGarr played the beam of his torch down the several bays of the garage.

"Gone," said Dromgoole. "Even the old Humber. Kept it shiny as a staff—" He did not continue the thought.

"You mentioned that and the P&T van. The 'K. C. Confectionery' bread truck. What else, Art?"

In a small, defeated voice, Dromgoole said, "A bloody big Land-Rover. Olive-drab it was. British Army specs, I'd say, though at the time he told me he'd got it at an auction of superannuated equipment at the McKee Barracks, Dublin."

It was a facility of the Irish Army.

"When was that?"

Dromgoole sighed. "Before. Well before." He meant well before the bombing in Strabane.

"Any others?"

"Well—there was a new Ford. Gray."

"An Escort?"

Dromgoole canted his head. "I'd say, though I don't follow the models much anymore. Seemed to me he was working on it, when I stopped by. Over there." He pointed to the nearest bay. "Under the bonnet he was."

"When?"

"A month, six weeks past. Maybe more. It was cold, and he asked me to close the door. Had the place warm as toast. Handy, that man. Not much . . . beyond him, I'd say.

"And there was an old Fiat he'd park in here from time to time, but I think it belonged to somebody else. Northern plates."

"You didn't happen—"

"No," the older man said in a tired voice, "though there was a time when nothin' got by me. A bucket, it was. Red. Rusty. A wagon. Belfast plates, I'm after thinking.

"Sure, even his tools is gone. Who would've suspicioned it with him so . . . innocuous, like. *Seamus* Rhines. Like father, like son."

The back gate was more easily jimmied and the garden door as well. But as McGarr swung the beam of his torch into the kitchen it passed across the interior jamb, which had been painted, of all colors, black.

"Small kitchen for these parts," observed Dromgoole, after

O'Shaughnessy switched on the overhead light. "And have I been drinking?" He pointed to the ceiling, which diminished in height, and the walls, which narrowed, as they approached that which divided the kitchen from a long sitting room. All appurtenances there—a divan, two stuffed chairs, a mantel replete with familial mementos, and an eight-day clock that in the silence beat like a metronome—were covered with a thick layer of dust, though the kitchen (McGarr stepped back in to check) had little.

Concluded O'Shaughnessy, "Your man isn't much of a sitter." With a handkerchief he reached for the shank of the handle of the door that led into the hall. There they heard noise—the scrape of a chair, a thump—from the room opposite, though no light appeared under the door. His Walther came up, and he glanced at McGarr, who nodded.

Stepping back, the larger man raised a foot and kicked out at the door, leaning his considerable weight into the thrust. With a crack, the door popped open, and McGarr, rushing in, dropped to a knee, the barrel of his automatic pointed at the forehead of a woman who was bending over what appeared to be a surgery table.

Startled, she dropped the rag in her right hand.

"Now place both of them on the table, palms up. Slowly."

"If you're friends of Seamus's, I'll have you know—" But she saw Dromgoole in the doorway, and her expression hardened. She then complied with McGarr's order, turning herself away from the door: a strong but fetching woman of early middle age—reddish-blond hair, fine skin, dark blue eyes which, McGarr imagined, could become soft.

"Have us know what?" McGarr asked. Then, "What friends?"

Said Dromgoole from the doorway, "Roisin Johnston—does your father know you're here?"

She bent her head, causing waves of hair to gather about her face, but McGarr thought he heard her laugh. Yet when

150

she straightened back up, he could see her face had taken on color. Embarrassment? Anger? Guilt?

She reached down for the rag and stepped to the night stand beside the bed, which she again began to wipe down.

"Stop that," said McGarr.

She kept on, faster now and with purpose.

"I said stop that."

When she continued, McGarr moved quickly toward her and yanked the cloth away, her right hand whipping up from her waist and catching him across the side of his face. It rocked him, and his hat flew off. His left ear was suddenly hot and ringing.

She was wearing a white hospital-type smock, the front thigh pockets of which were bulging. He shoved her back into the table and reached into one, to pull out what appeared to be an unmarked aerosol canister attached to a jar filled with— this time he caught her hand, which he twisted down to her side until she cried out—a powder, though darker and not uniform.

"Dust," said O'Shaughnessy. "Shouldn't we leave the lot to McAnulty?"

All the other rooms were covered with it; in Roisin Johnston's smock two canisters remained unspent.

"Show me the cellar, Art," McGarr asked, after O'Shaughnessy had taken the woman to the kitchen.

"None here. There's not a house in the street has one. Boggy hereabouts. Wet."

Certainly nothing that Seamus Rhines could not deal with. With Ward, Delaney, and Sinclaire to help him, McGarr discovered a door concealed behind paneling at the back of the closet in the sitting room. Below, all had been removed but for a diesel generator, a yoke of thick cable that led up to the room above, and an outlet behind the bookcase.

"And to think," said Dromgoole, "right under me nose."

Said McKeon, "Sure and I thought your nose had retired along with the rest of you."

Hours later and well past midnight, when the Technical Bureau had departed, McGarr phoned his office on the off chance that something might have come in.

Said Bresnahan, "Yes, a negative from Interpol on the prints."

"From the Yard?"

"Nothing."

"The RUC?"

"Not a thing. Not even an acknowledgment. Will I keep trying?"

"In the morning."

They had gotten a match on the fingerprints: the partials on the barrel of Duncan's .357 magnum with a full set, left hand, on the top of the night stand. They were not, however, those of Rhines (or Ryan or Rheiner).

But it was the car that was bothering McGarr most, the Escort. Why all the preparations weeks before in the garage at the back of the house, only to abandon it stripped of all that would make its identification possible in the short run? Eventually that too would come to light. Or would it?

"Tell me," he said to Bresnahan, "would you have the Technical Bureau report on the Escort handy?" She had, of course. "Is there any mention of its paint being new?" He waited until she said, "No, but, then, there's no mention of the paint having been examined. Particularly. Should we—"

"Yes," McGarr said, and he rang off.

What was left? Apart from interrogating the woman, Roisin Johnston, which would take yet more time, he imagined, there was only the hat from MacGonigall's, Belfast, and an oddity at size 10. It was yet another matter that would have to await the pleasure of the RUC. McGarr thought back on the session he had had to endure with the assistant commissioner the afternoon of the day now passed. Every trying moment was still painfully alive to him—the frustration, the feeling of impotence, the specter of failure.

"Coming?" O'Shaughnessy asked. They were standing in the adumbrated kitchen of the Monaghan house, a stage set to be viewed from the windows in the back garden.

"No." McGarr lifted his own hat from the table and stared down into its pearly silk liner. "You take the boys back."

"And what about you?"

"Sure"—McGarr glanced up, though he avoided O'Shaughnessy's hard hazel eyes—"there's Mick and Terry and Maire to see. I'll catch a bus back in the morning."

"I'd prefer you to come along now," said O'Shaughnessy, and when McGarr did not reply, he turned to the door. "I'll say this only once—it is wrong, and you know it."

"Yes," McGarr said.

O'Shaughnessy left.

9

With fear, with a loathing of himself and a hatred that made him want to crush, Carron had weeks earlier entered the Belfast neighborhood of tall, gabled Victorian houses where Blount lived. Cautiously. Probing the bonnet of the Escort down the tree-lined streets. He had noted the spiky knobs of cast-iron fences around lawns that were obscene in their length when compared with the stoop-fronted row houses that had been the dwellings of his youth and in which he still passed his restless, solitary nights.

"Fairclough and Blount, Ulster Risks Ltd.," the sign on the side yard gate said, "Security. Protection. Please Ring," though Carron did not. It was why he had waited until nightfall, knowing that Blount would be working late of a Friday evening. If he was going to be dressed down, it could not be in public, for his condition was such that he could not allow that to happen.

His condition, which was what? Passing through the halo of the tall dwelling set on chipped granite blocks, hearing the sounds of domestic contentment through a partially open window—the low voice of a woman; the click of a plate on a counter—he nearly stopped and turned back to the car for a sup, which would be a mistake. He had timed his last, he had, having taken just enough to steady him. Twenty minutes before.

But though the door to the office in the carriage house was open, nobody responded to Carron's call of "Robbie." He waited by the desk that was usually occupied by the secretary, who treated him with the surplus of deference that told him he meant little or nothing to their operation, and he tried again—"*Robbie?*"—listening to the sound of his voice and knowing from the guilty ring of the one word alone that Blount would know.

And then he began moving through the rooms in a kind of fearful daze, knowing where Blount would be but wanting— like a child; it was a feeling he hated—to put it off as long as he could. But on seeing him Blount said nothing, only remained behind the desk, his age-spotted hands clasped over a knee, the leg crossed over the other, regarding him.

Carron began by removing his hat, the new one, which still smelled of the shop—MacGonigall's—though he could not bring himself to look down into it, as he was wont before superiors. How had they come by it and when? Before Dublin or after, when he'd been recuperating? Before, he had a feeling—which made him believe he needed Blount and what he represented even more, though he could hardly say why.

"Slipped, I deid. Bahd," he blurted out. Murder, he nearly said, but—thank God!—it stayed in. "Been"—on the mend. No!—"straightening out." He paused, chancing a glance at the blue blazer, the regimental tie, the thin sallow face and beaked nose. And finally, Blount's brown eyes, which were the deadest he'd seen since— Carron then buried his own in the bright liner of the hat. "The week."

Still Blount said nothing, nor did he change his position. Above his head an old clock, taken from a barracks in Malta where he had done "his best work," he had once said, was ticking, each beat a hammer throb as the minutes ground on.

Carron began to sweat. He wanted to ease a finger under his collar and pull his tie free, and the wound now became apparent to him, itching, then stinging, then burning almost as though it was being seared in Blount's pitiless gaze.

And Carron had misjudged his need. Already he felt light-headed, quaking, and his stomach had begun to roll, yet the clock above Blount told him he'd been there but seven minutes. In his mind he played over saying, "He's back, I trust." "Who?" Blount would ask. "Geer." But, then, that had been his own duty, hadn't it, and he had "slipped," he had.

"Ballinamore. County Leitrim," a voice that wasn't his own then said, a voice dripping with what Carron had had occasion to hear from others and hated. "He ended up there." No, Carron had ended up there. "The button box. A pub," for Carron himself. "And all."

And all, Blount thought, easing his leg down and standing. Carron was drawn, haggard, his skin the color of scudding, dead flesh; he looked worse than he had at any other time in their acquaintance, and there had been some "bombs," as it were.

"The *Slieve Na Eireann*," Carron replied too fast.

"Really, now. *Really.*" Hands behind his back, Blount began circling him, surprised at the alacrity of the reply. "Sounds like a right 'Paddy' kip for a soldier, now doesn't it, Mr. Carron? A *right* kip." The pants were pressed, the shoes shined, the overcoat—a dour gray, like the skies over the shipyard, Blount thought—freshly brushed. Carron had gone to some pains, though it would do him no good. "And you 'recuperated' where—?" Blount nearly called him "sergeant."

"A coopla places, surrh. I, you know, moved around, like always."

"There or here?"

"There, sir. I was . . . sick, like I said. Ill. I think"—a large hand, the fingers thick and spatulate, came up, and then plunged into an overcoat pocket—"I've got here a receipt from one. No," Carron as much as shouted at himself, and although his hand touched the receipt in his pocket, he did not draw it out. "Had it here some place, I thought, but—"

But you're a drunk and I'm a fool to have had anything to do with you, thought Blount, who had taken Carron on only as a matter of pity. And, then, he reminded himself, he had not gotten where he was—which was where?—by ignoring anything that might cost him. The part-owner, he averred, of a damn good operation. Yes. At least as good as, and far more profitable for Blount than, any SAS. "Names?" he nearly shouted.

"Names of what, sir?"

"Names of the places you put up. Names and addresses. Names of the owners, the desk clerks, the proprietors, the maids, goddamn you, and if you're lying to me, George Carron, I'll have you gibbeted and roasted, and by that I mean your pension and more and you know it. One word. One proper noun in the right place—"

"Corduff House, sir. I stayed there . . . mostly."

"*Mostly?*" Blount's shouted question lifted him off his feet, and in contained increments he let himself down.

As he reeled like a tethered bullock before the knacker's maul, Carron's great, balding head jerked, a shoulder swirled. One of his heavy calves, as though hawsered, began to struggle and flex. "Exclusively, sir."

"Exclusively? What does *exclusively* mean, George?"

"I"—a knee buckled, and Carron snapped it back—"I let them nurse me back."

"Which means?"

"They're Austrian. They have a bar. I . . . I tapered off."

Blount, having circled round Carron, now stopped exactly in front of him. "So you lied to me, George. 'A coopla places, surrh. Ah, y'know, moved aroond, like al'ays,' " Blount, who could no longer help himself, mocked. "What else did you do 'like al'ays,' George?

"Billfold," he shouted up into Carron's long, tired face, which, though sweating, remained impassive, pouchy, and drawn from years of every sort of abuse. "You heard me, George. I said your personal effects." Pivoting, Blount snapped a finger at the desk, then tapped a fingernail on its gleaming surface. "Your wallet, your 'journal,' the contents of your pockets. Perhaps whatever you're hiding is in there."

But when a blood-muddied stare rose to Blount, it was plain that there would be no such abasement. "Very well," Blount went on, "in this extraordinary case we'll settle for your hands," one palm of which Carron raised, his eyes still regarding Blount, and closely.

For a whole minute—Blount paced it off—he waited, but when he returned to Carron's side, that great, gross appendage which could kill was as steady as when Carron first held it out.

"Over," said Blount, but even when, in turning, Carron revealed a great, scabbing scrape across the knuckles, no explanation, which Blount demanded, was offered. Only his eyes—and were they truculent? they were—searching his face, and the slight jut of his chin, which preceded the lumbering, condemned swing of his head and shoulders toward the door when Blount demanded to see the car.

A gesture, it was, no more, but Blount, whose indignation now ruled him, ignored it and failed to remind himself of the fact that above all else, Carron was dangerous. He suspected only that the balance had tipped, and it was now he who was grasping for justification. Why?

The car. It was with relief and a quickened, distracted pace that Blount, on seeing it parked in the deep shadow of lindens a block and a half from his house, stepped round Carron and made for the door. For days the rental agency had pestered

him about it, complaining that Carron had rented it only for
the weekend, that his deposit was too low, and—a week later—
that they intended to notify the RUC. Finally Blount himself
had had to journey to Aldergrove and—by God!—splash out
270 quid, to say nothing of his time and the apologies, which
he had never made easily and for a sot at that.

"Keys." Blount held out a hand, into which Carron dropped
them. After opening the door, he reached for the glove box
to search for the interior bulb, which the agency would require, and when he had twisted it home in its yoke, he then
checked the mileage, comparing it with the figure he'd had
to grovel for at Aldergrove and quickly deriving its total. Figures were Blount's strength.

One hundred forty-eight. Enough to get there and back
but little else. The truth? Perhaps, but it had been Blount's
experience to observe that drunks invariably told lies, either
to themselves or to others, and which had been Carron's?

Sliding out of the car, Blount handed back the keys. He
noted a chill to the wind blowing in off the Lough; it would
rain by morning. "You're to return this car, George Carron,
if only to take Ulster Risks off the chit. What you do with it
or yourself after that, I don't give a damn. Two hundred and
seventy quid," he nearly shouted, "I've already paid for your
gluttony, man, and I'll not pay more. That sum will be taken
from whatever Ulster Risks owes you. You'll receive the balance, your revenue slips, and a formal notification of termi-
nation in the mail. I'll not support you and your problem any
longer."

And then, "God*damn* you, George, you're a bloody sot!
You've no grasp on reality. This isn't Kenya or Cyprus or the
Kesh. There is no army, no easy billets, no free rides. Everything you do comes down on you and therefore me, and
as of this moment we are quits."

Slowly Carron, who was standing with one hand slung over

the open door and the other on the top of the car, raised his huge, hatted head, which was swimming with a blinding, breath-snatching anger that was all the more intense because he believed at least for the moment that it was futile. His heart was beating wildly, and the drop of sick, greasy sweat that had been clinging to his left ear lobe now caught on his collar and leaked down his neck.

Blount, who was standing in front of him, his back against the car, eased his hands to his sides, only now realizing his mistake. Desk man. An officer. Yet Carron could only admire his command; he did not pull his eyes away or even blink. Even though in Carron's power, which was total, Blount refused to recognize Carron's authority. He—not some army or Britain or the Queen or even the man who was now struggling with every atom of his being not to kill him—was right, and there was a lesson in that.

Feeling the distance that he always experienced before losing control slowly diminish, Carron realized that it was more Blount than he who failed to grasp the reality of the situation. It was not the same Escort that had been rented, mileage that had been recorded, hat, coat, or suit that he had been wearing or, in fact—Carron there decided—the same man who had left Belfast on Blount's bidding nearly a fortnight before.

But it was a difference which Carron was not allowed to appreciate in depth, for although the intensity of Blount's gaze did not falter, his body jerked or quivered, and his hand came up to his chest. Only when he opened the palm, which bore a small spot of blood, did a single furrow appear on his brow. As he lowered his head to look down, he jerked again and again, and it was then that Carron heard low muffled pops, like the release of pressurized gas from a hydraulic valve. A rosette now flowered on the pocket of Blount's blazer. His head came up and his eyes met Carron's, but they were shallow, depthless, and dead.

Without taking his hands from either the door or the roof of the car, Carron merely moved his feet to keep Blount's body, which crumpled, from falling on him. He then lowered his head to check the narrowness of the gap through which the shots had come, knowing full well that if he himself had been a target he would have been long dead. Two inches, three at most, and the pattern on the pocket was tight, a small fist of blood. Blount's tongue had lolled from his mouth, and with the toe of a shoe Carron now tried to nudge the jaw shut.

But, raising his head, Carron was struck by the revelation that Blount's death had suddenly changed everything for him. Ulster Risks, which had a partner, would have to make a strong showing in order to survive. Again lifting a foot, Carron shoved over Blount's thin left shoulder and examined the back of the blazer for penetration. Some low-velocity slug. A .32 short, he was betting. So that . . . nothing could be found in the Escort and Carron himself might depart, if he was of a mind?

Turning and lowering the bulk of his body over Blount and in behind the wheel, Carron glanced across the street at the car from which the shots had to have been fired. An old Humber, it was, but in good shape. A heavy, quiet, secure motor.

A moment or two later a light appeared there, a flame from a match that was held to the end of a small cigar. In its momentary flash Carron saw a face which in the shadows seemed thin, the skin rough, the hair an abiding red and wavy. The Humber moved off in a hush.

A drink Carron needed, but he settled for a smoke. Whatever it was, he was now in even deeper than from the murder in Dublin. A setup it had been, right down to the change of clothes. Why? What did they want from him?

But he'd be needed now by Fairclough, the surviving partner—guardian, shepherd, and (how had the Tinker said it, though he was obviously not Tinker?) "highly skilled." Yes, he was that, all right.

And Geer? With him Carron would just continue on, like nothing had happened; they'd be in touch, of that he was sure, and pay him for once in his career what he was worth? He'd see, though he suspected he now had no option.

He removed a match from the box that he had gotten in the pub in Dublin and struck its phosphorescent flare into the dark mixture. He opened the door. He then snatched up Blount's collar and like a sack of coal dragged him across the street toward the lights he could see in the distance.

10

Belfast. In the half-light of early morning weeks later it was a steel trap strung taut with metal barrier grids, electronic gates, checkpoints bristling with weaponry, and the prowling, angry purr of knobby rubber tires banding the city in a grid of kinetic force.

Driving the Austin of a cousin whom he resembled in every way but age, McGarr had twice since the border been stopped, told to get out, and then been frisked and had the car searched. And a third time, in the car park beyond the battlements of the central shopping area, into which no unauthorized vehicle was allowed.

Finally, at the iron mesh of a windowless storefront that advised prospective customers to "Please Ring and Await Service," McGarr stood at a grated door while he was scrutinized from within. Turning from the slit window, two of the three women there conferred. When they returned for a second assessment, McGarr, as if impatient, removed his bowler and raised the liner, which said Cavanaugh, to the glass.

It was greeted by two smiles, though it was the third woman who began throwing the bolts to open the door. "Beggin' your pardon, surrh, but yeh cahn't be too careful these days," she said, her one movable eye fixed above McGarr's head as he entered the shop. "Is it a hat you're after?"

" 'Tis that," said McGarr, thinking of how in his youth it had been Belfast, not Dublin, that had been the friendly city. He handed one of the two smaller women his hat and allowed the other to help him off with his Chesterfield, the label of which was also—he saw in a towering, arched, three-way mirror that dominated the front of the shop—duly examined. The piece matched a ponderous curly-maple chair, cushioned with fraying chintz, that had been positioned in front of it. "Have you anything like that?"

"Like what?" the tall woman, who was obviously blind, asked. Placing her hands on McGarr's shoulders, she eased him into the chair.

The hat was reached to her, and as her long fingers, which in the haze of the old mirror seemed almost blue, worked over the hat—assaying its line, feeling its bevel, drumming across its crown—the youngest of the three explained, "Mildred's the hatter here. Caps is Margaret's line. I keep the till." A small furrow appeared in the shiny arch of her brow: fifty, perhaps fifty-five, she was a slight woman with a cheerful face, as round and as bright as an apple. Over the knitted puce dress, which was what they all wore, was a starched linen apron. Her thin legs devolved to heavy kitchen shoes that were flecked with flour, and from the rear of the building came the aroma of something baking.

"Although almost totally mass-produced," concluded the tall woman, "it is, I suppose, an adequate hat."

At just under £100, McGarr hoped so.

"Mend that," she said, keeping a finger on a small tear as she passed the hat to the woman named Margaret, who was a match for the first in all but age. "We're not Cavanaugh's, Mr.—"

"McGarr."

164

"No *Martinis*, no *young* ladies for pamper and show, and not—mind you—Cavanaugh's high prices, though I'm sure you'll agree one must pay for quality. We can, however, offer you a cup of hot and a fresh-baked scone, if you'd like."

McGarr liked, and the heavy kitchen shoes shuffled off down a shadowed hall.

On his head her hands felt like soft, stinging ice, searching out, as would a phrenologist, its contours, the fingers playing over every lump and line.

"Seven and an eighth. A busy life you've had, Mr. McGarr. With your head. A bearer perhaps?" Her smile was thin, and she now held his head as in a caress.

"Of nothing but sad tidings," said McGarr, having decided that it was best to misrepresent himself even further.

"Which explains the bowler," she replied, removing her hands. "Not many men these days will wear one, except on the Twelfth." She meant the July celebration of the Battle of the Boyne. "And then all most want are—what shall I call them . . . ?" The one eye searched the ceiling, while the other remained fixed on McGarr's image in the mirror. She was a stately woman, whose long, bony face in no way resembled those of the other two. On the appropriate finger was a wedding band; the sign outside said "Henry P. MacGonigall."

"Replicas," McGarr supplied.

Her face lit up so that she seemed for a moment almost pretty. She cocked her head. "Yes. Exactly. Though"—the smile cracked—"you're from the South yourself." Her hands were now grouped below what had once been an imposing chest, and McGarr imagined that in her time she had been a handsome woman. A tuft of ginger-colored hair imperfectly concealed a glaze of scar tissue on the side of her face near the glass eye.

"Dublin," said McGarr.

"Do you like it there?" Though masked, it was the question

165

which was inevitable even in the most casual conversation in the North—that of McGarr's religious persuasion.

"I suppose it's much like Belfast was a few years back."

"Peaceful?"

"Within reason," said McGarr, sensing that the drift of the conversation was contrary to his purpose.

"Tell me—do people there often think of us here?"

Only when forced to, McGarr thought, but then, "With pity and fear."

Said the woman who was mending his hat, "I'm sure it's not the kind of peace I—"

"A *single* bowler, is it, sir?" the tall woman asked, cutting her off.

McGarr, who was always in need of hats, had felt the touch of competence in her icy fingers, and certainly the hat that they had found at Herbert Park House had been well made. "Actually, I was thinking of the bowler, and then a hat for the out-of-doors. I do a bit of fishing."

"Bream?" she asked, which was considered "coarse" fishing.

"Salmon," McGarr corrected, and she tilted her head, her wan smile reappearing as though she were concluding that although most probably Catholic it was a gentleman she had on her hands. "Then, a cap or two—one in green houndstooth, I should think, and another navy-blue. There are times as well that I find a fedora indispensable."

Ah, yes—a *fedora*, she as much as crooned. The smile grew more complete, forming delicate knobs of pleasure on her cheeks, the one movable eye searching for McGarr below her. Her hands moved back onto his shoulders. A pat. Another.

Then: "You realize, I hope, that this is a custom house. We build hats prepaid to order."

"Miss—" McGarr began to say.

"Mrs.," she corrected, her thumb running over the gold band on her finger.

"Mrs. MacGonigall—I would not be here otherwise."

It was then that the tea arrived, and McGarr, using the excuse of the excellent scones—light, airy, hardly there at all; they had been made with lard—mostly listened. He learned that the two smaller women were MacGonigalls as well, sisters of Henry, who had been killed in the car crash that had blinded his wife; that after the several IRA bombing campaigns in the center of Belfast, trade had dropped off to next to nothing; that they had considered moving, as had their custom, to some distant suburb of Belfast or Bangor, Lisburn, or (Margaret's choice) Ballyclare, but had not the means; and finally that they had also considered "building" ladies hats and (in utter desperation) contemplated, if briefly, "emigrating" to Dublin.

Did many men there still fancy hats? Were rents dear? What would be made of a name so obviously . . . "Scottish" (a euphemism for Protestant) there? Slathering a scone with sweet whipped butter and tangy lime marmalade, McGarr opined that Dubliners would make nothing more of it than one recognizably Catholic, "though at the proper address your name might even be advantageous." He then revealed the fact that his own wife's family's business—Frenche Galleries of Dawson Street—had been a going concern for generations. "The carriage trade," Margaret said into her teacup, which she had grasped in both hands like a chalice.

The fact that McGarr was in some way a "hybrid" cast a new and an even rosier light on him, which in silence they appreciated severally until the tall woman—Mildred by name—spoke up. "Tell us, sir, how you came to hear of us?"

It was the question McGarr had been waiting for, and he explained that a hat had been left in his ". . . establishment. Light green, it is. Alpine in shape, with a small spray of feathers in the brim. Although not to my taste"—he regarded them over the lip of his raised cup—"I could see that it was a lovely thing, well made and to custom. Peering into the liner,

I found your name, though not—as I expected—that of the owner. Being a man in need of the odd hat and preferring (I hope you'll take this as it's meant, which is Irish) to trade with my own, I decided that while up here on business I might stop in and order a few things. London is . . ." He let the silence carry whatever assessment they might have of that city.

And it was only after he had given them his address and paid—"Cash. No," he averred, "I insist. Why put the banks, God *bless* them, to any bother"—that Mildred inquired of the hat.

"I don't understand," said McGarr, who was being helped on with his overcoat.

"Did you manage to find its owner? Every liner is mono-grammed before it leaves here. It's a service we offer, free of charge."

"But this one wasn't. No name, no monogram. Nothing in it. And with the bereft coming and going . . ."

"Size?" asked Mildred, her hands held out before her as though grasping a head.

"Ten, of all sizes. Huge. I—"

McGarr glanced up to see the two sighted women exchange glances and the third nod her head once. "The big fella. The one who comes in here and pays, like you, sir, cash in advance, then returns to pick the hat up himself. No mailing to—"

"Mildred!" Margaret interrupted. "There's some—and he's one—who prefer anonymity."

"Oh . . . that." The blind woman's hand came up, as though to touch her left breast. "Though what's the difference, Margaret? There's probably not a man on the streets, now, without—"

"And, then," Margaret again cut in, "how do we know it's his?"

"Whose else would it be? Even the last we built like that was a present to him, sure."

With a histrionic disgust that told McGarr that she did not often get the chance of giving out to the taller woman, Margaret said, "Now, how could we know that? What makes you think—"

"Who else, I ask you? In all the years—forty-seven, count them—that we've been here, have we had an order for a size ten green Alpine *without* a monogram?"

"Twice by two different men."

"And the second with a hat size of seven and a half, if that. No fitting. No presentation. A gift, it was, from one to the other."

"But we don't *know* that."

"We do."

"Ladies, ladies," said McGarr. "Please, now. I'm a man of business, and I'm only after wanting to put that hat back on the head of the man who lost it. A name, is all I ask. An address. Anything. If the first of those two men wishes to remain anonymous, so be it. I'll try the second."

"A pained silence followed. Finally Mildred explained, "That's impossible too. He gave us the order and paid cash, like yourself. Returned one afternoon and collected it."

"When was that?" McGarr asked.

"Last month."

"Well"—McGarr looked down into the liner of his own hat—"I suppose that's that. Sure, I tried my best. Now I'm in possession of a lovely green hat, size ten. A veritable sombrero." He laughed, reaching for the door handle.

"You could, of course, send it up here to us, and we—"

"Mr. Paddy Geer was the second man to purchase a hat like that," said the cashier, who was called Madeleine, without looking up from her account book. "Lives in the Short Strand on the Albertbridge Road. His is the modern house, the only house left in the row. I went to school with his father, bless him. Killed in the war. Dunkirk."

169

11

"**B**ody is that of a preadolescent female child showing marked postmortem decomposition with strong putrefactive body odor. Body cool—covered by maggots and rodent feces. Scalp moist—covered by thin, moist blond hair. Hair loosely attached—easily plucked from scalp. Right posterior parietal scalp, upper swollen and bruised, discolored dark reddish-black. Right eyeball marked postmortem decomposition—left orbit marked by moderate amount gray-white mold. Nose missing. Skin covering upper jaw and right lower jaw missing—bones exposed. Lips soft—marked by postmortem decomposition. Mouth—maggot-infested. Tongue missing. Teeth . . ."

The voice of the compact blond man droned on, as it had now for—how many days? two, three?—since they had finally realized that she would say nothing: supposedly (for it had only ever been proven by Garda memoranda) revealing to her the litany of crimes and the description of the victims of J. Rheiner or James Ryan or Seamus Rhines, so many now that Roisin at once could no longer believe them and suspected at least some might be true.

But the man who was sitting at the graphic projector with a torch pointer in hand—"Dt. Sgt. B. McKeon" by pocket tag—had kept returning to the autopsies of two people, a father and daughter who, while berrying in a Leitrim field of a Sunday afternoon, had, it was assumed, witnessed the mining of an RUC checkpoint on the Fermanagh border. "Your Seamus Rhines, dear," he had said, "he leaves no witnesses. Scrupulous, he is. Absolutely. Heedless of age or"—in the near darkness of the interrogation room, he had tried to collect her eyes—"innocence."

The screen was large, and the images impossible to ignore. With hands trussed behind them, they had been stuffed into the boot of a car that had then been concealed in a hayrick and only discovered a month later. And there they were above her, like twin grinning and hideous fetuses—mouths gaping, facial bones protrusive—contained in a brimming caul of maggots and slime.

"Entrance of the bullet wound, as you can see"—clicking a switch, he then brought up a picture of the little girl laid out, like a gutted rabbit, on a pathologist's steel table, the structure of her decomposed face turned to the side to reveal how she had been slain—"is the right side of the head, centered at a point eight inches posterior to the glabella, seven-eighths of an inch to the right of the midsagittal line."

With the addition of articles and auxiliary verbs, Roisin glanced over at the man to discover that he had placed the copy of the autopsy on the table, though he continued to speak from it, as if from memory. "The wound is round, measuring three-sixteenths of an inch in diameter. The edges of the wound are hard, frayed, crusty, inverted, with apparent blackening and scorching of gunpowder burns. The wound perforates the dura and the brain parenchyma. The brain tissue— look at it—is soft, pasty, grayish-pink, with marked post-mortem decomposition. The anatomical markings are completely obliterated, and a large, irregular, distorted lead bullet is lodged in the decomposed brain tissue." He again changed the picture to show the skull stripped of its scalp and then opened, like a clam. There in the jell that had been her brain was a lozenge-shaped chunk of lead.

"This wound was lethal. It perforated the right posterior parietal bone and linearly fractured the left orbital, frontal, and sphenoid bones, and came to rest in the left posterior fossa at the base of—"

"That's enough," she said in a small voice barely audible over the whirr of the fan.

McKeon glanced up from the page. "You said something?" And when she did not repeat it, he reached for the thick copy of the autopsy, as though to begin again.

"I said that is enough," she now repeated with angry authority.

In the slit of light produced by the projector, his small, dark eyes flashed. "Is it, now?" But for its truculence his tone matched hers exactly. "Certainly it was enough for this wee"— when his voice cracked, she glanced up at him, and, like stones clashing, their eyes met—"lassie who had her life ripped from her. And maybe enough for a nurse used to the gore of surgeries and gunmen and thieves. But here's the question— and listen up, sweets; you'll not leave this room until you tell me—is it enough for Mr. Seamus Rhines or James Ryan or J. Rheiner or whatever the hell he calls himself when he's off on a bombing run?"

"Whatever that is," she bit back without thinking, "it's surely better than whatever it is you're being paid for here."

"Which is?"

"What is?"

"Whatever he calls himself—patriot and soldier one day, terrorist and assassin of wee children the next."

"We don't know that," she said.

"But we do." Quick for all his size, McKeon was suddenly on his feet, searching through the stacks of papers on the table. "It's in the bloody song, you know so yourself. Bragged about it, he did."

"But you"—she shot out the back of her hand, her eyes blazing because she had been forced into speech, only to embrace a position that she held neither easily nor well—"fat and happy here in Dublin, not knowing or caring what's happening to your own people in the North and, in fact, conspiring—"

McKeon's head came up.

"Yes—*conspiring* in the repression of those who are actually doing something about the situation there. What would *you* prefer to have done about that—nothing? Or something?"

Slowly McKeon straightened up, his hands moving to his hips, his eyes to the sordid scene pictured on the screen. He then appeared to shrug and cock his head once, and in turning to her he seemed suddenly old, the paunch of his belly repeated in the pouches of his face.

Pulling his chair closer to her, he sat and placed his hand, palm up, on the table. "Miss Johnston—take my hand."

"I will not."

"You will." When she hesitated, he insisted. "Go on, now—take it." His eyes were not small, but rather closely spaced, which made them appear so; she glanced toward the stenographer in the corner before touching her palm to his.

"Something," he said, looking down at their hands, "because something must be done and all things are possible. But if that something invariably results in death, then what can we say about that something?" His tone was low and contemplative; it was a subject, she believed, which he had considered before. "*That* something is wrong. Categorically. No two ways about it.

"Then what can be done? Well, since force is wrong, we must try reason. What is it about"—he touched the tips of the fingers of his other hand to his breast—"ourselves that

173

makes all those people in the North think we're ogres? The 'hatred of generations,' the 'curse of history,' some 'tribal animosity' beyond explication? I don't think so, since neither of *us* was born with any of that—were we?—and we know that we're both people of good will who want nothing more than to live and let live.

"Then perhaps it's the way we appear that makes them want to do anything—fight, die, kill us, kill themselves—rather than become part of the Greater Us that so many think is a geographical imperative. We profess toleration, equality, and democracy, but why do you think our own Protestant population, which, if my memory serves me right, was seven percent of the Twenty-six Counties in 1921, has now all but evaporated? Could it be because we've allowed our institutions, which should be separate, to become so confused—constitutionally, administratively, personally—that the one must seem (to them, now, not to us, who *know* better) merely the public-affairs bureau of the other?

"And I'm not referring just to the abortion issue or divorce or censorship. Or to the fact that over ninety-six percent of our schools are Catholic. Or even to the bloody *Constitution*, which for thirty-five years all but conferred official status on the Catholic Church. No. I'm referring to Irish life, from football of a Sunday afternoon to the necessary pint after, that Catholic attitudes, but, more, Catholic practices, do not pervade.

"I'm not blaming the Church—mind—which must plump for its own interests, but could it be they've been a mite too successful? From the cradle through school and marriage to the grave, we've allowed one institution and one alone to tell us how to think. Life, work, duty, guilt, and death. 'Home Rule Is Rome Rule'?" he concluded, quoting a pre-Partition Loyalist slogan.

On his palm her own was frying, and her hand had begun

to shake. Off in the room, the dull click of the recording machine had grown suddenly loud. "They weren't far wrong, were they? Nor those others who wanted to make this place into 'The Holy Isle.'

"And to what purpose? An end to Northern Ireland?" Still staring down at their hands, McKeon shook his head, his graying blond locks stirring gently on his forehead. "Neither the Catholic Church nor the great mass of the politicians it props up want that, and why should they? A monopoly they've got with no unified opposition, and gone suddenly would be the . . . tension that people like you and Rhines"—she tried to pull away, but his fingers now crimped over her hand— "have maintained over the years to keep the many, who would prefer to think of others as individuals and the great group of others as humanity, thinking instead of sides. Our side. And *their* side. And in such a way, my dear, you and 'poor' Rhines have been dupes.

"No—with opposition like that right here on this side of the border, it's hard to fault you for doing *something* up there in the North. For instance, shooting that little"—she struggled harder to free her hand but could not budge it—"lassie, but, you know"—McKeon shook his head, then raised to her a face sagged with a sadness that she herself had never known, his eyes, which were filled with tears, fixing her gaze—"I do."

Having ceased her exertions, she said, "But it wasn't me."

"As much as if you pulled the trigger," he replied.

Perhaps a quarter hour after he had left, Roisin reached for the copy of the autopsy he had been reading from. "Case No. LEIT GS 80883. MOIRA MCKEON, HOMICIDE BY SHOOTING. BULLET WOUND BACK OF HEAD. LACERATION AND HEMOR-RHAGE OF BRAIN." The second autopsy was that of her father.

"Related?" she asked of the Ban Gharda, a large woman with bright red hair who had remained seated at her machine. "Related to who?"

"To him. Detective Sergeant McKeon."

"His son and *their* daughter, if you can appreciate that."

Roison, whose family before Seamus Rhines had been the most and perhaps the only important aspect of her life, could indeed. And to have him, Seamus, the little boy with whom she had grown up and with whom she had now decided she would have (and probably had now even begun) her own family, responsible for those deaths? The Seamus Rhines who seemed, beyond all else, a gentle man with quiet talents and a respect for life so . . . integral to his personality that he had gone out of his way to help any and all? Impossible, she thought, pushing the thick, stapled folds of paper aside. It was just a police ploy to get her to talk.

But she thought of him on the stage, as she had seen him in Canada. He was an actor and accomplished, she reminded herself, but how . . . totally? And what McKeon the detective had just said to her was no act, of that much she was sure.

Turning her head to the darkness of the window, she wondered where he was now and what *exactly* he was doing. Seamus Rhines.

He was in the ambience he most enjoyed, no more than two hundred yards from where Roisin was sitting in Dublin Castle. Leaning back against the studs of what had been a temporary dressing room when he himself had used it twenty years before, he breathed in the pungent, musky, ancient reek of greasepaint, so long in the bright glare of the bare bulbs that surrounded a horseshoe mirror that it had worked its way, like oil, into the wood of the table and the floor.

And he smiled, thinking of Duncan, who, in addition to freeing up the position without which none of what they planned would have been practicable, had also programmed and processed the tape, supplying them with the names of six . . . surrogates. From that list Rhines had selected just one, and it was with a profound sense of contentment that he now peered across the dressing room at his choice, who was perfecting his face before a performance. He had, he believed, made the best selection. The age, which was somewhat advanced; the weight, which was a bit heavy; the height, which was about average; even the baldness was right. And then the little hair that remained could, like Rhines's own now in disguise, be changed, and other telling characteristics created, for that was the talent of the man before him. It was, however, the facial features that were correct. Dead on, Rhines thought. Yes, he had found his man.

Casting director, stage manager, director, and producer—Rhines had been and would be them all again for the last time. And now what was he? Agent for an *agent provocateur?* The thought rather amused him.

"But—it's only suicide you're asking of me?" said the man at the lights.

"No, John, you didn't listen to me. I told you, we'll get you out. The last thing we want is for you to be discovered there, and we'll have provided for that."

"So you tell me, but the SAS? And you know so yourself, Seamus, it's not like the stage. Once the thing goes off, anything can and probably will happen, and more than likely for the worst."

The actor shook his head. He was fluffing a great bush of white eyebrow, which would be perfect when dyed black. Pozzo of Beckett's *Godot*, apropos of which Rhines judged it was time to offer the stick, the carrot having failed.

"I must tell you, John, it's now tantamount to suicide, should you truly say no."

The hand came down from the brow, and a face that looked as if it had suffered an eternity of abuse turned to him—lined, creased and puckered, a large nose dominant. "You're coddin' me."

Rhines shook his head. "There's a time for jokin', John, and we've had ours. I've been given the task, and I chose you.

"The money. I know you and—what are their names?"— Rhines, reaching into a suit-coat pocket, removed the computer printout—"Moira, Siobhan, Padraic could use it. And, John, I know you're fadin' and fast." He opened another fold of the sheet and read, " 'Arteriolar nephrosclerosis. Malignant.' How long have they given you—six months or a year?"

The man's shoulders fell, and he lowered his head, so that he appeared yet more world-weary, which Rhines had thought not possible. "Six, if that. It's why I'm working as much as I can." There was a long and noisy pause, in which the stage manager banged on the door and shouted, "Places. Places."

Finally, the man said, "But *how*, Seamus—can you tell me that?"

"You'll have to play Lady Macbeth, I'm afraid, in the 'dunnest smoke of hell.' "

His head went down, and he sighed. "I never enjoyed the killing. You know that. And, Christ, how will I manage that? The security there— "

"You'll carry it in."

The dark eyes came up. "You must be mad."

Rhines smiled. "There're some who think so, but I'll assure you this—you'll scarcely know it's on you yourself."

Again the door received several insistent blows. "Places!"

"Jesus." The man used both hands to push himself up from the dresser, then turned to Rhines. "You don't suppose I could have an advance?" In his eyes was the resignation that Rhines had sought.

"What part do you have in mind?" Rhines reached for his billfold.

12

From afar, through a thin fog that now, as the day declined, seeped in over the Short Strand, Geer's house rose in dark, staggered tiers, phoenixlike and solitary from the surrounding rubble. Four floors it was, and fronted in the Strand with a sunken and walled "back" garden running down to the Albertbridge Road. Before the wall stood a grimy glass-sided and opaque-roofed bus stop, which was all McGarr had to see to know it was possible.

Having phoned ITN and been told that Mr. Paddy Geer would be away on assignment for the next several days, McGarr had taken a taxi up the Albertbridge Road to scan the tight pack of mean four-room row houses and narrow streets that was the Strand. There, he knew, security would be, as in the other Catholic areas of Belfast, at once more total and less obvious than the arrangements the British Army had made in the city center. Eyes mostly, and ears and memories for faces, dress, deportment, even the way one walked. Surrounded and embattled, theirs was a consciousness that no army of occupation could hope to emulate and no one man breach—at least from within—and the less he was seen the better.

Thus he had returned to the central business district and

checked into a hotel, where he pulled his cousin's Austin into the car park. From the phone in his room, he then called the Belfast Board of Works and, pretending to be a photographer, learned that the lights along the Albertbridge Road were not switched on until 10:35 of a glowery late-spring evening.

At two different hardware shops he purchased a diamond-bit glass cutter, a meter-long metal T-square, and a roll of clear tape. At an auto-supply agency a rack for a car top, with four stout suction cups. He returned to his room, where he rumpled the bed to make it look slept in, and left by a back stairs, a dining room, and a bar. After what had seemed to him an interminable wait in a city-center pub, McGarr boarded at 5:10 an eastbound bus, sitting, as he had planned, on the upper deck, where he could look over any walls into the tired brick and sagging slate of the Short Strand.

And through a thin rain wrung from the char of a lowering sky, the slogans that had long been a facet of the Belfast experience appeared to McGarr, as they had throughout the day. Years old and faded and nearly gone were "SUPPORT THE 5 DEMANDS," "DON'T LET THEM DIE," "SUPPORT OUR POWS," and "POLITICAL STATUS NOW." But stark and splashed on the rain-wet walls were newer, more strident demands: "SHOOT SOLDEIRS [sic], NOT HEROIN," "GOD MADE MAN AND THE ARMALITE MADE HIM EQUAL," then James Connolly's observation, which, if accurate, had been in his day premature, "THE WORKER IS THE SLAVE OF THE CAPITALIST STATE, THE WOMAN IS THE SLAVE OF THAT SLAVE," and finally "GIVE THEM THEIR RIGHTS, NOT THEIR LAST RITES."

Shouts, they were, imprecations from the rubble of lives passed in the knowledge that on principle they could only be in some crucial way poorly spent. Cries from this patch of slum cramped onto a low corner of a riverbank near a gutted bus works and an all-but-abandoned shipyard which even in its prime had offered few Catholics work and then as navvies alone. McGarr looked out over the burnt-out husks of trashed cars, discarded fridges, bottles, cans, a busted pram, paths footworn through a desolation that their fathers had trudged before them, and he wondered why? Why was this ground and the many other unlovely "islands" of Catholic population —the Bogside and the Creggan in Derry, the Divis and Unity Flats across the river—so important to them?

Because, simply, they would not give it up? No—for through need or emigration many already had. The distinction, he believed—looking out at the sentinel of Geer's house down the street—was brutally finer than that. Here a people (or, rather, a tribe) had made a stand and, short of annihilation, would not be driven from this spot. Collecting his parcels and pushing the button for the driver to stop, he remembered the other slogans that he had seen earlier in the day, in Protestant sections farther to the east. So much retouched that the white lettering seemed like a veneer of calcified stone, they said, "HAVE YOU BEEN SAVED?," which meant, Are you *truly* one of us? And "THIS WE WILL MAINTAIN," which meant, We are prepared to die. And yet another now appeared to him on the side of a bus going the other way, "IF YOU HAVE INFORMATION ABOUT MURDER, EXPLOSIONS, INTIMIDATION, OR ACTS OF TERRORISM, IN COMPLETE CONFIDENCE CALL BELFAST 652155."

Two tribes, one locally dominant, being played off against each other by the third in Westminster, which now had all but tired of the game. Hatred blinded them, he concluded, lurching off the bus and under the canopy of the stop in front (or, rather, in back) of Geer's house. He then looked down the Albertbridge Road, as if for a bus with a different route number, and waited for the other people there to board the one he had just gotten off.

After it had departed, he placed his parcels on top of the wall and stepped back out to peer around the dirty glass, noting that no other pedestrians were approaching in either direction. He checked his watch. Five thirty-two. Drivers had flicked on their fog lights; given the street lamps, it was, he imagined, about as dark as it ever got along the Albertbridge Road.

Passing back under the canopy, he reached up and shoved the parcels over the wall and—mindful of the devices that had been discovered in the culvert by Herbert Park House—he waited, listening. Hearing nothing, he then paused further for a break in the traffic there in front of the shelter, and when it was clear, he placed one foot on the bench that was shackled to the wall and thrust himself to the top, to slide off into the deep shadows on the other side. The fall was longer than he had imagined, and his heels, plunging into the soft humus that formed a margin around the back garden, made his knees thump on his chest.

There too he waited, but briefly, then picked up the parcels and stepped resolutely across the shaggy lawn to the sliding glass doors of the patio. Without looking behind him, McGarr set down the parcels and in the encroaching darkness tried to determine if the double-glazed panes had been wired, which was unlikely. He unwrapped the largest parcel, removed a single throw of the rack, and, after spitting on the cups, fastened it to the glass. Then with the T-square and glass cutter he scribed out a square cut large enough for him to duck into and also reseal the cut once inside. He had to work over and back over the track—the cutting wheel squealing in its groove—before, with a tap and a tug, the section came free.

The second cut, which was necessarily somewhat smaller and more difficult to make, took longer, but once it came clear, McGarr gathered up the bottom of his slicker and with extreme care contorted himself into—what was it?—the dining room of the house. Once he had pulled in the parcel wrappers, he concentrated all his attention on the delicate

182

manipulation of turning the first section, so that the rack was now inside, and fitting it into the aperture. It took precise pressure to keep it from coming too far; and then he could not be sure if the cups would hold.

Minutes went by, and finally, when securing the corners with the clear tape, McGarr found that he was sweating. Only as he was about to draw the curtains across the door did he look out into the back garden, the wall, and the Beersbridge Road above. The cadmium-vapor street lamps had just begun to glow; in five minutes the area would be bright. A bus, its second tier packed with commuters, lumbered to a stop. McGarr waited and, after it had left, pulled the drapes to. He reached into a pocket for his penlight.

The kitchen satisfied the definition but minimally—a sink, a cupboard, a table with a white, cone-shaped, porcelain lamp-shade above it, two chairs, a two-ring cooker, and a tiny fridge meant for a one-room flat or the galley of a small boat. In it were two cartons of Jaffa juice, a tin of half-eaten bristlings, a puckered, sagging tomato, seven uncapped rolls of film for a still camera, and three reels for a movie camera. In the cupboard were several forlorn groups of canned goods and a pot, a kettle, two plates, two glasses, two cups. McGarr did not need to see more. Bachelor digs. Geer did not live— indeed, he probably hardly ever ate—in his kitchen.

The ground-floor room beyond was a kind of urban mud room, used for storage, and contained mainly items used in the man's work—tripods, stanchions arrayed with braces of lights, drop cloths, wheeled dollies—with a few jackets, some rubber boots, three umbrellas, and a battered case (McGarr touched its clasp, which sprung open to reveal the green folds of a button-accordion bellows); in all, a place to drop things, once inside the door.

The rooms on the upper floors were for the most part similarly Spartan: a sitting room with a single easy chair drawn up to a circular, cast-iron fireplace with a hood, like a mushroom cap, and a shiny green stack that ran up to heat the two upper levels and changed in color in the bedrooms to white and in the study on the top floor to orange, completing the colors of the Republic's flag. It was there, in a kind of penthouse, that McGarr discovered where the man lived.

The room had been divided in three sections: what appeared to McGarr to be a library/museum, roofed with glass panels, like a conservatory or a greenhouse, a small projection room with four actual theatre seats; and a darkroom with film-editing facilities.

But it was the library that attracted McGarr first. It was stacked with books, pamphlets, magazines, and newspapers, almost all devoted to Ireland or to what McGarr deemed was the Ulster experience. Under glass in display cases located throughout the large room were arrays of colorful and various Orange sashes; a collection of what appeared at first to be bars of fudge but were, in fact, the several and often lethal varieties of rubber (plastic) bullets that British forces had fired in the North; cameo brooches of the fifteen men whose deaths in the Maze Prison hunger strike of 1981 had galvanized Catholic sentiment, north and south of the border. On one wall were displayed blackthorn sticks—the choicest collection McGarr had ever seen—and on the other were silver-handled swords in their bucklers, appropriately and eerily lit through the windows above by the orange cadmium-vapor lamps along the Beersbridge Road.

Then patches of all the British forces that had served in the North since the outbreak of hostilities in 1969: the Black Watch, the Royal Regiment of Wales, the First and Third Light Infantries, the Queen's Lancashires, the Green Howards . . . it went on and on.

McGarr then viewed a collection of party favors, buttons, pencils, and caps embossed or printed with unlovely sectarian sayings. Next came a phonograph-record collection, audio tapes, reels of movie films stacked upright on every shelf of a deep closet: "NICRA Marches," "The Stormont Collapse," "Loyalist Walks" for the years 1972 through '85, "The Abercorn Restaurant Blast Aftermath" . . .

And all was—McGarr discovered as he continued his perusal, checking his wristwatch and seeing that three and a half quick hours had passed—referenced on index cards in a master catalogue. In it he learned that Geer had also compiled a "Personalities File," with extensive biographies on nearly every person who had figured in the politics of Northern Ireland from its founding in 1921 to the present: John Andrews was there, as were Neil Blaney, Alexander Boyd, Basil Brooke, Charles Butler, Isaac Butt, Edward Carson. . . . McGarr's eyes returned to the name of Blaney, who could be considered a "Northern Irish" politician only in the broadest sense of the phrase, hailing as he did from Donegal, which had been part of the ancient Celtic Ulster but was now within the Republic.

David Lloyd George, Tommy Lyttle—it went on and on, with subheadings (personal life, political offices, religious and fraternal affiliations, etc.) for the major political figures such as James Craig, William Craig, Terence O'Neill, Ian Paisley, whose file took up nearly an entire drawer, and dozens and dozens of other figures.

McGarr worked through the night and most of the next day, marveling at the man's—Geer's—obsessiveness and piecing out as much of the material as his eyes, tired by the thin light of the pocket torch the night before, could tolerate. He was startled in the morning by the rattling bottles of the milkman, and later by the rap and shout of the postman.

But it was only in the afternoon of the following day, while waiting for a tin of soup to come to a boil, that he discovered something which he had missed on the earlier search and which of all the extraordinary things in the dwelling attracted

185

him most. It had been concealed in a compartment that had been fabricated into the end of the concertina case, which he had found in the ground-floor storeroom: a reel of film. Unlike all the other reels that he had seen, it was sealed in a watertight case that itself was sheathed in a plastic, zip-locked pouch. McGarr wondered what Geer had thought so valuable that it should be given such care.

In the fourth-floor studio, McGarr fixed the film on a sprocket and snaked its end through the projector, then switched it on and adjusted the volume until it was just barely audible. He took a seat by the door, which he left open.

It began with a series of stills that pictured a tall, "mountainy" farmer who in the 1920s came down from the Antrim hills to preach in Ballymena. "A Baptist," the rich voice of a narrator said, "he married a Scottish governess who bore him two sons, the younger of whom, like his father, tried farming for a time, only to turn to religion."

Performed by his father, Ian Paisley's ordination into the Christian ministry did not conform to the practices of the Northern Ireland Presbyterian Church and remained under a cloud. At the time, it seemed, the young minister could not even manage to conduct a mission of a Presbyterian church that was temporarily lacking a minister, and when the presbytery objected to him, he and a handful of followers broke away, forming the Free Presbyterian Church of Ulster.

It was, the film suggested, Ian Paisley's first step toward his eventual success. Contemptuous of rules, he here decided he would make his own. Even if cramped into a chapel near the Harland & Wolff Shipyard and ministering to the unemployed and working poor, Paisley suddenly found himself not merely a reverend or a minister or even a canon, but, rather, the moderator of a church body entire, answering to nobody but himself. "It was a lesson that Paisley would take to politics, when he broke from the Unionists to form his own party, and he wielded his moderatorship with pride, though nearly two decades of virtual obscurity were to follow. The year was 1951."

By 1962 Paisley was desperate for public attention and—McGarr was made to conclude—power. It was then that he launched upon a virulent, anti-Catholic, anti-Pope, antiecumenical campaign. Not satisfied with abusing the half million Catholics in his midst or the four million south of the border, Paisley twice flew to Italy to berate "Old Red Socks" on his own soil. The second time he forced his way aboard the Archbishop of Canterbury's plane, which was bound for Rome and discussions at the Vatican, only to have Italian police hustle him onto another, which flew him straight back. It proved to be just what he wanted, however—media attention in a world forum—and McGarr now watched a young, trim Paisley with a great, dark pompadour being trundled along the tarmac of Fiumicino, while he railed against "That Scarlet Woman" (the Roman Catholic Church) and the Archbishop of Canterbury, who was "slobbering on the slippers of the Pope."

Yet when his first efforts to make political capital of his growing religious support produced little, Paisley's genius showed itself. The lesson that he had gleaned from his years of obscurity was clear: events, not issues, would make him, and he would have to force events. The year was 1964, and Paisley protested the flying of an Irish tricolor above a Catholic housing project during a British general election. Claiming it violated the "Flags and Emblems Act," he demanded that the RUC take it down.

But when the police, armed with Sten guns and riot gear, arrived there, fighting broke out. Sticks, stones, and petrol bombs—the first seen in Ulster in thirty years—were thrown, and Paisley got just what he wanted: not the removal of the tricolor, which began appearing in every quarter of Catholic

Belfast, but, rather, media coverage that put him on the front pages of the newspapers and on the television screen north and south of the border, in Britian, and in much of the Western world.

Said the narrator, "For three decades prior to the Divis Street incident, Northern Irish Catholics had maintained an uneasy but steady peace with a Stormont government that had consistently ignored their needs and conspired in the abuse of their rights. Paisley shattered that."

And as Paisley had learned from failure, so too did he learn from success. And the lesson? McGarr cocked his head, realizing what indeed had become the point of the film, for in the casuistry of what from 1964 became Paisley's standard stratagem there was an artfulness that was demoniacally sublime. If paradox depended upon the contradiction of received opinion, then Paisley was a study in paradox.

In what McGarr considered a brilliant collage of quick clips that capsuled three decades of history, he watched Paisley state flatly that if, since 1950, the IRA had seemed to grow weak, it was only because they were rearming, training untold hundreds of volunteers and infiltrating the nascent civil-rights movement. If Catholics with their demands for reform were seeking to bring about evolutionary change by peaceful means, they had to be dealt with harshly, "with gas, batons, guns, and bullets."

Though decrying violence from the pulpit, Paisley was now shown calling himself "Adjutant of the First Battalion of the Ulster Volunteer Force," the ranks of which paramilitary group were filled out with hoodlums and toughs. After the UVF man who confessed to murdering four employees of the Malvern Arms Hotel was shown saying, "I'm sorry I ever heard of that man Paisley or decided to follow him," Paisley denounced the killings and "the criminal element of any stamp." Yet when Paisley himself was released from a second jail sentence to

188

conduct a political campaign and found his support considerably enhanced with the "God-fearing, good people of Belfast," he proudly returned to jail to serve out his term. Prison, McGarr was made to conclude, was a tradition that Paisley's hard-core supporters obviously respected.

Having accused Prime Minister Terence O'Neill of being soft on dissidents, he then criticized O'Neill's successor, James Chichester-Clark, for asking the British to send in six thousand additional troops to deal with the increasing lawlessness. He said Chichester-Clark had capitulated, not to the British or the British Army or even to the civil-rights movement or the IRA, but, rather, to the "Roman Catholic Church". His vituperation was such that he in large measure helped bring down the Chichester-Clark government and that of Brian Faulkner, which led to the dissolution of representative government in Northern Ireland and to direct rule from London. When Britain later threatened to withdraw its troops, however, Paisley demanded that they remain "on British soil, protecting British subjects." At the same time, he kept demanding that the power to govern be returned to "the majority in Ulster." He seemed to want it every way—self-rule with the army and with chaos—for in political deadlock a well-armed majority could resist every change.

"For by that time Paisley had correctly perceived and had totally identified with the single purpose of the Ulster statelet—the maintenance above all else of privilege. Not once did he endorse a solitary practicable step that might lead to a settlement of the issues that divided the two communities. On the contrary, speaking from pulpits, from barricades, from a back bench in Westminster, and to Orange halls convened with armed and hooded men, Paisely succeeded in making the demands of Loyalist ultras impossible for any Northern Irish politician to ignore and primary to any British devolution of the status of the province.

"He also succeeded in making himself the most visible, popular, and charismatic leader in all of Northern Ireland. And while other sectarian politicians, such as Roy Bradford, were murdered on their doorsteps, the more highly visible Paisley . . ."

Thinking he heard something from below in the house, McGarr got up and moved quietly out to the stairs, where he listened for some time before deciding it was his imagination. In what was now nearly complete darkness he returned to the studio.

". . . Paisley's two hundred thousand zealots, and the other three hundred thousand who at one time or another had voted for the sectarian chieftain, would take to the streets. Without forewarning and a definite plan of defense, the ghettos of Belfast and the other pockets of Catholic population scattered throughout the Ulster countryside would be overrun. Sectarian bloodletting would begin."

The film then began to detail—as history?—nearly down to the phrase the language that was currently being used to describe the planned round of discussions between Charles Haughey, the Irish Taoiseach, and Margaret Thatcher. Even the main elements of the agenda, which in the pub a day earlier McGarr had read had been released for the first time, were included.

"By July 1985," the narrator went on, the month being a week away, "relations between Protestant ultras and the British government had deteriorated to such an extent that . . ."

Sensing danger behind him, McGarr spun around, instinctively throwing out his left elbow, which struck something solid but was held for a moment in a grip that hurt before it was cast aside with a careless disdain that knocked him from his seat.

Pivoting and rising from the carpet, McGarr saw a tall,

broad-shouldered older man wearing a light-green Alpine hat, whose eyes—dark and deadly calm—flickered toward the screen even as McGarr launched a punch.

It was caught—McGarr's fist—in a large palm that came up, like a wicket, and held on for a moment before a crushing force was applied that bent McGarr down in front of him—slowly, inexorably—with a severity of pain that brought his entire presence to the palm of that hand. He writhed, he kicked out. He tried to push off the anchored base of the theatre seats and yank, jerk, thrust his hand free, but he was held.

From the screen, which was now behind him, McGarr heard a shout, a cry of outrage, and then a scream that seemed—given his pain—to come from his own throat.

"The Big Man's down! He's fallen!" a voice said in disbelief.

McGarr wrenched his arm, trying to pull away from the man, but it felt as if his bones were being pulverized.

"There's blood everywhere."

On his back, McGarr tried to kick out at the man, who spun him around, jammed an elbow up under his chin, and snatched him to his feet. Something hard was then rammed against his back.

On the screen, which McGarr now faced, pandemonium reigned. People were crying, shouting, cursing—everywhere, it seemed. The camera then focused on the crazed, reddened face of a silver-sashed, bowler-hatted man whose arm was cocked and mouth tightened into a bloodless white line. In his hand was a heavy blackthorn stick. "Look out there," said another, curiously disembodied voice, and a vicious swipe knocked the camera from focus.

Pinioned now, like a fly on a tack, McGarr squirmed, the pain in his lower back excruciating.

"Bahs-tuds!" Somebody—obviously the figure on the screen—began to wail. "Yez rotten Romish *bahs*-tuds!" Until the screen

191

went dark or McGarr lost consciousness or was suddenly released.

When he came to, soldiers filled the room. They had seized the other man by the arms, which he raised, shrugging them off, as another emotionless voice said, "Not the sergeant major, the other one," and McGarr was hauled to his feet.

At the top of the stairs stood a man dressed in plain clothes. His clean-shaven face was pink, the skin like that of a baby, his eyes the color of blue steel.

"What's to be done with him?" a voice behind McGarr asked.

"He's to be processed and put back over the border where he belongs," said the man. "But mind the face."

It was then the baton was slipped between his legs.

Carron waited until the others had left, watching the end of the reel of film snap on the projector table, thinking about what had happened and what he had seen. Replaying it in his mind, struggling and failing to gather up all the strands. Finally he merely reached down and pulled the plug.

Out at the small bar, he debated as fully as he was able the question of a drink, which by the time—two full days later—Geer returned had become three bottles.

Having heard the old Fiat pull into the garage on the Strand side of the house, Carron met Geer in the storage room, where he might remain concealed, were Geer not alone.

"Paddy?" Carron asked, stepping out from the shadow of a locker there.

Surprised, Geer started. "George?" he asked, reaching out to steady himself under the weight of the two cameras that he was carrying. He looked worse than Carron had ever seen him. "I heard about the trouble here. Was it you?"

"Paddy—it's time we talked."

In straightening up, Geer swayed under the weight of the equipment, and Carron moved forward to help him.

When, back up in the study, Carron finally spoke, he said, "But it would make me a Lundy," meaning Robert Lundy, the Protestant governor of Londonderry who in 1689 attempted to surrender the city to the Catholic King James II rather than await the arrival of the Protestant King William III. In Loyalist circles the name had since come to mean a particularly loathsome type of traitor.

"Ah, *no*, George," said Geer, who had made sure that, together now, they had drunk drink for drink. "Don't you see that when . . . passions have died, history will see you differently.

"And for that it won't all be just tea and crumpets and the promise of a pint at the end of the day. There's that figure"— Geer motioned toward the slip of paper in Carron's large hand—"which is real, and it all will be yours. That's a promise from me. You want half now, you'll have the half."

Carron turned up his palm and glanced down at the number, which Geer had written out when he had had trouble comprehending the amount. "And who would pay . . . this?"

"Men who believe, as I do, that we owe it to future generations to clear the stream. Men who would like to see relations between our two peoples flow again. And the Big Lad— you know so yourself, George—has become the snag. As long as he lives, it's impossible."

"Republicans?" Carron asked without taking his eyes from the paper.

"Not all of them," Geer said, "but, to be honest, that's the point. But it's an inevitability, you know so yourself. Even the British intended it that way all along, and they with their Parliament and their compromise and all the endless dickering and rant, both sides, will only muddy the waters and prolong an agony which—George, we both know—we've supported far too long."

"But—" As if he were a bullock shackled in a yoke, Carron's large head swirled, his eyes sweeping the glass of the ceiling; it had grown dark again, and the orange phosphorescence there made it seem as though they were locked in an amber flux.

Geer thought of their mutual blood pooling in the rainwater by the back gate of Herbert Park House. "Yes." He nodded. "There'll be losses. Carnage. But . . . with it we'll make an end, once and for all, and settle down to the business of being one nation. At last."

After what Geer perceived as the longest time, Carron asked, his deep voice filling the room, "But, Paddy . . . why me? And why you? We were . . ." He waved an empty glass at the study walls and the swords and blackthorn sticks clustered there.

Just going through the motions, Geer concluded.

Handing Carron a refill, Geer said, "Well, George—it's not as if we were asked."

Carron folded the paper and slipped it in a pocket of his coat, and for perhaps a quarter hour they drank in silence. Finally, Carron said, "Can I see it again?"

"The film? Certainly—as often as you like." Geer stood.

While fixing the end through the machine, he asked, "I wonder—how much of it did our man see?" He meant the person that Carron had told him about earlier, the one that the soldiers—and who had alerted *them*, he wondered—had taken away.

Enough, thought Carron, though it would hardly matter, with all who seemed to be in on it. And now Fairclough, who had been Blount's partner and was now himself Ulster Risks, Ltd.

Paisley's protector.

194

IV
Close-up

13

"**T**OP COP SACKED," read the banner headline in the newspaper O'Shaughnessy had raised to conceal what he believed must be a bulge under his right lapel, though an hour before McKeon had assured him there was none. The story described how McGarr had broken into a Belfast house, where, after a struggle, he had been apprehended by security forces.

Continuing on a back page, the article enumerated what had been made to seem like a compound crime but was—at least from O'Shaughnessy's point of view—that which McGarr had had to do, once having launched upon the foray in the North: the presentation three times of false credentials to officials, a fourth to the desk at a city-center hotel, from which he had been seen leaving by a rear entrance. After having visited two hardware shops where he purchased a glass cutter and then a T-square, ". . . Mr. McGarr slipped the surveillance." Those items were later found within the house, along with a single span of a car rack fitted with suction cups.

"In a statement relieving Mr. McGarr of his Garda Siochana commission, Minister for Justice Suilly said, 'We can allow nothing to disturb an atmosphere of improving relations between South and North, Ireland and England, and the Garda and the RUC and security forces there. The way of the gun, the bullet, and the bomb has been tried. Thankfully, it has failed. We can tolerate nothing but the rule of law devised by reasonable, dispassionate men. We condemn all acts of violence, but especially an incident as uncalled for as this, wrought by a man whose sworn duty was to uphold peace.'

"It is expected that McGarr will be released shortly."

Disgusted, O'Shaughnessy shook out the paper, though he now heard his name being called. To be fired peremptorily and without a hearing on the uncorroborated word of the RUC, the ranks of which organization—he believed—were filled out by bigots and toughs, or the "security forces," a phrase that stuck in his craw, was a gross disservice. And that after years of dedicated and often inspired service. Now he himself had been summoned by the Minister for Justice, who was both Ireland's *top*, if nonprofessional, cop and the very man who had wielded the sack. O'Shaughnessy would keep a record, he would.

He stood, then lowered the newspaper and nodded to the advancing receptionist. Only when she had turned to lead him through the most official gloom of dark oak and deep carpeting did he button his coat. He slid the newspaper onto a desk before entering the Minister's office.

Suilly was sitting at a gleaming expanse of desk in his shirt-sleeves, staring down at a file. A countryman, like O'Shaughnessy himself—where was he from? Donegal. As Duncan had been, a protégé of Neil Blaney—he kept his steely gray hair combed back in tight, glossy finger waves that bunched on his neck. His skin was well tanned (from a winter holiday in Crete, O'Shaughnessy had read in the papers), but it was the shirt—silk and ironed like glass, its blue stripes bordered by pin lines of red—that caught O'Shaughnessy's eye. The cuffs, like the collar, were brilliant white, punctuated by dull gold tacks in the shape of fiddles with crossed bows.

Suilly's fingers, which were ringless, drummed on the blotter, as though he was struggling to come to a decision. He then drew in a breath and let it out slowly. The room was filled with some costly scent—some lotion, pomade, or cologne.

"O'Shaughnessy, Liam Malachai," Suilly read in the file before him. "Superintendent of detectives. MURDER SQUAD; born, 1919 . . ." And his eyes quickly scanned the page, noting the man's rural beginnings in Galway, his early entrance into the Garda—eighteen years old, just—and then his many similarly rustic postings throughout the country, until, at his own request, he transferred to plainclothes ranks and was assigned to Special Branch in Dublin. After ten full years, again at his own request, he moved to Homicide and Dublin Castle, having been passed over for the head post when McGarr—an interloper, as Suilly (who had not built his own career by forgetting much) now remembered—was hired in from some place on the Continent.

A "Culchie" undoubtedly, Suilly concluded, appropriating the snidely urban term of abuse that he had never minded hearing applied to himself, but there was more to the large man who was now standing before him. He glanced up. Calm, yes—that was it—a composed, imperturbable, perhaps even a serene older man who, after some early success, had built his career in patient, quiet, careful steps. A survivor and perhaps both easier and more dangerous to deal with than the less orthodox McGarr.

But there was something else about him too. What had he just seen? Allowing his eyes—as yellow behind the glinting discs as barley in autumn, O'Shaughnessy thought—to flicker up once more, he took in the carefully tailored dark suit, the large hands folded in front of him, the light-blue eyes, which were very clear and were regarding him without a blink—"A moment, please. I'll be right with you?"—was it priestly?

It was, Suilly decided, turning back to the first page of the file. The man had never married and, unlike some others, who might have used the controversy a decade before to transfer to greater position, O'Shaughnessy had stayed on at the Castle in the second spot. Why? Because the Garda was not simply his job but, rather, his vocation, and the Murder Squad the elite corps.

But would he want the job? Suilly asked himself, closing the file. No—that wasn't the question. Could he *possibly not want* it and would his appointment, coming so close on the heels of McGarr's dismissal (the details of which would be hotly discussed in Garda circles), offend his . . . sensibilities? Pushing himself back from the desk and raising his head to O'Shaughnessy, Suilly tried to empathize with the figure before him. A year from retirement, the elevation would cap and make sense of a forty-seven-year career. For the rest of his days he would be known as "Chief." His pension would be nearly 20 percent greater.

Smiling, Suilly stood and offered his hand across the desk to the man who was nearly twice his size. "Superintendent O'Shaughnessy. Des Suilly. D'yah know Joe Johnston here. He's a friend of mine."

And the father of a terrorist, throught O'Shaughnessy, as you are a canny man. Well, it was out now—the source if not the reason for McGarr's having been fired. He stared down at the owlish, but not unhandsome, man, and allowed his hand to fall when it was released, turning only slightly to Johnston, an older working man who, though uncomfortable in a suit that had grown too tight, regarded O'Shaughnessy coldly.

"Ah, gents—for Jesus' sake," said Suilly, stepping lightly around the desk, like a publican to his custom. "Let's talk this over, like reasonable men. Take a seat, please, Liam—may I call you that?" he asked, flashing the smile again and drawing two chairs in close to Johnston, who had not taken his eyes from O'Shaughnessy. "Julia," Suilly bellowed at the closed door. "Drinks! Jesus, these women," he continued, smiling up into O'Shaughnessy's face, "will be the death of us all. And it seems now it's a lady who's brought us together this morning. You *do* take a drink, Liam, while—"

Carefully and without unbuttoning his jacket, O'Shaughnessy sat.

"We could make it tea."

O'Shaughnessy only met and held Johnston's gaze.

"Y'know, I'd scheduled this meeting with your—" Suilly ran on.

A lie, thought O'Shaughnessy, who'd checked.

"—and I'd like to discuss that with you, after . . ."

I buckle on the chance of a promotion. O'Shaughnessy had not maintained a spotless record for forty-seven years to cave in now, and by his own standards, which were exalted, he would never sell out a comrade, much less a friend.

"Of course, I myself have got nothing to say in the matter."

Cock, thought O'Shaughnessy. And shite. No Minister for Justice in recent history had so consistently involved himself in the affairs of the Garda Siochana. He had forced Fergus Farrell's resignation; he had personally selected a new commissioner and had influenced the appointment of that man's two assistants.

The drinks arrived, after which Suilly said, "Well—business. Joe here tells me that nearly a week past now you detained his daughter. Why?"

O'Shaughnessy again raised his eyes to Johnston's. "Because she was discovered trying to dispose of evidence left by the perpetrator of a crime we are investigating. Because she has since refused to help the police."

"But I've known Roisin Johnston all my life," said Suilly, "and she's a good woman."

Then, concluded O'Shaughnessy, you've probably known Seamus Rhines for as long, and in his case guilt by association is enough.

Johnston only continued glaring at him.

"But what is the evidence?"

Saying, "For the record," and swinging his head as though to look for a stenographer behind him, O'Shaughnessy then detailed what had happened: the Duncan murder, Dromgoole's tip about the P&T van, the safe house in which Roisin Johnston had been discovered wiping down the furniture in the surgery.

Said Suilly, touching his lips to the glass but taking none, "I'm no barrister, but that's pretty thin stuff. Your arriving there—as you admitted yourself, on the tip of a pensioner. Her just happening to be there at the house of a friend who, if all that you say can be believed, without a doubt would have kept his identity from her as well. The house, you tell us, was dust-covered. 'Could you give the place a bit of a go, Roisin. I'd appreciate it,' I can imagine the man saying. And, Liam, they were just passing friends, no more.

"The 'dust bombs,' as you call them?" Flaring the tight mesh of wrinkles which was his smile, Suilly piped a little laugh at the ceiling. His eyeglasses again glinted. "Well, I suppose everything's possible, but a very good case could be made for her having found them there during her clean-up. Her destruction of evidence? She was, after all, cleaning up, wasn't she? And finally, even if we grant you the hypothesis that the Rhines address may have been a safe house—though I've never heard that owning a diesel generator and having a surgery in a house that was built by a man who was a doctor are illegal acts—your jump from Seamus Rhines to James Ryan and then to the infamous Jay Rheiner is unwarranted, to say the least.

"And you've been holding Miss Johnston for how long now?"

O'Shaughnessy only kept his eyes on Johnston, a man whose anger, he guessed, was concealing a mortification—at his daughter's arrest but, more, at his own involvement now—that he would never forget. He then said, "I'm wondering if M. Johnston takes any pride in all of this."

It was the prick Johnston needed. His hands came down on the arms of the chair, his jaw firmed, he began to pull himself up. "Ya dirty, blue-coat—"

But Suilly was now between them. "Joe. Now, Joe." The publican again. "Easy, now. Go easy. We tried it my way, now we'll try it yours." He turned on O'Shaughnessy, "Can I have a word with you on your way out the door?" He pointed to it as though showing O'Shaughnessy out.

Leading him past other offices toward the foyer, Suilly remarked, "A hot man. Volatile. But, you know, a spotless record. Absolutely pristine—not even a motor violation in all his years." He stopped and looked up at O'Shaughnessy. "I checked." They took a few more steps, and Suilly then asked, "You'll be speaking with—" He meant McGarr; it was as though he could not bring himself to say the name.

"When he returns, of course."

Suilly seemed to consider for a moment—the gold-rimmed glasses swinging to the side; the yellow eyes searching the carpet; he then squared around on the taller man, staring up into his face. "Then you should know this. There's more at stake here than meets the eye—in the Duncan case, in your man's dismissal. No"—he raised a palm, the head again moving to the side—"I can say no more than that. Now. Eventually it'll all come round, you'll see—the identity of Duncan's killer and a kind of exoneration of . . ."—he pretended not to remember McGarr's name—"*without*"—two fingers again touched O'Shaughnessy's sleeve—"the position which, from this moment forward, I'll consider yours and yours alone." The round yellow eyes now rose to meet his; Suilly nodded;

203

the eyes blinked. "I'll have one of the gir-ls," he waved back at the office proper, "draft a letter this morning.

"Now, apart from the release of Roisin—who we both know has no more to do with the fuckin' Provisionals than she has to do with the fuckin' Pope—what I want from you and what I sensed I could not get from . . ."—again he glossed over the name—"is some fuckin' breathin' room—two weeks, three, for Christ's sake—and then—I promise you—you'll get everything you want. You've got other work, I'm sure, that . . ."

You can crawl under, concluded O'Shaughnessy, for whom all abuse began with the abuse of language, that is, thought.

"—and I can't impress upon you enough the . . . moment of this t'ing." Suilly paused for a moment and then, glancing up, asked, "What d'ye say?"

O'Shaughnessy considered for a moment: they had, after all, gotten as much as he believed they would from the woman, and, then, she could be enjoined from leaving the country and watched. At the same time, it would serve nobody— McGarr in particular—for O'Shaughnessy to remove himself from whatever purchase he might gain through Suilly on what he now firmly believed was some larger and unfolding . . . was *conspiracy* too strong a word? O'Shaughnessy judged not. And finally there was the tape which—please God—was still running. No technical man, he had no faith in any machine whatsoever. But, if not by the same means, O'Shaughnessy had in his long service been down such a road before.

"For the record, I say that this is not a proper conversation for a Guard to engage in." But he held out his hand.

"Well, yes. You're right, you are," said Suilly, beaming as he shook it. "And I must say it's been a pleasure meeting you, Liam. I look forward to a long and cooperative relationship. I can tell Joe now that he can expect his daughter's release within the day?"

You can tell Joe anything you wish, thought O'Shaughnessy, turning from him. But I will not say one other word. For the *fuckin'* record, he thought.

"By the way," Suilly asked to his back, "when you speak to him, I'd keep a fair distance, were I you. A house is none the worse for cleaning twice. And you're too old for a resurrection."

Stepping out onto the sidewalk, O'Shaughnessy tightened his homburg on his forehead and glanced across the street into St. Stephen's Green, where crowds had gathered to bask in the hot summery sun now, at noon hour. Perhaps, he thought, but too old to kiss any man's arse, and, then, could he live with himself now, knowing that McGarr had been set up?

He considered the years of hours that he would spend in retirement wondering why and how, and how he himself did nothing. He stepped off the curb and walked across the street and into the park, in an office on the other side of which a solicitor was waiting to affirm that the seal that had been placed on the tape recorder in O'Shaughnessy's pocket two hours earlier had in no way been broken or tampered with.

From his office window, where he could see O'Shaughnessy moving along the flower-lined walk of the Green, Suilly reached for the phone and dialed a number from memory. It rang a long while, as he knew it would, and when it answered, he said, "Neil—how was Portugal?" They then discussed the several matters of mutual interest. Finally, Suilly said, "Listen—have you found somebody to replace poor Jock?" As he again listened, Suilly's features brightened and for a moment he felt the thrill of an excitement for which he had worked and risked his career during the three years since Geer—a brilliant chap; they had gone to university in London together—had first come to him with his proposal.

And the next step?

As he now spoke glowingly into the phone, he thought of the Haughey/Thatcher talks on the North and the summer Exercises of the Irish Army, which for the first time in a decade were being held near the border in Monaghan and Donegal. And he thought of the whistler's words and the fact that now all would indeed dovetail and be made to seem—how had it been phrased?—"plausible . . . and inevitable." In that, Suilly now concluded, they would find their cover.

Momentum—they now had it. A time car packed with explosives and hurtling toward the Twelfth of July, which was just slightly more than a fortnight away.

"Really? I thought as much, your having been away and all. Then—come closer now—I've got just the man for you. Sharp as a bloody tack, he is, but, unlike Duncan, you'll hardly know he's there. Low profile. The lowest, yet known to the Taoiseach himself, he is." Suilly's smile was wry; his eyes were glinting. "His name?"

Jesus, he thought, reaching for the center drawer of the desk. What was it, now? He'd had so many.

Searching, Suilly found the memo with the ITN logo at the top. "Hines. Tim Hines. From Monaghan, though you'd hardly realize it. Savile Row suits. American-trained, he is. His dossier here says he was the executive assistant to the president of an international corporation. All business.

"Shall I have him stop round?"

14

Like so many of the housing estates that in recent years had been built on the periphery of Dublin, the unit that Ruth Bresnahan lived in had been designed for another purpose. The architect had envisioned it inhabited by a young family with at most two small children, and not the half dozen young and poorly paid people who, because of a housing shortage reported as the worst in Europe, now found themselves cramped together in modern, suburban, and domestic discomfort. The rawest of these *arrivistes*, of whom Bresnahan was one, had to take what was offered, which was a "child's bedroom," if it could be called even that.

But, given her native Kerry concern for the few pounds at her disposal, Ruth had on that first day viewed all—the modern bathroom with its needlepoint shower head that, she discovered, was always in use; the "piped" telly with a choice of six channels, seldom her own; the kitchen with its capacious fridge that was always packed with other people's food and from which anything that she had boldly labeled "BRESNAHAN" with indelible marker vanished like a joint on a haying-time table ("Pinched it from the Guards," she once heard the loudest of the others bray before belching loudly)—through the unduplicable saving of £15 per week all found.

Now, however, with a party at full bore in the sitting room downstairs and herself exhausted from her day at the office and evening at the computer center, and with the room itself so small that she could scarcely roll over without coming up against something, Bresnahan would have gladly, if she could have summoned the will to get up and dress herself, paid £15 for one decent night's sleep. "I would not," she said audibly to the door.

And then there was the matter of the transom, which flooded the room with a light from the stairs far brighter than any at the office. It was on all night, most nights, with the last in invariably forgetting the switch. In defense, Bresnahan had spread one of the only two nonuniform blouses that she possessed here in Dublin (Kerry being now, as it would the rest of her days no matter where she went or why, her true home, please God) over four hooks which, unseen by the householder, she had secreted at the corners of the transom. But it was pink and sheer and it swathed the tiny niche in a rosy glow that made her think of the toilet-accessories department in Switzer's, a pricey Dublin department store.

In the room now, balanced on what passed for a bed, she fingered the horny beads of a Celtic rosary—a gift from her eldest sister, who was "a religious"—and tried to make her husky, big-chested whisper both lull her to sleep and drown out the hooley below, but she was distracted.

She thought of the office, where Superintendent—now *Chief Superintendent*—O'Shaughnessy refused to assume the desk chair but instead continued to sit day after day where he always had, at the side of the desk, reading every newspaper, it seemed, published in Ireland and recently the U.K. ("Ruthie—take this"—20 quid—"and make sure the news agent across the road has this list of papers for me every day"), and nodding or saying nothing whenever anything was brought to him, but insisting that they bend every effort to the Duncan case. "Crack this, we'll crack the nut." And now, with Sergeant McKeon a holy terror with what had happened to the chief—the *real* chief, Mr. McGarr—and what he thought (she had overheard him discussing it with O'Shaughnessy) was shaping up, Entry E, second floor, Dublin Castle, had become a kind of war room. The staff spoke with lowered voices and mostly in monosyllables; the tension could nearly be touched.

On one level, she suspected, it was loyalty (". . . Holy Queen, Mother of Mercy, our life, our sweetness, and our hope . . ."), and on another anger at the government's duplicity. But, then again, the both of them—O'Shaughnessy and McKeon—were, like McGarr for all his Sphinx-like inscrutability, good men who always made it clear where they stood. And in Bresnahan's world, in which people ended up paying, sooner or later, for every transgression (". . . as it was in the beginning, is now and ever shall be, world without end, Amen"), men like those three were necessary to thwart evil, which was rampant everywhere. A cry went up from below, and Bresnahan raised her eyes to the rosy glow of the ceiling, beseeching her God to grant her patience.

Where, then, had she gone wrong? What had she done that was keeping her from making something out of the tape, the first bit of actual police work that she had been given at the Castle?

Perhaps (". . . pray for us sinners, now and at the hour of our death, Amen") she had gone about it wrong from the start, wanting to solve everything bang off and concentrating on the tape as a whole and not, as McGarr had explained to her on her first day when handing her that card, the sum of its parts.

The card. Bresnahan threw back the sheet, applied a palm to the ham of a calf, and, grunting aloud, prised herself from the tiny bed.

Another crash and whoop came from below—she recognized the voice: the little gurrier who kept nicking her chow—

and she was flooded with a hot if momentary anger. But, rummaging through the pink haze that now seemed as thick as velvet, she at length came up with the much-thumbed and dog-eared card, which was titled "The Method of Descartes," a writer whom, McGarr had told her, he had studied while at the Christian Brothers School in Synge Street. A fine organization. "The foinest," she said aloud, after her own Loretan Sisters, of course.

And, seated on the edge of the bed, from which she could reach most objects in the room, elbows on her thighs, the card close to her face, she said in the same hoarse and prayerful whisper, "Accept nothing as true which you do not clearly recognize to be so; accept nothing more than what is presented to your mind so clearly and distinctly that you have no occasion to doubt it.

"Divide each problem into as many parts as possible.

"Commence your reflections with those items which are simplest and easiest to understand, and rise thence, little by little, to knowledge of the most complex.

"Make enumerations so complete, and reviews so general, that you should be certain to have omitted nothing."

There was a different piece of advice altogether printed on the other side of the card, but that was the man (McGarr) all over—never saying one thing and meaning just that, always taking things back, and she began with the undoubtable, plain truth of the parts of the problem with which she had been presented.

The tape. Magnetic it was and mylar, made in America for use with an IBM-360 or some other compatible machine. After a three-week bout of trial and error she had found that at least some of the information contained in the tape had been names. She had discovered that simply by assuming that names would be a central part of most tapes important to most organizations and by making a list (extracted from the phone book) of all possible Irish names, and then running a program which matched all the fragments to all the names.

It had been an utterly exhausting task, which had taken weeks, and what had she gained? Nothing but the fact—undoubtable as it was; how many common nouns began with "O'Fao-" or "McNaugh-"?—that at least some intelligible snatches contained names. But what else she might assume, what else she could productively ask of it, she had not a clue.

"Divide each problem into as many parts as possible," she said aloud.

Right. If her problem was just the tape, then her parts were: the tape itself; the computer language; the information itself, which was in bits; and whatever set of assumptions she might bring to a search of what remained. But if—she glanced up into the magenta haze; somebody downstairs was banging something hollow, like a head, against the wall—the tape *as used by Duncan* were considered, what parts were there? The tape, the IBM-360, the computer terminal at Duncan's desk in Consolidated Irish Bank, the modem with its telephone, the devices in the culvert designed to defeat the transmission, and, *and*—Bresnahan began to rise to her feet—whatever system Duncan himself might have had on the other end in—was it?—his apartment in Milltown. Might some of the information that would give her a clue as to what was being done with the tape have gotten through? Had anybody—McAnulty or that cursed boy Walsh—checked?

"*No*," she nearly shouted at the transom. If they had, she would have read of it in a report. And why not? McAnulty did not know byte one about computers, and Walsh, for all his brains, had not cared. But would whatever system (another IBM but smaller, she remembered from Ward's report) still be untouched? Better, could it never have been switched off and whatever had been sent it still be in the computer itself? Why would it have been switched off? Ward, who had sealed the place, would have had no reason to switch it off, would probably not have known how. She reached for her uniform.

Thundering down the stairs toward the telephone box in the hallway, Bresnahan plunged a large hand into the pocket of her jacket and came up with only a fifty-pence coin and some coppers. Blast. It was 11:45 P.M., and she had missed the last bus. She'd be shattered if she had to hoof it into town, and without 20p. in two tenpenny coins she could not phone for a cab.

A gust of laughter now rattled the French doors that separated the sitting room from the hallway, and, without thinking, Bresnahan tugged it open.

There, swaying drunkenly in the middle of the room, was the little gouger who had stolen from her, having stopped whatever pantomime he was about. His head rocked as he turned it to her, the others looking on aghast. "Is it a raid?" he asked mildly.

Taking two strides into the room, she grasped him roughly by the ear.

"Ow!" he hollered. "I'm being lifted."

Lowered, Bresnahan thought, bending him down until he writhed before her on the floor. Grabbing him by one ankle, she then snatched him up and began shaking—"Christ, somebody—get Amnesty International! It's torture, it is. I'll lose all me drink"—until coins spilled from his pockets onto the rug.

Gathering 20p. in two tenpenny coins, she said, "Pinched by the Guards," and left the room, which was locked in silence.

As she made the call, she heard first a titter and then another and then a chuckle that exploded in a burst of wild laughter. "Pinched *by* the Guards!" somebody howled.

In the taxi she remembered the other side of McGarr's

card, which she had studied perhaps more, trying to ken just who the boss was, that he would think it important:

"Consider that the heavens, the earth, colors, shapes, sounds, and other external things are naught but illusions and dreams.

"Consider yourself as having no hands, no eyes, no flesh, no blood, nor any senses; yet as falsely believing yourself to possess all those things.

"If, by this means, it is not in your power to arrive at the knowledge of any truth, you may at least do what is in your power, namely, suspend judgment, and thus avoid belief in anything false and avoid being imposed upon by this arch-deceiver, however powerful and deceptive He may be."

"He?" *Capitalized?* What did it mean?

15

Perhaps more than at any other time in his life, nineteen days later McGarr had some idea.

In the kitchen of his house he had backed himself into the warmth of the Aga and was looking out at the neat, planted rows of his garden, which had burgeoned in his absence and was illuminated by lights at the eaves. He was still sore from the drubbing he had taken on being detained, and exhausted from the days-long rounds of interrogations that he had endured, the seemingly interminable ride down from the North, and the near dozen phone calls he had made once he had gotten back. And now the details of his debacle in the North, which he had just related to Noreen, who was seated at the table. McGarr had his hands in the pockets of his overcoat, the collar of which was turned up. His hat was still on his head.

At length, Noreen broke the silence. "But *Paisley?* Doesn't this Geer know what that would mean? The people who support that man are the worst sort of . . . zealots."

Was there a best sort? McGarr thought of all the Tartan gangs and death squads, the Shankill Butchers and the Orange and even more arcane Black lodges that had amassed arms and made plans for "any emergency" as Paisley had once phrased what he went on to describe as civil war. On the other side was a spate of terrorist groups, like the INLA (Irish National Liberation Army), which the preceding two decades of "troubles" had generated.

But what disturbed McGarr most were the sheer numbers. Hundreds of thousands would be involved in the disruption that would inevitably follow the man's death, and some twelve thousand British troops, even if "supported" by the ten-thousand-man Irish Army and a like number of Irish reservists, would be hard pressed to do much more than defend themselves.

Said McGarr, thinking of all the records and files he had discovered in Geer's house, "He knows, sure. Maybe more than others."

"He must be—" Her green eyes flickered up at him. It was early in the morning, and she was dressed in a house coat. She looked tiny, delicate, and vulnerable—like a precocious child, there at the end of the large table. "—daft."

McGarr cocked his head. Certainly what Geer planned was daft, but the man himself knew what he was about with a clarity that few others enjoyed.

"And he's not alone in this," she went on. "From what you've told me, from what we know, he's got the man with the hat with him and this Rheiner. You said the British officer who lifted you called the man 'sergeant major,' and they left him there." She inclined her copper-colored curls to one side and looked down at the floor, as she always did when she was thinking. "That means he either saw what was on the end of that film, or could have looked at it again, after you were taken away.

"And why did they keep you all this time, and why incommunicado?"

Upon his return, McGarr—who had been followed from the border to Dublin—had phoned his office to warn the

215

others off him. If he were to do anything about Geer and Rhines and his own personal predicament, he would need some official resource—for information, for technical assistance—but it would be unfair to jeopardize the positions of any other of his former colleagues. After O'Shaughnessy had taken himself to a public phone, they had spoken at length. McGarr had then called in some favors that were due him. But he not only owed his wife an explanation, it was their practice to discuss all matters of moment in their lives. He was also waiting for a call.

"And if Rheiner is the Provos, and the man with the hat is the Brits, then what is Desmond Suilly but the government of this bloody country? Why?"

"Why what?"

"Why . . . *everything?*"

McGarr, who had had nearly three full weeks to consider it, said, "To foment civil war. To create the conditions of August 1969, but without Jack Lynch." He meant the Irish Taoiseach who had first threatened and then, with the British waiting two full days for him to act, failed to send Irish troops into the North.

"And what would that solve?"

"As you said, *everything* for all parties but the Orangemen." And those who would bear the brunt of the fighting, thought McGarr. Those who would die.

Again her head canted to the side. "We must read different newspapers." She reached for the one on the table before her, which pictured Margaret Thatcher and Taoiseach Charles Haughey shaking hands. The morning of the day before, they had begun their scheduled round of talks. "It says here that the mood of this thing is conciliatory, that the North will be discussed. Isn't that what Paisley himself has been running on about for"— she raised a hand —"the last couple of months? A sellout? I'm no student of politics, mind, but my reading of the situation is that they're planning to withdraw as it is."

"As they were in 1921," said McGarr, who had redirected his sight out to the garden. He wondered if it had been dry in Dublin during his absence, and if she had remembered to water the slips. "And withdraw, how?" he went on. "With what guarantees, to and from whom? They—the British— would have to offer to resettle all those Loyalists who'd prefer to emigrate rather than live in a united Ireland, and at what cost? And it's that that's galling them right now: the over two billion—think of it!—that they're splashing out in direct aid and security, to say nothing of what internment without trial and juryless courtrooms and their shoot-on-sight policies have run them in international regard.

"Better a . . . *fait accompli?*" he continued. "The Irish having 'sorted it all out' amongst themselves? By all means. No. By *every* means. If she plays her cards right, she might even get to keep their military installations and naval bases there, or—even better—get us to toss in our neutrality as an act of . . . solidarity with the rest of Europe." He was alluding to the fact that Ireland had never joined NATO; the possible "Cubanization" of Ireland was the practical reason given to explain why the British remained in Northern Ireland. "That would mean a deep-water port or two, perhaps an airfield, in our 'blighted' Southwest. It'd mean jobs and revived tourism and, say, a financial packet from London for our huge national debt."

"And a Churchillian coup for Maggie," added Noreen. "She'd go down in history. The Iron Maiden who bowed to historical inevitability and turned the other check, while gaining a basket of concessions that would keep her in office until mold set in.

"But . . . Dublin would have to be prepared for it?"

Glancing down at the telephone, to be sure the receiver was in its yoke, McGarr stepped to the table, where he turned over the newspaper. In the pantry he poured them two weak drinks.

The paper described the "Summer Maneuvers" of the Irish Army, which for the first time in over a decade was conducting exercises right along the border with the North. The training would begin in three weeks. "Monaghan and Donegal," McGarr said, placing the glass before her, where they could pincer in, taking Derry on one flank, Belfast on the other, and cutting off Antrim and the "Orange" far to the north.

Noreen only sighed, ignoring the drink. After a while, she asked, "But would Dublin want that?"

It was an old argument: that since the Revolution the two major political parties in the South had so monopolized wealth and power that only three percent of Irish people now possessed 72.5 percent of Irish wealth, and any change—especially one that infused a million Protestants and six hundred thousand radicalized, Six-County Catholics into the electorate—was to be avoided.

McGarr shrugged. "Far be it from me to explain politicians, but a good bet could be made for their wanting it now. None of the parties has been strong of late. We've had coalition after weak coalition. And a Dublin government being forced to 'take' Ulster to prevent a pogrom of Irishmen and -women is a different scenario from a negotiated settlement, altogether. The guilt that the Loyalists would be made feel might eliminate any need to offer them 'terms.' And, then, the legacy of having finally united Ireland would carry a raft of politicians through many a stormy election. Remember, the gang at the tiller now don't call themselves Fianna Fail for nothing." The "Soldiers of Destiny," McGarr thought—a grave, romantic title which could corrupt. "Then, Haughey with Blaney and Kevin Boland have tried before. Their only remorse was at having been caught." McGarr raised the glass.

"Then why the talks?"

"A smoke screen. An alibi. So they can cast the first stone. So they can say the settlement that they were negotiating was never given a chance. So they themselves can remain lily-white, though there'll be blood enough to go round among the lowly."

A minute went by—two, three—while McGarr continued to sip from the drink and stare out the window. Finally Noreen said, "Well—we can do nothing about it at the moment, and you look a sight. Are you comin' to bed?" she asked, her green eyes glinting less in challenge than reproof.

McGarr pointed to the telephone.

"Who from?"

He shook his head.

"About what?" she demanded, and when he only continued his vigil at the window, she added, "Ah, Peter—haven't you laid yourself out already enough for one month, and for who? Some schemers who don't care how many of somebody else's family they kill. It'd be far different if any one of them was actually from the North, but, no, it's just a way of keeping them and their sons and their sons' sons in office. The tarnish won't quite rub off the Revolution any longer, and the big majorities from the lads their grandfathers fought with down in the country are just not coming in. So at last, now that it might prove expedient, they'll put the rest of it through. But how? With as little risk *to them* as possible.

"You're lucky to have been shown that while you still have the best part of your life before you. But for Jesus' sake, take the lesson. Don't let them rub your nose in it. They'll only get you—and *not them*—kilt."

Her eyes were now blazing, her face flushed. She had one hand on a hip. "And, sure—there are plenty of things we can do: expand the gallery, buy a farm, start a little security firm, a consultancy. You don't *need* them."

But for McGarr it had gone beyond that. Yes, he didn't

need them, but, yes, he needed to see them fail, if only as a matter of pride. Any other concern—for life, his own and those of the others who would die—was now secondary. His injured pride now ruled him at least as totally as sectarian hatred ruled so many others in the North.

Shaking her head, she left the kitchen, and he heard her on the stairs to the bedroom above.

Several hours went by in which he received three phone calls, all of them negative: No, there was no possibility of identifying a retired British Army sergeant major by an unusually large hat size and the other physical characteristics, at least not by one junior officer who had only limited access to those files. No, at ITN Patrick Geer had no subordinate employees: he usually worked alone. And no, Seamus Rhines had no consistent MO. He used whatever was best suited to his task—a bomb, a gun, he had garroted two, gored another.

It was then he heard Noreen's foot on the stairs. He glanced at the clock: 4:17. She appeared in the doorway, her bright hair disheveled, her eyes darkly ringed. "I couldn't sleep, thinking about this thing." McGarr waited while she sat. At length, she went on, "It'll appeal to the bloodiest-minded, both sides. They'll tell themselves—because they'll want to hear—that it's the end, and they'll rush out to do as many others in as they can before they get done in themselves.

"And they'll care damn-all about the innocents who'll get killed—babies and wee ones. The elderly. That whole place is . . . atavistic and barbarous. There'll be firestorms, like before, and"—she shook her head—"mayhem.

"Peter"—she looked up at him, her eyes glazed with a light he had not seen before—"I know it's easy for me, who can do nothing, to say, but this is bigger than just your career or our momentary happiness or even—" She looked away; tears suddenly flooded her eyes. "And I know it's probably impossible to stop anybody from murdering anybody else. But if you could know *how* they were planning it, couldn't you do something to at least make people aware of what was on the cards?"

How? McGarr thought. It was the question that had occupied his every conscious thought from the moment he had understood the intent of the film at the house in Belfast. If their purpose was to achieve the maximum effect, then certainly it would have to occur in some public forum, at some central event, when media attention was most intense. And soon, given the fact that they had already drawn some attention, and purposely. Why else have murdered Duncan?

The phone, ringing, startled him. A familiar voice said, "Carty, Joseph or Joe."

"Thanks, Bernie," said McGarr, and rang off.

At the door to the cellar, the moist funk of the few slips which she had still not yet planted rose to him. It was the time of morning when the first house lights made a surveillance team feel most tired and the first activity—the buses, the few cars speeding through the empty streets of the city—put them off their guard. And, then, they would not be expecting him to make a move his first night back.

McGarr turned and there at the top of the stairs drew Noreen to him. "Be careful," she said, "and remember that it matters not the fallout here. Sure—"

He completed her thought: gossip being what it was in the country, his reputation was ruined already. That he had been sacked would be the only thing people would remember until he died.

"And I love you."

Before opening the garden door, which under a leafed trellis would lead him to a stile in the wall, to the Viners' back garden, and then to that of another neighbor, where he could wait in shadows until he saw the rocking imminence of a lighted, double-deck bus up the road, McGarr said, "I love you too. Mind the garden."

"I will."

And once in the shadows, listening to the traffic on the other side of the garden wall, McGarr considered the parts of the problem before him:

Geer, who was their exposure. Since the incident at his house, he had been allowed to come and go, McGarr had learned. He had not even been questioned. And he would remain conspicuous, McGarr believed, right up to and through the moment of the attack.

But what of the man with the hat? Sergeant major and known to the security forces, yet for some reason—guard, protector, co-conspirator?—he belonged in the house, though McGarr knew that only Geer lived there.

Lastly, there was Rheiner, the experienced professional. Would he be responsible for the actual killing? "Reason" would dictate as much, but who was McGarr to presume to ken their motives?

How, for a maximum effect? No bomb, which would be too impersonal. A bullet? Perhaps. A—McGarr turned his head aside, even to think of it—back-snapping?

But something about the attack would have to be . . . manifestly identifiable, either by agent or by means. Paisley's supporters would have to know who killed him, though the *why* could be assumed.

Seeing the lights of a bus in the distance, McGarr lowered himself down onto the sidewalk and held out a hand.

It was what Rhines was doing at that very moment to indicate what he wanted, not far distant from Dublin city center, where he would have to report on time at least for the balance of the week.

And where he now sat was the strangest and probably the most fascinating place that he knew of. To it he had had to return from time to time, whenever an assignment required some specialized apparatus—a ramped building, the ceiling netted with trapezes, the floors laced with the track of a monorail. On it rode a full-bearded man with a wide, powerful torso, titanium arms, and no legs. A bomb, it was said, had gone off in his lap, and he was now—too late—the island's most careful man.

"Two of them," said Rhines. "The same size and identical. I want them secured by either pressure snaps or Velcro, but bulk is the factor to keep in mind. It's crucial that they neither create a bulge nor be perceived as anything more than, say, a watchband. At the same time, length, strength, and edge are important."

The man thought for a moment, then reached for the teacup on the workbench before him. "Spring-loaded? Quick-release?"

Rhines nodded.

The metal fingers crimped around the handle, and pulleys hummed as the cup was drawn slowly up to his mouth. He drank. "But why two?" he asked as the cup began its descent. "Once it's used you'll not get a second chance."

"Call it insurance," said Rhines from the door. "Three days?"

"For the money you're paying, you could have them in two. Your last, you say?"

And yours, Rhines thought as he closed the door, should you breathe a word. But, then, once it happened, nobody would claim even the least responsibility for what followed.

Of the props, all that was needed now was the vial of blood, which he could pick up on his way "home" from "work." Then on to the performance, the first act of which would be played in two days that seemed to him two centuries off. Stage fright? Not a bit of it, he thought. If anything, just the reverse.

16

Bresnahan was in a quandary, lacking the courage to proceed. She glanced up at the round-faced clock, more fit for a bar than an office, and read the time: 7:53 A.M., God bless her, and she not daring to take the final step. And, sure—she thought, her mind again slipping away—the place had the feel of a bar, with Delaney at McKeon's operations desk playing cards with Greaves, Sinclaire and Finn. They had airboard cups of "coffee" before them, which were replenished from the bottom left drawer of the chief's desk. "Don't be so judgmental," Delaney had said. "We plan to replace it." In seven minutes the day shift would be in, and Bresnahan would have to apply herself to her regular tasks.

Plans. Hers was to pick up the touch-tone telephone in front of her and tap in the number listed for the Milltown flat of Mr. Jock Duncan, which had been sealed by Ward, who nowhere reported having switched off or in any way touched the computer found there. Ward was at present in Monaghan, commanding a surveillance team that was watching the Rhines safe house and the woman Roisin Johnston, and, short of traveling there, contact with him was out. O'Shaughnessy had decreed that any intercommunication, apart from Ward's daily calls to the office, was ill-advised. "It's best to assume that in these matters their sophistication is greater than ours, and the fewer the chances the better."

Sophistication. With quaking hands that were usually as steady as two pink rocks, she lowered the report, folded down and smoothed the front page, drew in a breath, then reached for the telephone and placed the receiver into the modem by the side of her desk. It was undoubtedly—she believed—the most important moment in her life to date, and if she botched it, she would be shattered. Destroyed.

She glanced down at the dog-eared card that she had placed squarely on the desk before her. "Make enumerations so complete, and reviews so general, that you should be certain to have omitted nothing."

If, she thought, Duncan had tried to transmit the information from the larger tape by telephone to the computer that was discovered in his apartment, he would not have had the opportunity to switch it off, having been murdered.

If Duncan had been given the tape for the purpose of accessing—extracting—some specific information from it, either he would have had to program the tape himself to fulfill that purpose, or the tape would have been given to him preprogrammed, which she thought unlikely. *How* would they (whosever tape it was) have accomplished that, if not on a machine such as the IBM-360 at Herbert Park House, and then why the need for Duncan?

And if Duncan *had* programmed the tape, then the electronic safeguards that had, it was assumed, been built into the "informational" files of the tape would not have been a part of Duncan's program.

If Duncan had attempted to purloin the information, sending it over the wire to the computer at his flat, then the program which he had written would have gotten through, as well as whatever part of the informational aspects came before whichever "defensive" check it had been that had alerted the device in the culvert in the street beyond Herbert Park House.

If, finally, Duncan's computer had not been switched off, and barring any power failures (and there had been none—she had checked), then its memory capacity (quite substantial at 352K) would have absorbed and would still hold that information, provided the machine itself was of good quality, in working order, and sufficiently ventilated to keep itself from overheating and losing some or all of what had been sent. It had been over five weeks since Duncan's murder, but the machine was the newest of the IBM personal line, with a host of accessories and an expanded memory capacity, and Duncan himself had been a computer expert. He would have kept all in tiptop shape.

Why hadn't she thought of it immediately? she now asked herself. And here she was hesitating even now. Courage. All she had to do was dial Duncan's number and examine the current contents of his computer's memory as they had been sent from Herbert Park House, and—if her assumptions had been correct—she would pull it back to the IBM-compatible modem beside her desk and the computer that ran it.

And, "If, by this means," she thought, "it is not in my power to arrive at the knowledge of any truth, I *will* at least do what is in my power, namely, suspend judgment, and thus avoid belief in anything false and avoid being imposed upon by this archdeceiver, however powerful and deceptive —————may be." For in the end, what would she be out if she failed? A night's sleep alone; blasphemy was, after all, a cardinal sin.

With a quaking finger, she reached toward the buttons of the telephone and began punching in the numbers and then ("Hail, Holy Queen, Mother of Mercy, our life, our sweetness and our hope . . .") the program. There was a pause that

226

seemed interminable, and her heart sank. But then—yes!—
through the voice monitor on her desk she heard the familiar
aviary sound, like birds gone mad. The contents of the memory dump began to display on her monitor, while the disc
drive whirred, recording the information.

The call had gone through, Duncan's computer *was* on,
and, rising from her desk with both big fists clenched, Bresnahan turned her joyfully reddened face to the ceiling and
said, "T'anks. T'anks very much," such that the men at McKeon's
desk looked up.

"Rut'ie," said Delaney, "you'll break me concentration and
with it me luck."

"Sh!" she insisted, now blocking the glare on the video
screen with her hands. "Oi t'ink Oi've got it."

"And what has she got?" Greaves asked. "If it's a deuce, a
one-eyed jack, or four aces, I'll have some."

Delaney, however, put down his cards and got up to see
what she was about.

She was typing in a few short commands that would activate
the memory-analysis program and pull up the listing. Soon
came the file name, "PROVIRAMEDINACT." Then a series
of program instructions interspersed by interpretive docu-
mentation:

/BIRTH: 1920–1925/
/WEIGHT: 13–14 STONE/
/HEIGHT: 5' 9"/
/EYES: BROWN/
/BALD/
/WORK: THEATRE/
/OCCUPATION: ACTOR/
/TERMINAL/
/AMBULATORY/
/DEPENDENTS; AGES/

Then the jamming came on, and Bresnahan felt at once elation and despair. She had retrieved something, but what? "Is it the tape?" a voice asked over her shoulder. It was McKeon, who had just arrived, his hat still on his head. The men beyond Bresnahan had put away the cards and were beginning to leave.

She nodded. "The program that Duncan wrote."

"But what's it mean?"

"I think—that they were searching for a particular person."

"How do you mean?"

Bresnahan pointed to the screen. "The birth date. Somebody between sixty and sixty-five years old. Somebody about thirteen or fourteen stone in weight. Somebody with brown eyes, who's bald, who worked in the theatre, who was an actor.

"This next part I can't make sense of. If we can assume PROV-Oi, Ar, Ay-MED-INACT means what it says and we're dealing with those people again, then they were looking for somebody who was . . . terminally ill. Whoi?" she asked. "Whoi in God's name would they want a poor sod like that?"

"Never mind, sweets—you just work away. Dependents?"

"Family," she said. "Children, parents, in-laws, and so forth. History means whatever the file contained about the man's 'career' before they destroyed it. The blood group with 'ALL RESPONDENTS' means that that question was asked not just about the person the first eleven questions were seeking, but of all persons in the file."

"Shall I notify Special Branch," she asked, meaning the department of the Garda that dealth with unlawful organizations.

"Don't you dare. We'll handle this ourselves. And, Rut'ie—you're a gem."

The rush of blood—from her chest to her neck and face—was like a hot, welcome tide, and suddenly tears filled her eyes. Turning away, she stared down at a crumpled sheet of paper that had been collecting dust under a nearby desk for weeks. Her head felt as though it would burst.

Jesus, Lord, God—whatever it was, she had done it.

17

Mornings bothered Geer most, and the spot on the sheet of the bed, which was growing daily larger: the seepage from the rank, pus-filled crater in his shoulder, the stench of which had now permeated most other rooms of the house. And what to do with the linen, which he kept having to buy more of? A rag fire would stink, the binmen checked for anything valuable, and the darkroom, in which he was hiding them from the cleaning woman who came in once a week, was already unusable.

The yoke of the camera, it was. On it day in and day out. Said the doctor, "If you don't give it some rest, you'll find yourself down with gangrene." But how to take even a day— he now asked himself while trying to ease the crusted bandage from the drain of the wound—after what had happened with the plainclothes Guard. A reassuring normality was required, as much for the authorities as for Geer's neighbors in the Strand. They had yet to ask him for an explanation, though the query was not long in coming, given the fact that his old red Fiat would not start.

It was a hot, close day with a heavy fog, soft as wet felt in off the Lagan. Geer had scarcely raised the bonnet to look inside when another figure appeared beside him—the youngest Glynn, Francy, who lived across the street—and Geer straightened up, wary now in spite of the dressing, the pad, and the cologne he used to mask the odor.

"Trouble, Paddy? Aye—Ah can see she'll no' start." His hair long, hanging in greasy twists as he peered over the engine, Glynn held out a hand, only the palm of which was bright. In it rested a rotor from a distributor arm. "You're to follow me, Paddy. We'd like a word with you."

"But . . . my work."

"You'll have little of that if you don't come along."

"I'll have to phone—"

"In the pub."

It was where he would have had to go for the neighborhood's only mechanic. Appearances, for the sake of which Glynn now led him down the street, hands plunged deep in the pockets of a tattered slicker, his stride the unambitious amble on runners that branded him as urban and Catholic and poor. Nonchalant. All the bloody time in the bloody world—to be frightened, unemployed, and watchful for anything out of place. But not, say, Carron, who would be where he belonged at the head of the street, waiting for Geer to rattle by.

The game, Geer thought, a crucial action of which they began after he had made his phone call: a back alley, a garden, and then through house after house—like Tarzan through a special stretch of sordid jungle, Geer thought, with each house a swing until they were deep within the Strand. But it was a transit not so thrilling by half. At a clip they ducked under a low door, passed down the threads of a frayed carpet to foot-blackened linoleum, squeezed by a missus at a cooker here, at a fridge there, under a line of diapers in the next street, a clutch of "wee wans" running riot ("A few bob, mister. A few bob for some sweets. Pleece. Pleece"), wide of a lunging, chained mutt in the next.

And the reek of it, the want. It was an acrid smell, especially in wet weather, like grease from pale, worthless puddings—there was a bucket of it, it seemed—in the final house that they entered. There a group of mostly older, poor men had squeezed themselves around a table, which the two women attending them quitted as soon as Glynn and Geer arrived. In their wake they left a grim, smoke-filled room lit only by the tarnished rays of a steely light from the transom of the back-garden door. The yellow plaster of the walls had been whorled three-quarters of a century before. The ceiling was tin and patterned.

"Paddy," remarked Joe Carty, the old man who ran things there in the Strand. "How are ye t'day?"

"Fine, sir. Fine," said Geer, smiling and then turning to the others so they could see that his teeth were not better than their own. None returned the greeting; of the ten men there, Geer knew nine.

"Will you take a seat?" Carty seemed lost in a stiff woolen greatcoat—the collar like the deckled edge of a shell, his neck a withered reed—and his hand quavered as he gestured toward the only unoccupied chair, at the other end of the table.

"I would, sure." Geer glanced at the clock on the wall, his features glowing. "Sure, I will." He sat and looked up at them.

"Tea?"

"Love some."

Glynn poured Geer a cup, skidded the rotor down the table to Carty, and left.

"Paddy—I knew your father, back when we were lads. I liked him. We got along. There was the difference then, but nothing like now. For his sake and for yours"—he paused, a little old man whose left eye was dead and looked like the belly of an oyster—"I'll come to the point, so you can see where we stand. Not all of us here agree on that, but until we decide otherwise, this is how it'll play.

"It was us who called in the Brits, after yer mahn was seen

232

going in your place. Now, him we knew about and understood, but the other man, the Guard who was found inside and got lifted—we'd like to know what he was doing there, and"— he paused to accept a light from a man by his side—"I'll tell you why we ask." The smoke crabbed over the top of the table, curling back on itself. "About a month ago we were told by those who can ask such things to keep an eye on you, son, but after having satisfied our curiosity and gone in there and seen for ourselves . . ." Carty lowered his good eye. "Well— it's not for us to judge. You've been a good, an uncomplaining neighbor. And you did the university and do the telly, and a good job, from all we hear. We're proud of you, sure, and your difference from us? Well—that too most of us believe is your business. But we'd like some straight answers. You should know some think your living here—your house, your . . . contacts—can only hurt us." He paused a moment, then: "They tell me they'd prefer you gone, and"—the bad eye blinked, it was the color of dirty slate—"not just from the street."

Carron, Geer thought in a panic—he'd been talking. But he just kept looking at Carty, knowing how any sign, the slightest, might make him dead in minutes.

"Now—why did your man think he should go into your house?"

Said Geer, "Who am I to speak for him? Drunk? Possessive of what I represent to him? A . . . job. Obviously he knew the man was in there, with the contraption on the sliding doors in the back garden. When I got home a day later and some . . . well, he'd guzzled three bottles of whiskey, and it took me another to get him out the door. He kept babbling about his pension."

"But the policeman, Paddy. The one from Dublin. Why was he in there in the first place?"

"A film, I think," Geer replied without hesitation. "There

233

was one in the projector that he'd gone through. Some others on the floor by it. My files had been ransacked. There were clips all over the cutting-room floor. I think maybe he believed I either filmed something I shouldn't have or there was something he wanted to see."

Another, younger man spoke up. "But why'd they tail him, the Guard, until, here in town, he either lost them or they let him go? Did they know he was in there? Your house."

"I won't attempt to explain the British. I'm an open book. I work for ITN, for myself in my spare time. If you care for a second look at my invitation, just ring the bell. Better"—he fished in his pocket—"I'll give you a key."

When he looked up, Carty was raking a hand back through hair that had gone beyond white to yellow. "Paddy—*why* were we asked to keep an eye on you. *Why* was Blount, your man's whip at Ulster Risks, slain? *Why* then did Fairclough show up with the Brits? He was there, you know. There're some right here who saw him themselves. And'll tell you something else"—Carty glanced around at the others, including the man by his side whom Geer did not know—"which is not to go further than here, and I don't care what your profession is—cameraman, journalist, or whatever the hell it is you do up in that little room. Understand?"

Geer nodded. He blinked. Carty was angry in the manner of a man not used to being thwarted here among his own. But he only twined his hands before him, his one good eye on the plaster of the wall beyond Geer's head. And in a voice so low that Geer had to strain to hear him, he said, "For the past five, nearly six weeks, and not *exactly* from the time we were given the word about you, Paddy, we've been getting presents. In the first week it was a lorry-sized load of ammunition, much of it suited to weapons that we did not then possess. The second week it was more of the same. The third we were given"—Carty again shook his head—"man-portable, anti-armor weapons with RMX- and HMX-shaped charges. Then came medical stocks, canned goods, formula for babies, of all things.

"Since then, each of us not already having one got a driver's license in the mail and—listen to this close, Paddy—the keys, the tax stamps, the registrations, and then the location of a car or a small truck or—are yeh hearin' me, Paddy?"—Geer nodded, his face (he hoped) suffused with wonderment—"a feckin' school bus with St. Columba's in Gaelic print on the side. And another. And another. Four in all parked in back of the rectory, and us—who are supposed to control this place, can tell the priest only to look the other way.

"Now"—Carty slapped the pocket of his dun greatcoat, and a cigarette and a light were produced for him by another man—"we're not totally ignorant here, in spite of what might be thought of us beyond the Beersbridge Road." He exhaled a gust of smoke, blue in the gray light through the transom of the kitchen door. "We are being armed and supplied to defend ourselves. The cars? All near wrecks, like your own, Paddy, which with the lorries and buses are to make certain we've hulks enough for barricades, come time. And the British? They turned a blind eye to it all. Not one has been questioned.

"But, Paddy—most of us are not, like you, a bachelor. We have wives and children. And, Paddy—we are asking you, who are in your own wee, sweet way one of us, what time is that?" The eye, ringed in smoke, fell to meet his, and the Strand was then about as quiet as he had ever heard it.

He drew in a breath that the sharp line of his shoulders, swathed in the shiny leather of his jacket, made emphatic, and slowly let it out. He looked down at his hands, catching from the collar of his turtleneck a whiff of the rot below. He was sweating now and suddenly tired, as he had been in the past few days. He thought of the piper's words, "In the end—

235

seven quiet men, please God. . . . But, mind you, no more."
He shook his head.

"Right," said Carty, "if that's the way you want it. Paddy,"
he as much as shouted, "this man here says you murdered
Jock Duncan in Dublin." He meant the man beside him that
Geer did not know—short, stocky, red hair, gray eyes; the
Guard, it could be nobody else. He was wearing a cloth cap
and, like Carty, an old winter coat. "He says he's got proof
of that and the fact that you and whoever you're with will
murder Ian Paisley."

Geer had been wrong. It was now the quietest moment
that he had experienced in the Strand, and, standing, he could
feel the weight of their twenty eyes upon him. He was a
bit dizzy and he had to reach out for the edge of the table.
He reminded himself to take more of the pills he'd been
given.

"Yes, I am a bachelor," he said to his hands, "but I live
here and have, like you, all my life. Everything I have is tied
up here—in my house, which I rebuilt here and not out in
some suburb. With that came another decision that I would—
again, like you—do something to make the place right and
correct"—one hand jumped—"all that was being done to us.
But in my own way, which it's taken a dozen-plus years to
work out but which might just"—he sighed—"turn the whole
thing around for good.

"You were told to keep a friendly eye on me, and you were
sent those things and will get more, because I'm not alone in
this. The British want out—we all know that—but they'll need
a little prodding. I won't lie to you and say I can't tell you
what or *when*, but the fewer who know of it the better, though
we'll give you fair notice, and that's a promise.

"Now—if I can have the rotor to my distributor, I'll be
leaving. I've got my job to get to, which I must maintain at
least until then. Any further questions can be directed to

those you know. They'll corroborate everything I've said."

Carty looked down at the rotor in the palm of his hand, then placed it carefully upright on the table before him. "Funny how I'm after thinkin' this little thing here, that can stop you from coming and going, could mean more to us in the Strand than, say, an aitch-bomb. This decision of yours, Paddy—it scares me, as it does this man here." Again he meant the Guard. "He looks at it different than you.

"He tells me we'll be overrun and butchered. At best we'll be burnt out. Then, regardless of what happens in a general way, there'll be a year or two of confusion before anything is settled. And even if you have your way, what will it mean? A few thousand dead, many many more injured and homeless, the place ravaged, and then a million or so Orangemen who'll be thinking only of the worst sort of revenge. And it'll be *you* who'll have turned this place into a police state. You and whoever you're with and the British again."

Geer, quaking now, lowered his head. The stink of him was nearly overpowering; it would kill him, it would, he realized in a sudden burst of intuition. But he no longer cared. It was time, he judged, to challenge Carty, but not directly, time to appeal to the others and ask for a vote.

"Who?" he asked, his voice rising as he committed his last reserves of energy. "Who the fuck is he, this emissary from the Garda Siochana, to pass judgment on the purity of *our* aims. Where is it exactly that he's from, if not from the jails and internment camps that have kept *our* people and *our* problem bottled up for sixty-plus years. Him, from there. Him, from anyplace else but here, can't possibly know what it means to have been born and raised here into what? A lifetime of tyranny, poverty, and abuse.

"Does he think for one minute"—Geer raised his head, his gaze locking into McGarr's—"that if at one fell swoop any man in this room could end that tyranny—completely! irrevocably! for all time!—that man would hesitate one bloody second, regardless of the loss?

"And if, then, that man might know that the very power that enslaved us would, for their own reasons, help us keep our losses to a minimum, do you think that man would give a second thought to Ian Paisley, the UDA, his Third Force, or the sectarian bastards who sit in those lodge halls and on the county councils and dispense jobs and housing and dignity only to those just like them?

"Does he think we care fuck-all about what 'complexion' some new government might take or if, like a cancer, we would have to burn them out at some later date? *Change* is what we want. *Change* is what we've been demanding for sixty-five years. And *change* is what we have not, until this very moment, had a hope in hell of realizing, and if there's a man in this room who does not desire *change* from the very pith of his being, then I know nothing and will traipse happily after this policeman from Peace and Prosperity."

Geer tottered, the table listing up at him, so that again his hands had to go out to it. "For, yes—I helped murder Jock Duncan, though it's an admission I would make only here among *my* own. And, yes, I'll help murder that bastard Paisley. And, yes, it will—this time—bring gross, radical, glorious, wonderful *change*. Here in the Short Strand, the Six Countries, and Ireland. Yes—blood will be spilled, but not, if we can help it, innocent blood.

"Those buses you mentioned"—pulling his eyes from the Guard, Geer could not at first find Carty—"they're for the children or haven't you been told? They're to be taken with their mammies, if they like, on a bit of an outing in the South. Ballinamore, County Leitrim. A lovely place, I'm told. A certain Father Rheiner runs a health camp there, says the whole thing is being financed by an American philanthropic organization."

"Jay Rheiner?" one of the younger men asked.

Geer nodded. "The rotor," he said to Carty.

The old man glanced around, his one eye haunting the shadows there at the end of the table. Nobody spoke. Several were regarding Geer admiringly.

Dismissively, with the back of his hand, Carty struck the rotor, which skidded down the table to Geer. But before Geer could leave, he said, "Paddy—I don't like it."

Nobody believed you would, thought Geer, as he weaved down the hall past the two women, who had taken chairs in the sitting room. Glynn was at the door, and Geer could hear a sandwich of electronic sound coming from some room upstairs—shortwave monitoring the RUC, sideband the British Army, and citizens' band, which was their own means of communicating among themselves. Irish, somebody was speaking.

Out by the curb, as he expected, a car was waiting to take him to the back door of the pub. There he would ask for a glass of water for the pills.

Back in the kitchen of the house, one man asked, "What about him?" He meant McGarr.

Said Carty, "He'll remain with us for the moment. Until—" Who knows, he thought, they might need a witness to all of this. Somebody independent and once trusted by the powers that be and *would be*, he suspected. Nearly seventy years of experience in the Strand had leached from Carty the little optimism that he had ever enjoyed.

A day and a half later, in a low, filthy social club—no more than a partially reconstructed room in a gutted row house near the car barns in the Strand—all glanced up at the television when the bartender called for silence and reached for the knob that controlled the volume.

A news bulletin had come on, and an announcer was saying, " . . . through a spokesman, Blaney has stated that the Thatcher/

239

Haughey talks will only lead to a slightly more acceptable but a mortally more protracted Partition with 'risings' from two sides, not merely one, in years to come. Blaney has called for a new approach, which his statement describes as 'an ethnically monolithic Protestant state carved out of what is now Ulster.'"

"No!" several of the men in the barroom shouted but were silenced by others, who pointed to the screen. Since he was a politician who had been perceived as the Republic's conscience in regard to the North, the turnabout was both personally and politically radical.

Continued the announcer, "On the question of the status of Londonderry under the plan—"

"To hell with Derry," somebody yelled. "What about Belfast?"

Others agreed, and when their voices quieted again, McGarr heard, "'. . . it's time that all of us face up to the fact that the over a million Protestant people in the North are just not going to melt away. Nor will they tolerate total integration with the South or resettlement in northern England or Scotland.'

"The Blaney statement, which the Donegal T.D. plans to bring before the Dail, called for the resettlement effort to be directed and paid for by 'those who created the division, there in the North. Certainly a one-time, funded payment is preferable to the billions of pounds that they lose there every year. Some of the expense could be recouped by the sale of Catholic properties in the North,' the spokesman said."

Pandemonium broke out in the bar as commercial messages came on the screen, and Carty, who had been chatting with McGarr most of the night, seemed to sink even farther into his heavy winter coat. "Christ—the whole country's out of joint. Neil Blaney?" He shook his head. "I would've thought he'd be the last. The Loyalists—your man, Paisley—will jump on that like a sovereign in the gutter, which'll lead only to further 'protraction,' as he calls it. And then there's Geer." He raised a hand, signaling for more drink. "We'd best enjoy ourselves while we can."

Minutes went by, perhaps a quarter hour, in which McGarr tried to fit the disparate events of the recent past into some semblance of a whole, without success.

Said Carty, "But you're right, you know. Both you and Blaney." The dead eye, which was splayed and looked unsightly, like a lump of sputum, was flicking up and down as though searching McGarr's neck. "It's . . . lunacy to think that anything, apart from freeing a half million people and impounding a million others, will be gained by taking those people by storm. The young fellas there"—he raised his chin to the crowded bar—"go for it because they think it'll give them a future, and I can hardly blame them. But I think they'll find the hatred—the Prods for them and them for the Prods, once they get a chance to pay them back—'ll be unconquerable. And the thing itself. . . ." Carty shook his head. "Well—

"Tell me, Peter—could you stop it?"

McGarr had to strain to hear Carty, whose voice was scarcely a whisper. "I could try."

"And how would you try?" Carty's head turned as he scanned the room; the clamor was deafening now, what with the approach of closing and Blaney's statement, which was being hotly debated.

"The man with the hat," said McGarr. "Given what you've told me about Ulster Risks and Paisley, he's got to be a part of it."

"And how would you stop him?"

McGarr only shrugged and looked down at his drink.

241

"I could go to him. With a warning."

"But don't you think he's been warned of such things before?"

And often, McGarr thought. "But not by me," he said. Could he get to either of them—castle to castle, as it were—in a city besieged?

"You'll be lifted, you know," Carty went on in an undertone. "Either before or after. Fairclough won't let you off. You're too much of this thing as it is, and to them deadly. Can you put it together, you'll blow them sky high.

"Drink up, now. I'll nip out for a moment. I'll have something for you when I get back. Go on, drink up," he continued, squeezing past McGarr. "You're in no danger now. It's closing and the hour of our greatest vulnerability. The t'roat rules all, and you'll not be missed."

Said Carty, when he came back, "Your turn. Try the door on the left. The man's name is George Carron." Beneath the table McGarr felt something nudge his knee. "The gun is for him, and you'll need it. The rest is papers and your money, which you'll need. You'd best take accommodations out by the airport, where strangers are common, and be quick about it. The Twelfth is only four days off, and the town'll soon be flooded with every run of bigot and busybody. This time, I suspect, the more the merrier. For Geer and his bunch.

"Francy Glynn—you'll know him—has the proper sort of car and clothes for you. You're Mr. Samuel Pease Frenche for the duration. Gallery owner. Horseman. It has a ring to it, don't it, and should get you in. I suspect you know enough about him to carry it off."

It was McGarr's wife's uncle, who was only a few years older than McGarr.

"Ah—we've our sources too, Peter." He paused, then turned both eyes on McGarr. "And there're those of us who'll not forget, should we preserve the capacity to remember."

McGarr had to wait until the toilet was cleared, only to move into an alley so dark he had to guide himself by touch. Three steps in, the lock was thrown on the door behind him.

Glynn, his hair cut short and dressed as a chauffeur, was waiting in the street by an Audi sedan. "There's clothes for you in back. You can use the alley. Again."

V
Take

18

It had taken its toll: the sudden, distant civility at the bank; the burden of every stare in Monaghan Town; her father who would no longer speak to her or acknowledge her presence.

"Shamed us, you have!" he had roared when she had come to collect her clothes. "The whole town'll know you're 'living' with Seamus Rhines, and him a—"

"A what, apart from a kind, competent man with . . . resources," she had said, though she had even then begun to fear those resources, did not fully ken his competence, and (more the pity) suspected his kindness. "A man who's made me an offer and with whom—hear me, now—I will have *my* family."

"Resources!" His fist came down on the board over the set tub, which boomed. "You'd know that, wouldn't you? I'll tell you what Seamus Rhines is—like his father before him, he's a Fenian bastard, and if it's money he's got, it's blood money, and I'll not have that blood in my family.

"You're to decide this moment. If it's him, you're not to show your face here again, and that's final."

When she returned the next day, she found her belongings by the gate in the back garden and the kitchen door locked.

"Your father," her mother had said in a whisper through the window, which she opened only a crack, "he's beside himself with this thing. I've tried speaking to him, but, you know—"

She knew, all right. He was a man who was adamantly ignorant in his rectitude. *She herself* had not bombed or shot anybody, nor had she known—nor *did* she know—that about Seamus, except by the say-so of others, whom she could not trust. But without, of course, even a word from him, and in what had now become the utter . . . emptiness of her life, it had begun to work on her, a slow action, like time—the nearly four decades of her life condensed into the two weeks that had gone by since her return.

Trust. Was it that which was giving out in her? For there were only so many movies she could go to, so much television she could watch, so many books she could focus her attention upon until in the silence it came back to her, the voice. And then what little she had shared with him—Seamus—seemed so distant and so dimly remembered in comparison. What *had* he told her, what *had* he promised? The *last* "action" as he had phrased it, and then all that money to begin a new life with? Money from what beyond one man's murder?

And louder by far, like a skull full of maggots, the voice now filled Roisin Johnston's days and stalked the ten rooms of silence and dust, which were her nights in the Rhines house, with a baleful, deathly presence. By day, curiously, she had found, she could carry on, though the voice—monotonal and regular, like the beat of a clock—subsumed all other sounds until it had spoken to term. Then it seemed like a poem or a song or a jingle, of chains—a death rattle, it was, harsh and horrible—but tolerable while there were others about.

But at night, when she was alone in the house, it packed bodies cool and covered by rodent feces, scalps split open like clams, wounds "hard, frayed and crusty" from every shadow and dream, haunting her reveries, chilling her ease. Drawers opened brimmed with gaping mouths, eyes scudding with gray-white mold, closets were stuffed with thin, moist blond hair and ". . . lips soft—marked by postmortem decomposition. Mouths—maggot infested. Tongues missing. Teeth plucked easily, one by one." And all in the contained cadence of a countryman's speech.

Schooling it was, she first told herself when trying to shrug it off—hers by her father and mother. For failure. She had a chance here and her last to make a life for herself with a man she knew and could admire, a strong man who—by *his* report, which, she should value more than any other—was performing ". . . the one task, which, handled properly, might unite the country and permanently resolve the division of the North." And if he was being paid for that and enough for them to live comfortably, well then . . . all the better. He was, she suspected, nobody's fool.

But yet, welling up from drains, tumbling down stairwells, sticking on her fingers which she had slipped between the cushions of the couch to retrieve her glasses, was a slurry of scalps, "bruised, discolored, dark, reddish black," or a yellow cone of gore from which blood was trickling across a varnished table, or a bullet-fractured parenchyma encased in a soft, pasty, grayish-pink jell of decomposed brain.

Reaching for a jacket, Roisin told herself it was company she was in need of. Like nearly all other Irishmen and -women, she was a gregarious creature and required the company of others. Without it she languished and the absurdities, which were a part of every personality, became dominant. But in a lounge bar, she was made to wait and then served only reluctantly, with neither a nod nor a thank-you. Dromgoole, it was, she thought, and whatever it was that had happened in Belfast, to the other one, the Guard who had taken her in—McGarr, it had been in all the papers. Politics was bad for custom, and she wondered if they would ask her (politely, *of course*) to take her trade elsewhere.

Walking slowly "home," Roisin chanced to pass her family's house, and, standing in the street warm from the summer sun, which now at nearly eleven still colored the sky to the west, she on impulse rang the front-door bell.

Her brother, Michael, answered: "Roisin!" He glanced behind him, then, stepping out, pulled the door to. "He's home, he is, and—" He shook his head. "It's good to see you. I'd stop round, but he's told us all how he's having it." A handsome, dark boy, he had eyes, like her own, which were deep blue flecked with silver; he furrowed his brow and looked away. "We're to pretend, says he, that you"—he again shook his head—"died. If he even hears elsewise, it's us. We're out, and he means it."

Death, she thought, turning away. It was what had driven her from nursing. Life was what she had sought in returning to Ireland and university and then here to Monaghan and her family and the bank, where a steady flow of people sought her out for money or advice to help them grow.

Turning the latch, she opened the back door on twin, grinning and hideous fetuses—mouths dropped open, facial bones protrusive, contained in a luminescent caul of maggots and slime.

In the sitting room, she switched on the telly, and the logo for the late news flickered on with the headline of the day's major story, "BLANEY TO WALK IN NORTH." And while she tried to concentrate on the announcer's words, ". . . a Blaney representative, having contacted the Reverend Ian Paisley, has issued the statement that the Donegal T.D. and forever Member of the European Parliament will meet with Paisley on the Twelfth of July . . . ," the shadowed floor, the mantel and wall behind throbbed and heaved, like a compost of viscera. ". . . 'somebody has to take a first step and offer a friendly

250

hand,' said Blaney. 'If not a member of the present government, then a man from former governments, which have opposed . . .' "

Roisin stood and found the section of radiator which at the proper touch swung back to reveal the weapon concealed there. ". . . 'a man who before was blinded by his own prejudices. And then,' Blaney added, 'I'm from the Greater Ulster myself.'

"In other news . . ."

In the basement, surrounded by a charnel house of rotting human parts, she took over an hour to get it to fire. If she was to be a gunman's woman, she would carry a gun.

McKeon's reaction to the late news was far different. Sitting on the sofa which had been placed along one wall of his kitchen to accommodate the usually present friends of his immense family, he asked his youngest daughter to ring the Castle and hand him the receiver.

When a familiar voice answered, McKeon said, "Rut'ie—what the hell are you still there for?" though he did not wait for a reply. "I wonder if we could discover the blood group of the Reverend Paisley." He listened for a while. "Well, I don't know meself. Otherwise, would I be asking you? I'm sure you'll find some way, and I'll be here, now. Waiting."

When three hours later the phone rang, McKeon found himself for one of the few times in his life alone in his kitchen. Said Bresnahan, "It's AB, sir."

"What is?"

"The Reverend Paisley's blood, sir," she said indignantly. "You asked me to find out about it, oh . . . midnight, I'd say."

"Did I?" he asked without opening his eyes. "That's right, I did. AB," he mused. "That's the same as the question on Duncan's computer whatsis you dug up, is it not?" But before she could answer, he went on: "Listen, Peter's statement—

251

the one he gave Liam over the phone about the Geer house in Belfast—did we get it typed up yet?"

Bresnahan was about to give him a piece of her mind, but she reminded herself that hours meant nothing to McKeon, who often worked whole nights running himself.

"Good girl. Now, turn to the part where he's describing the room, the one at the top of the house. Could you read it to me? I'm interested in the bit about the sashes. That's right, the Orange sashes." When McKeon heard her say, " 'the most extensive collection I've ever seen,' " he said, "That's grand, Rut'ie. Thanks very much," and rang off.

A quarter hour later, the light in the closet of their bedroom woke Bridie McKeon. She sat up to discover her husband packing a suitcase. "What's that lot?" she asked.

"Ach—I thought I'd take a bit of a walk."

"At midnight? In your best suit?"

McKeon had lifted it off a hanger and now folded the black wool of the suit into the case. "Sure, I thought I'd upgrade me image. You don't catch the boss being fil-med in a rumpled jacket."

"The *former* boss," she corrected. Then, "It must be a trek you're planning. You haven't worn them trousers since Dympna's wedding."

"All the more reason I should give them some air." He winked.

"And where, pray, will this walk be taken?"

McKeon looked up from the case, the hard glint in his eye betraying the playful tone of his words. "Sure, I know the South. I thought I'd see the North now."

"Ah, Bernie—are we to lose more?" At the front door she added, "Remember—you've got *other* wee ones who need you. Now."

But by early morning, McKeon found himself in a rundown section of Belfast. Standing well away from any building, he

252

placed his case at his feet and kept his hands out of his tan slicker and in plain sight.

After a dozen minutes, a man dressed as a woman pushed a pram toward him, stopping a few feet away to adjust the bonnet. "You've got a name," he said. "Tell it me."

McKeon complied.

"And you're—?"

He told him that too.

"You're here for what?"

"A wee chat with Mr. Carty."

"Why?"

"I'll tell that to him."

"Sure," the man said, "I'm after thinkin' you will."

19

Even before taking the key from the lock of the door to his digs on the Shankill Road two days later, Carron knew it was a mistake. After all, he now had half of the money—hadn't he?—and right in the grip of his hand. Quite enough, thank you, to buy three dozen of anything, apart from the weapon, that the tiny flat contained. "You'll not need it, George. We want you for your hands," Geer had said when presenting him with enough preshaped and fitted Kevlar to make him an armored man. "We can't have you getting hurt. And after we come through this thing, I'll get you the bonniest piece our suppliers can come up with, and that, like the rest, is a promise that you know I'll keep."

Geer had not failed him yet, but it was the "coming through" that had Carron, who had taken only "maintenance" drink since the talk, worried. And the gun itself—a 9mm. Military Mauser machine pistol, which could spew out a clip that, fired at close range, would shatter any Kevlar. Hadn't Carron seen for himself in Armagh, when he was ordered to fire on their own troops to provoke an incident? Aimed down from a second-floor window, the low-velocity weighted bullets had chunked through the graphite-thread helmet, like stone through cardboard. Though an antique now, the Mauser had, as a close-quarters weapon, few equals, and Carron felt the need of it now.

Turning as though neither of the two other men was there, Carron in four strides reached the couch, on which he placed the grip where he might snatch it up quickly, if need be.

"Mr. Carron—might we have a word with you?" asked the little one, the Guard; he should have finished him when he had the chance. He was sitting in the reading chair by one window, which was open; the second man, who was wearing some type of uniform, stood by the other.

Yet Carron merely kept on with what he was about, reaching up for the small tab that he had glued to the corner of the wallpaper that declined with the slope of the roof, feeling the "cobwebs" he had carefully arranged there before pulling it back.

"They're using you, you know," the wee man went on, dressed again—Carron could see in the mirror on the table— in a bowler hat and a black jacket, but formally, as though he too would "walk" today. There was a shiny thing in his lap, a pistol, something—by the look of it—too small and with the silencer too weak to buck through the Kevlar, which was eight times stronger than the same thickness of steel.

Aye, Carron thought, they were, but at least for the proper pay. And with the Mauser, which—palming off the section of loose plaster that he let fall to the couch—he reached for in the shadows, it would go no further. Touching the heavy wooden stock of the weapon, inserting his index finger into the trigger guard, he asked, "Using me how?"

The Guard's hand was now on the gun but he did not raise it. Why? "For your background, who you are. Former SAS. A man with a bit of a problem—understand my drift? And whatever's in that grip or your pocket or some bank'll mean nothing to you. Your own people—Fairclough and the others—will make sure you're lost for good. And once you are, end of tale."

"But what if Ah wan' ta kill 'm meself?" said Carron, sliding the awesome weapon from its niche and turning to them. The other one—from the Strand; Carron had seen him before—had a handgun as well, but still down at his side. Why?

"But you're to kill him?" he asked.

"Dooz it mahder?" said Carron, suddenly realizing that the Mauser felt lighter than it should, his head bending to check for the clip, which was missing.

Very much indeed, thought McGarr.

But Carron, in a panic now, had spun round, his wide hand spading into the niche in the wall. Outraged, he turned back to them.

"Is it these you're after, Mr. Carron?" Glynn said, holding up the four clips that they had earlier found there.

A mistake, like a flag to a bull. Carron snatched up the grip and, holding it before his face, made for Glynn, who in the tiny room glanced round, as though trapped, then jerked up his gun and fired off a burst of four shots that thwacked into something hard and set ricochets thudding into the plaster wall behind.

At point-blank range Glynn fired again into Carron's chest, and then, raising the barrel at the grip, which Carron had held before his face, touched off another round, which jarred his hand and buried itself in the leather.

But Carron had Glynn now, snatching him up by the throat and shoving him through the window, which showered glass on some sheet-metal roof below. He then dropped him into three floors of darkness. Glynn uttered not a sound until he struck the roof, which roared, his moan mingling with the sound of his body rolling off whatever shed he had struck.

Carron snatched up a clip, which he jammed into the Mauser, and McGarr, half out of the window by the reading chair, paused only long enough to fire two shots at his head before consigning himself to the same fate as Glynn, though he knew—having checked—the back garden there was mostly lawn.

To the west stars were visible, though the day had just dawned, and already, somewhere off in the brickyard which was Belfast, he could hear the growling rumble of drums.

A clothes line, catching his shoes, his knees, and armpit and his throat, broke his fall, and he had scarcely picked himself up when Carron appeared in the window above and fired off a barrage that sounded in the contained space of the garden like a salvo of artillery and shattered the flagstones by McGarr's feet.

Lights were being switched on in the contiguous houses as he hurled himself at the man who had just opened his back-garden door a crack to peek out.

"RUC," said McGarr. "That man up there—Carron—he's running amok. Stay inside." He only just made the hall before the door upstairs was kicked open and Carron, aiming down the staircase, fired off a burst that shivered the frame and shattered the glass as the door swung back, the lead plowing into a car parked by the curb.

Gathering himself, McGarr straightened the brim of the bowler and the collar of the black jacket Carty had given him. He began walking calmly toward the corner, around which the Audi was parked.

The traffic was heavy along the Shankill Road even at this early hour as Orangemen by the thousands were making for the Carlisle Circus assembly area. They had slowed in one direction and stopped well away from the shattered door in the other.

Selecting one of the several picks on his key chain, McGarr inserted it in the lock of the long, gray car and, working it for a while, managed to open the door, climb in, and close it, just as Carron appeared at the corner, Mauser in hand, heedless of onlookers and—McGarr thought—the RUC or the security forces. In the distance he could hear the claxon of a patrol car.

Lowering himself down onto the seat so he could glimpse the ignition lock but would not be seen from the corner, he thought of Glynn. Considering what was at stake, Glynn was a dead man if he could not be gotten out.

Carron now turned in the only direction that he had not been able to see from the front door to his flat and began walking toward McGarr, the Mauser held before him but pointed at the footpath, like a man about to administer a *coup de grâce*. Five cars away. Four. Three.

The ignition lights flashed on but McGarr could not seem to get the wheel to disengage from its theft lock.

The engine started with a roar that startled Carron, but when McGarr jammed it into reverse and popped the clutch, playing the key and the wheel simultaneously, struggling to get it to slip free, Carron started forward, the machine pistol coming up.

The position of the wheel lock had swung the car out into the street abreast of the alley that ran behind Carron's flat, and only after he had slammed it into first did the wheel with a tug spin free. McGarr stomped on the gas and tried to catch Carron with a fender, as he careened past. But the man stepped back just in time, and the Mauser starred the windscreen, both windows on the passenger side, and the rear window, McGarr again throwing himself down behind the cover of the seat.

Gun still in hand, Glynn had propped himself against the back-garden wall and was keeping two men, who were standing near him, at bay.

McGarr braked to a sliding stop and threw open the door,

his own gun hand coming up. "Help him!" he shouted to the men. "Help get him in here, or that man behind me will kill us all. It's him he wants." In the exterior mirror on his side of the car McGarr could see Carron fitting his final clip into the Mauser.

It was then that an RUC car, its dome light pulsing, appeared in the alley ahead of them.

As the two men dragged Glynn toward the car, shoving him in, McGarr slid out of the car and propped his weapon on the roof, firing his remaining five rounds at Carron's head.

But yet, as he jumped back in and threw Glynn to the floor, he chanced to see Carron's hand coming up once again, and in front of them the RUC car was lurching forward at speed.

The Audi shot wildly backward, caroming off the walls of the narrow alley, the open door flattening itself against the fender and then swinging free, McGarr steering more by touch than sight. An arm was now out of the RUC car with a shiny object jumping from the hand.

A heavy slug from behind bucked into the instrument panel of the Audi, which showered the interior with shards of plastic and metal, and another imploded the glove box, inches from Glynn's head.

McGarr caught a glimpse of Carron's legs on the passenger side behind them and when, he judged, they were just by him, he pumped the brakes once, and the door—arcing with the momentum of their speed—struck something hard, driving it up against the wall.

But they were back out in the street again, the car in first, its wheels squealing, and McGarr only saw a figure sprawled in the alley in front of the RUC car, before they were off down the street. Away from the Shankill Road and the traffic.

Said Glynn, "The radio. How's that? We'll need it now more than ever, if we're to get out of here.

"Me leg."

At a glance McGarr could see that it was broken. The femur, right leg, was tenting up the material of the pants, which was sodden with blood.

McGarr reached under the dash for the microphone of the radio, which earlier he had seen Glynn use, and the small, red monitor light winked on.

20

Geer raised the sighting device to his eyes, then focused in on the large speaker's platform. It had been constructed at one end of Finaghy Park, Belfast, which, because of the large crowd expected, would for the first time in nearly a decade be the terminus of a Loyalist walk. Here, in the two-plus hours it would take them to arrive, over a hundred thousand Orangemen would be harangued by six of their own on this Twelfth of July. It was a celebration which Harold Wilson had once described as "a strange devotion to a long-dead Dutchman," meaning William of Orange, who had been the victor of the watershed Battle of the Boyne. Wilson, who had perhaps more than any other Briton tried to stop it. And now wee Paddy Geer, please God.

The seventh speaker—a lucky number, Paisley's *Protestant Telegraph* had today observed—was Neil Blaney, who had received, it was also said, several death threats from elements of the IRA. Security was tight. All around the edges of the park Geer could see British Army units in "sangers," sandbagged bunkers situated at key points to control both the field and any attack from without. A cordon of armor was idling watchfully around the perimeter.

And already the first lodges in the parade, having marched

261

through Belfast, were entering the park. With battered, ancient, but gleaming horns, with pipes and lambeg drums that made the earth beneath Geer's feet tremble, the Ligoniel True Blues, who had been chosen this year to march first, were blaring out "The Sash," while behind them the Temperance Dockers rendered a cacophonous "Kick the Pope." And behind them another lodge and another and another marched in two thin black-clad, sash-shimmering lines which, in the full summer sun and the camera's distant focus, seemed liquid and serpentine, snaking back into the city, Geer well knew, for at least three miles.

His hand rose to the focusing peg, and he again swung the camera around the park, if only to show the director in the ITN van in back of the stage that he was doing his job. Two dogs were coursing hopelessly after a third, a setter whose auburn mane flashed in the lens with each graceful stride. On the green verge of a rose garden some children had taken out a ball and were whooping with delight, as they kept it from an elderly park attendant who was trying to stop them.

In other places around the park, stands were selling flags, ices, jellies, hot dogs, and Yellow Man, the Ulster specialty that was, Geer believed, purchased on this day merely to maintain another distasteful tradition. There, as he had suspected, the first of the Ligoniel True Blues had gathered for their dollops of sugary confection, before filing to the front rows below the stage.

It was enough "setting," Geer judged, for the technicians in the van, and he again chose the longest lens and focused on the black-clad lines entering the park. He then felt in his jacket to make sure he had the tape that he had made from his film, and he dropped down off the scaffolding, falling to a knee and a hand. Shakily, he picked himself up and moved away from the camera, toward the stage and the clutch of emergency vehicles that had been parked beyond it: two ambulances—one with Irish plates, which had been a precondition to Blaney's arrival—and an old Humber sedan, the engine of which was idling to provide current for an air-conditioning unit and sounded deep and powerful for such an antiquated machine. In it, Geer knew, were three figures. He himself, however, stopped only at the stage, which he mounted ostensibly so he could understand the angles from which his camera would be shooting. Here and there—by the podium, center stage, the top and the bottom of the stairs—he paused, unobtrusively touching his hand to the undersides of various items at each spot. He then passed beyond the Humber to the ITN van and the Yellow Man stands in the distance.

There a black-derbied man, who was also wearing—of all things—a tan slicker, strolled round to the back of the stand and reappeared without the coat. Flicking a bit of lint from his blue-and-silver sash, which was brighter even than his blond hair, he joined the other Ligoniel True Blues who were headed toward the stage.

In the van, the director turned to Geer, who had opened the door. "Paddy—what're you doing here?" The man's eyes jumped to the monitor of Geer's camera.

"Look what I found." Reaching inside his jacket, Geer pulled out the tape.

"What is it?" the director demanded impatiently.

"The 'standby' tape," said Geer, meaning the footage of past Twelfth of July marches that would be shown in case all else failed. It had been missing from the ITN film library.

"Where'd you find that?"

"With that old rat of a camera you've got me on. Under the dolly. Sure, that yoke's not been used in a year, and must I remind you of my seniority. It's discrimination, it is."

Somebody at the monitors began laughing, but Geer made sure he reached the reel to the director himself, who stepped

263

quickly toward him, saying, "Why didn't you tell us over the set? We'd have had somebody fetch it."

"On a brilliant morn like this?" said Geer, thinking, I had to make sure you had it in your hands. "And, sure—we've got all the time in the world. It'll take the lads hours to arrive." He stepped back out into the sun and closed the door behind him, then scanned the crowd that was now beginning to mass before the stage.

In the very first row a man turned to the figure on his left, whom, surprisingly, he did not know. "Rather hot for this." He meant the sticky sweet that both of them were eating.

"Never for Yellow Man," said the other. "It takes me back."

"Are you new to the lodge?"

"Ah, no. An old hand. But you might say I'm new to parks and fresh air and the glorious sunlight." He looked up into the azure sky and smiled, before taking more of the sweet.

"Been unwell?"

"Oh, aye. Quite, though—thank the good Lord—it's gone."

"The cough?"

Smiling, the second man turned to him. "How'd you know?"

Pleased to have guessed right, the first said, "Used to be a smoking man and worse, myself."

"Were you 'saved' too?" the second asked, transferring the confection from his right hand to his left. "David Smythe's the name."

"Harold's brother?"

"The eldest but the only one left, I'm afraid. You know, of course, what happened to Harold . . ." he went on, although until that morning he had known none of it himself.

"You're to tell him who you are?"

If necessary, thought McGarr, though he possessed nothing to give that identity proof. The papers—those that Carty had given him with the name Samuel Pease Frenche—would prove counterproductive if he could get past the door. Credibility was needed most now.

"Let me ask you something," Glynn went on, his face sweating with pain, which he was struggling to deny. They had been met by men in another car, which was parked fifty yards from the detached Victorian structure which was Paisley's home. "What's Paisley to you?"

The two men in the front of the car stirred nervously, as four others, three to the front and one to the rear, got out of other cars and began to approach them. One held some snubby, modern weapon with a scimitar sweep of magazine.

Said McGarr, reaching for the door handle, "I could as easily ask that of you."

"Paisley to me?" Glynn tried to laugh.

The radio crackled. A voice was heard. Said one of the men in front, "Fairclough just left his house in Lurgan." It was ten miles away.

"I'd as soon see the bastard . . ."

McGarr closed the door.

He was searched, questioned, then searched again. He was asked why, if his name was Peter McGarr, he had papers that named him Samuel Pease Frenche, and whether he was the Peter McGarr that the security forces were now looking for. He said yes. Did he, then, realize they would have to call them? "Yes, but I'd like to speak to the Reverend Paisley, if I might." Why? "There's something I must tell him." He could tell them as easily. But not as convincingly, McGarr thought. "Please," he said, regarding each of them for a moment, "I've come here knowing what would happen. I'd like a word with the man. Five minutes, no more." Said one of them, "I'll phone." Don't bother, thought McGarr, he's on his way. Fairclough, a co-conspirator, for all he could know.

Minutes went by—ten, a quarter hour—in which McGarr sat on a hard chair, guarded by an older man with a hand inserted in the open leaves of a briefcase. He heard a strong voice say, "Mr. Fairclough is *not* my social secretary. You say this man came here on his own?" McGarr could not make out the muffled tones of the other voice, but he then heard footsteps, and the French doors leading into the hall were opened. With his head, another man beckoned him, and McGarr was directed through a long, somber sitting room to an airy glassed-in porch that looked out on a garden effulgent with summer flowers that were basking in the midday sun.

Paisley—an immense man by any standard—was breakfasting at the head of a glass-top table, staring down at a newspaper which, with a pile of correspondence, had been placed before him. His face was—as Geer had caught it in his film—helmetlike and hard, a construct of dour points (a sweep of forehead, high ridged cheekbones, a lantern jaw) that made his eyes seem oval and recessed. Dark, they flickered up and assessed McGarr.

"They tell me you're a rebel, Mr.—is it McGarr?"

"It is, sir, and you're misinformed."

"Am I, now?"

The man with his hand in the briefcase was standing beyond the open door, in the shadows of the dining room.

"And about what, may I ask? Weren't you involved in an incident along the Albertbridge Road? And something else today, I'm told. The first thing was at—"

"Paddy Geer's house," McGarr said.

Paisley let his eyes—almost Oriental in appearance—meet McGarr's for a moment, only to take in the black coat, dark tie, and morning trousers which were no different from his own, before returning to the paper. "So I understand. And you're here to tell me why, aren't you? Is it"—raising his teacup, he looked out into the back garden—"that Paddy is planning to kill me?"

"Today," said McGarr. "In the park."

The teacup did not stop on its ascent to Paisley's mouth. "Well, I should enjoy my meal, it being my last." Yet again he directed his sight to the newspapers. "And tell me, how is he going to manage this . . . feat of bravery?"

"I don't know, but it won't be Geer himself. Or Carron, though Carron will play some part. Or anybody"—McGarr had begun to pace, thinking of Fairclough and the British Army and Geer and Carron and whoever else was with them who could have killed Paisley any time, anyplace, and by virtually any means—"*distant* from you."

"George Carron?" One of Paisley's eyebrows arched. "The plot thickens."

From the front of the house McGarr now heard a deep voice raised in anger.

"It could even be your Mr. Fairclough," said McGarr. "His partner was murdered because he was not in it."

"Robbie Blount? Really?" Paisley laughed, raising a napkin to his lips, though his eyes had suddenly become distant. He cocked his head. "Now you're really running on."

"It began with the murder of Jock Duncan in Dublin," McGarr said quickly, but Fairclough had already appeared in the doorway.

Said Paisley, "Which, I suppose, led you to Paddy Geer's and accounts for your extraordinary activity there."

"I injured nobody. I found a film—"

"You're a criminal," said Fairclough from the doorway. "You were involved this morning in a shooting incident in the Shankill Road. A policeman was injured, and you're to come with me. A court will sort you out."

Lowering his head, Paisley pushed the teacup away and turned to Fairclough. "Derek—what have I told you before? I'll *not* have you—"

"This man is wanted, he's dangerous," said Fairclough, his face as expressionless, his eyes as steely as they were on the third-floor landing of Geer's house when McGarr was detained.

"Only to what you're planning."

With deliberation Fairclough's hand came up and slipped beneath the lapel of his jacket. The man standing behind him removed a chrome automatic from the briefcase.

"That's quite enough," said Paisley, discarding his napkin and standing. "You can take yourself off, Derek. Now. And with you him." He meant the man in the shadows.

Loathedly, Fairclough and the other man withdrew. After a short wait, Paisley took four angry strides to the door and shouted, "The hall!" Only after that door had closed did he turn to McGarr. "Well, sir?"

Said McGarr, "Look—I'm no . . . devotee of yours, and I never was. But you've chosen what you are, like I've chosen to come here, knowing what it would mean. And thirty years of police experience, which I'm here abandoning, tells me that an attempt on your life will be made today by those closest to you and best able to know your . . . vulnerabilities."

Paisley began to speak but McGarr stayed him.

"Maybe in the past you've been able to protect yourself with the magnitude of your political identity, but those conspiring against you now have changed those conditions"— again McGarr held up a palm—"just enough to make it all possible, and they'll not be among the injured themselves.

"Tell me—the Thatcher/Haughey talks. What did you first think when they were announced?"

Paisley's head turned to the garden beyond the windows. "That it was curious, given her former intractability."

"And Haughey's being willing to discuss the Republic's neutrality?"

Paisley shook his head and advanced on the table, where he picked up his teacup and moved to the window. "Extraordinary. I had always thought the issue dead, their enmity for the British making any accommodation politically impossible.

"Then . . . there's the troops in Monaghan and Donegal," Paisley went on, as though musing.

Torn by the probability that he was breaching a trust, McGarr said in a small voice, "And now the Provisionals in Belfast and most likely elsewhere have just received more money and more modern arms than they've seen in years."

Paisley turned his head to him. "You know that?"

"For fact."

Somewhere in the house a phone was ringing, and claxons could be heard from out in the street. At length Paisley asked, "What do you have in mind?"

"You'll still speak—?"

"Of course, I must. I couldn't—I *wouldn't*—have it said . . ."

McGarr glanced down at the papers and the empty breakfast dishes. "Two things, but for them we'll need somebody in the RUC you can trust. Some senior official. One of your"— he rejected "staunch supporters" and said—"adherents."

21

The crowd was vast. And now, as the rumor of the Big Lad's arrival spread through the throng, a shout went up, which was followed by a roar of approval that quelled the fifth and last of the Loyalist speakers scheduled before Blaney and Paisley and what was being described as their "historic handshake."

And it frightened Geer, made him feel weaker than he had at any other time in his life: the wound and the prospect that at last, after his years of effort, it would finally happen, and the fact that five minutes before, the Guard—the one who had broken into his house, McGarr—had appeared with an older RUC officer and a squad of constables, and now, as the speaker quitted the podium in dismay, began mounting the stairs of the platform.

Geer turned the camera to the first car, a black Rover packed with six men, which swung into the cleared green emergency laneway and moved slowly toward the platform, the emergency vehicles, and the old Humber that was idling nearby. Snapping in his longest lens, Geer focused on the windscreen and was relieved to see Fairclough in the passenger seat of the Rover, his eyes on the platform and the activity there. Geer then moved to the second car, which would contain the Big Fella, and finally the third car, which provided security from the rear, and he could not keep himself from observing that with all the black enamel and men in black coats, the proceeding looked like a huge funeral cortege.

Swinging his long legs from the back seat of the second car, the Good Doctor hoisted his great frame to a stand, his arms rising skyward, his palms outstretched, and again the crowd reacted. Immediately he was surrounded by Fairclough's security staff, who, quickly now, began moving their charge toward the stairs to the platform, though Geer kept his eyes on one man alone: Carron, who, as planned, hung back for a moment by the emergency van with the Belfast plates, having brought in with him the one item that none of them could. The stage, the area around it, the two emergency vans, and even the old Humber had been "swept and secured" earlier.

And Geer felt a profound sense of relief, knowing that all was on track and his own function, by agreement, over. He sighted in the podium, twisted down the securing lever, and straightened up. Saying, "Jakes," to the BBC cameraman, he dropped down off the scaffolding into the crowd, where he began to move away from the platform toward the trees and the street and the housing estate he could see in the distance. There he had parked a rental car that he would return to Dublin, could he make it. The padding, the bandage, the shirt and jacket he was wearing made him feel as though he was coming apart, and at the stink of himself he might swoon.

Planning, he thought—knowing he'd doubtless be fully out of the Six Counties before the major clashes began. Could they have considered too much, he wondered? What part would moment play in it all? Chance and luck?

Carron actually had two objects to dispose of in the backs of the emergency vans. Saying "Security" he flashed his Ulster Risks ID which he had clipped to the underside of a lapel, and pushed through the several ambulance attendants who had gathered to watch Paisley pass by. He wrenched open the back of the one with the Belfast plates, and climbed in, then slipped the vial from a breast pocket and placed it under the pillow of the center litter so it could be got at easily. Climbing out, he eased the door nearly closed, allowing a two-inch gap for, say, three fingers or the toe of a shoe.

In the van with the Irish plates, he hefted the substantial bulk of his Military Mauser and slid it, along with two additional clips, under the pillow there, though after climbing out he closed that door. It would be reopened for him before he returned. And having caught sight of the wee Guard—the one who had thumped him with the car door in the alley—he knew he'd need it later.

The Guard was standing by the stairs of the platform where, with some RUC, they were frisking all who went up, and it could not be found on him. Only the Harrington & Richardson automatic that he'd been issued, and—something made him suspect—he'd not be allowed to take up. It mattered not, he told himself. His hands would be busy enough, and he himself "shielded" certainly more than others.

With swift, sure strides for a man of his age and size, Carron returned to the rear of the Paisley entourage. Not seen, not missed, he suspected, his eyes peering over the heads of all but one man in front of him and seeing the Guard, the RUC—was it a commissioner? It was and that was good. An expert witness—speaking to Fairclough there at the stairs.

Said Fairclough, his eyes fixing those of the commissioner, "All our weapons are licensed, David, and registered. You know so yourself. My staff are either former policemen or members of the security forces. They have been selected after most rigid security checks. Not one of them has the slightest smirch on his record"—the gun-metal blue eyes turned to McGarr—"like this man."

"You'll hear it from himself, then," said the uniformed officer, turning to the figure of Paisley and those with him, who had now reached the foot of the stairs to the platform.

"Without their weapons my men will not go up," Fairclough continued.

"What's this?" Paisley asked.

"Without them, I remove Ulster Risks from any responsibility."

Right, thought McGarr, seeing Carron behind Paisley. Better, why not remove them from the stage? His eyes then met Carron's and the sear of their gaze made one thing patently clear—without the others there, only one of them would leave the park alive. Why? Why not, McGarr decided, having succumbed to the ——— of the moment. There was blood in the air, he could sense it, and he judged he had little choice but to give himself up to the occasion.

Said Paisley, "There'll be no guns on the stage today. But we'll all go up"—he turned the almond stare of his dark eyes on McGarr—"George Carron included.

"Where is George?" he went on, turning back to his retainers. "Ah, yes—there you are. George, you first. Let us demonstrate how fearless Ulstermen can be."

Said Fairclough, "Then Ulster Risks refuses to accept—"

"I'll take responsibility, Derek. And we'll talk about this later—"

And while McGarr watched Carron and the other members of the security staff meekly surrender similar automatic pistols and submit to a thorough search, he wondered how the attempt, if any, would now come? Any attacker from the crowd below would be ripped apart, and could Carron be that brutally deft that he could dispatch a man of Paisley's size and evident strength in the mere seconds it would take others to get to them? And why Carron?

It was while he was so musing that McGarr for the first

time noticed the soft, rounded lines of the sparkling, forest-green Humber with the Irish plates that was parked near the emergency vans.

In its quiet, air-conditioned comfort, Rhines—courtesy of the miniaturized microphones, the size of a sixpence, that Geer had placed around the stage several hours earlier—had listened to the exchange. He now turned to the figure beside him and said, "Well, Mr. Blaney, it would seem that you're on." The two front seats in the Humber had been independently positioned on ball-bearing axles that could rotate 360 degrees. They had been turned, and now the two men were looking out across the back seat, where sat a third figure, and the rear window toward the stage and the stairway leading up to it.

"*Eee-ahn, Eee-ahn, Eee-ahn,*" the entire park was now chanting, their one voice penetrating even the sanctum of the Humber.

The man turned to Rhines and offered his hand. "Big moment for me. My biggest."

Rhines looked over at the dark eyes hooded by shaggy brows and the folded and creased lineaments of the face. "It's a crowd, I'll say, and not the best part of it." He meant the television cameras, some of which they could see at a front corner of the stage. He thought of his own final task, which would require the diversion that would be created when Paisley and Blaney mounted the stage.

He took the man's hand. "Bad luck. I hope you break a leg."

And he continued to watch closely, as anxious now as he had ever been in his life, while Blaney was greeted by Paisley, who explained the procedure there before the stairs, and Blaney nodded his agreement. "Certainly. I understand. Crazies—" He shook his head and took out his pipe, into which he struck a match. His eyes moved around the circle of figures as he raised his arms for the RUC constables, who performed the search with careful deliberation.

In the Humber, Rhines eased his back into the cushions of the seat and lit a cigarette.

Paisley stepped aside to let Blaney mount the stairs first, but on the platform Blaney deferred to Paisley, solicitous of upstaging him. It was and would be, after all, very much Paisley's day.

The applause was deafening. It struck the stage in a gust that staggered McGarr and caused the others there to trade glances in a kind of awe. All but Paisley, who, with arms raised, was drawn—as by a magnet—to the front of the stage.

"*Eee-ahn, Eee-ahn, Eee-ahn,*" they had again begun to cry, and Paisley, beaming his pleasure, turned the toothy radiance of his smile back on his retinue, as if to say, Oh, see how I, the man accused of hatred, am loved. His security team had assumed key defensive positions about the stage, though they could protect him with their bodies alone. Carron—McGarr saw—was about nine feet from the podium, scanning a section of the near crowd, as he ought. Blaney, a smaller man, was as good as lost behind the others at the back of the stage.

Paisley dropped his arms. The crowd—immense as it was— silenced with a peremptoriness that, McGarr judged, was ominous, were anything to occur. Pausing dramatically at the podium, Paisley looked out upon the crowd.

"Fellow Ulstermen!" he boomed, his voice rolling over the sea of upturned faces. "I come here today with good news"— a flurry of clapping broke out, but he silenced it with a hand— "very good news indeed. I come here to tell you that though we're embattled, not all the world is arrayed against us. Yes— we have foes. But, *yes*, we also have those, perhaps even of contrary backgrounds and faiths, who perhaps in the past have even wanted to attack us, but who have finally, with the maturation of their vision, recognized the legitimacy of our right to Ulster"—again clapping intervened, which Paisley had some difficulty quelling—"and who have the courage, though threatened with bodily harm, to come forward and embrace the curious notion of an Ulster state for Ulstermen and -women."

Laughter, which began on the stage, now spread through the crowd. The thought was a paraphrase of a statement that had been uttered over sixty years before by Lord Craigavon, Northern Ireland's first prime minister.

"One such man," Paisley went on, "is the Donegal parliamentarian and former minister in several governments of the Republic of Ireland"—a hiss, begun near the stage, insinuated itself throughout the crowd—"who in the past sat with me in the European Parliament and who comes here today as *my personal guest.*" Paisley paused, his eyes scanning the crowd, so they would understand. "In itself," he went on, "it is an act of personal courage for him to be here. But he has come to expand upon an idea, of which, I'm sure, you're all aware, and which he broached last week.

"Good men of Ulster, you who are as righteous as you are loyal, as steadfast as you are strong, and as fierce"—he nearly shouted—"as you are forgiving, I want you to welcome Mr. Neil Blaney unto our midst. He is a brave man of rectitude and foresight."

Struggling under the weight, Rhines, who though strong was not a big man, was relieved to find the door to the ambulance with the Belfast plates ajar according to plan. With the fingers of his right hand, which for a quick moment he removed from his charge, he swung it open, and, bracing himself, thrust down first the right leg and then the left, and—

276

teetering on the welded stairs—the right again, before he found he could deposit his burden in the sweltering, antiseptic interior. He reached for the door, which he drew nearly to, and moved directly to the litter.

Using a knee, which he swung up onto the table for leverage, Rhines then reached down and slid his hand under the appendage that he had let loll over the edge of the litter. Grasping his left wrist with his right hand, he paused for a moment. It was not so much strength that was required as dexterity, he told himself. He then jerked up suddenly, twisting to one side and away. feeling through his knee the frightful snap.

He dropped the weight, and drew the vial of blood from under the pillow at the other end. It took him a moment or two to discover the spring release, but once the probe had appeared he impaled the membrane that sealed the mouth of the vial, stepping back quickly so as not to splotch his clothing. He had to tug to free it from the shaft of the instrument, and he placed it in a plastic sack he had brought along for that purpose. He would discard it, once well away from Finaghy Park and Belfast and what would soon be—he judged, and not without passion—the bloody Six Counties.

After dropping back down onto the grass outside, he closed the door fully, but opened that of the van with the Irish plates. Again, a crack. The requisite two inches.

Ambling, basking in the roar of the crowd, he moved with all the decorum of a funeral director toward the cool of the customized Humber, believing his career of two decades at an end.

Placing his prop—the pipe—in a jacket pocket, Blaney stepped through the cordon of taller men toward the front of the stage and the crowd, which, on seeing him, responded as they had only for Paisley himself. And, allowing a light smile to crease the corners of his mouth, Blaney, like Paisley, raised both arms high, turning in one direction and then another.

The gesture delighted the cameramen who were clustered in a thin crescent below the stage. "Neil! Neil!" some shouted in attempts to get the Donegal politician to glance at their cameras, most of which they had raised above their heads and with motorized drives were triggering off, like automatic weapons. But they shouted without success. It was as if, McGarr concluded, Blaney had rasied his arms not like Paisley, to acknowledge and return a greeting, but instead to embrace an approval that was necessary.

For, watching the fine blond hairs glimmer on the backs of Blaney's hands, McGarr judged that he was holding the pose rather long, and, nearly embarrassed for the man, he turned and looked behind him to see the old Humber rocking slightly, as it moved down the green verge of the emergency laneway toward the exit from the park. Blaney's car? Why would it be leaving without him? And a Humber, such as Dromgoole said Rhines had had in the garage in back of his Monaghan house.

It was then that the anomaly struck him—Blaney's hands, the hair on the backs which had been dark and thick on their first interview in Dublin but was blond here.

But when McGarr turned back there was more than just that difference to peruse. He only managed to take one step toward the stage before "Blaney," reaching over with his left hand, touched the wrist of his right hand, and something bright and shiny but very thin appeared in a flash above "Blaney's" right hand. Again he turned to either side of the stage, as though to display to the crowd whatever it was.

Consternation broke out among those in the front rows who could see the hand, which now began forming a fist as he turned toward Paisley for what loomed as The Handshake.

One man in the crowd shouted a warning. Another started forward. The press jerked their heads from their cameras to see the long and thin stilettolike object more clearly.

McGarr was now rushing forward, pushing, shoving the others out of his way. But "Blaney" suddenly lurched toward Paisley, his left arm hooking the taller man's neck, while the right cocked back and then knifed into Paisley's torso, the blade thwacking into the bleached brilliance of Paisley's white shirt.

Again and again he struck, sending bits of shirt and button and wool up over their heads, as Paisley—trying to push him off—tripped over something and began to fall.

"He's fallen," somebody there near the edge of the stage was fairly shouting. "The Big Fella's down. There's blood"—the knife, glancing up, traced a yellow line up his chin and cheek that quickly troughed with blood—"everywhere."

It was then that McGarr caught a glimpse of the man in the front of the crowd who, using both hands on a large-bore handgun, squeezed off a powerful round that struck "Blaney" in the side, driving him back into Carron, who had appeared there. And while all others on the stage now scattered—some throwing themselves down, others dropping off the stage—the man kept firing steadily, walking toward the stage, round after round into "Blaney," whom Carron had snatched up and was holding in front of him, like a shield. It was only then that McGarr, who, like the others, had dived for cover, recognized the man with the gun in spite of the bowler hat and sash—McKeon.

"Paisley has fallen," the voice was screaming now to be heard over the pandemonium. "Blaney has assassinated the chief."

"No!" McGarr himself now shouted, rushing forward to Paisley. "He's not. He's—" But others were there, bending to Paisley, whose face and head were splotched with blood, though his eyes were open. He blinked. Below his rent shirt, the beige gleam of a Kelvar jacket showed.

McGarr stood and spun around. Carron. Where was he? And "Blaney" or whoever it was? As he tried to work his way back through the crowd, which now packed the stage, he saw somebody tall—Carron, yes—opening the rear door of an ambulance, "Blaney" under an arm like a bundle of old clothes that he consigned to the darkness. At that instant, it seemed, the engine started, Carron tumbled into the back, the dome light flashed on, the claxon sounded, and the van began moving off, slowly at first, through the black-clad Orangemen who were rushing here and there, aimlessly it seemed, but mostly toward the stage.

McGarr broke into a sprint and, like a scrum half on a rugby pitch, jinked through the others who flitted by him. Catching hold of the handle of the rear door, which was swinging open, he pulled himself up just as Carron touched off a burst from his Military Mauser that flowered the sheet metal down one side of the ambulance interior and shattered the other door. The gun then drooped and fell from his hand.

He was slumped against the rear wall of the ambulance, having fallen and pulled the center litter table over on him and "Blaney," whose eyes were open and shallow in death. The weapon had fallen from Carron's right hand, which now kept sliding off the flap of his jacket pocket, as though reaching for something inside. His breathing, through a hole in his throat the size of a small fist, sounded like the gurgle of old blood down an open drain. In the pocket McGarr found only a tobacco pouch with something hard—a box of matches—inside.

McGarr then staggered and fell back, nearly tumbling out the open door, as the driver, clearing the park, geared up to speed.

Scrambling back inside, McGarr snatched up one of the skittering clips and slammed it into the Mauser, which he turned on the section of wall that, he judged, was directly in back of the driver. The burst nearly deafened him and filled the interior with the sweet reek of gunsmoke and hot metal, and he stumbled forward and fell on Carron as the van slowed suddenly, veered to one side, bumped over a curb, and came to rest with a scrape and a clump against a wall.

With caution McGarr stepped out into a neighborhood that was alive with distant shouts and curses. Cries. Somewhere doors were banging, dogs barking. Automobiles were being started. In the far distance, from the direction of the park, he heard what sounded to him like some great, wounded beast breaking free from its cage.

It had been Fairclough behind the wheel. The front of his head was spread in a kind of paste over the interior of the windscreen.

Neil Blaney, the Donegal T.D., was found in the back of the other emergency van, the one with the Belfast plates. He was dead. His neck had been snapped.

For Carty, the binoculars that he now eased over the top of the barricade made it look like the men and boys—clutching their bowler hats in one hand while brandishing long, silver-handled swords or pistols in the other—were running in place down the narrow Belfast street. Their new leather soles flapped in the shimmering heat, and their bolts of silver cloth, worn shoulder to hip, flashed like strokes of lightning.

And, given the brilliance of the high summer afternoon, it seemed only a harmless exercise until you noticed their faces, flushed with both their exertions and the special glow of religious hatred which Carty had been observing for most of his life.

They knew where to turn in—a house here, another there.

At one an old man, attracted by their screamed curses, had just opened the door. Newspaper in hand, pipe in his mouth, he was pulled roughly from the doorway and thrown out into the street, where he fell. As two others charged past his wife into the house, a forest of black legs gathered round and kicked him across a narrow circle, like a slow, docile, and mute dog. When his wife tried to come to his aid, she was abused, shoved, her apron snatched off her, her hair pulled. After she was tripped, a foot was then raised to her hip—"The fookin' slime," a man at Carty's side observed—and she was shoved into the gutter, where she struggled to right herself but fell back.

But the crowd was scattering now, continuing down the street toward the barricade yet heedless of it because of the distance. And the two men who had rushed into the house now shouted a warning as they began to leave. In the kitchen—Carty, who had been burnt out himself, knew all too well—they had ripped the cooker from the wall and kicked the cock from its pipe, flooding the two narrow first-floor rooms with gas. Flicking in a lighted cigarette was enough, and the final man had hardly closed the door when the blast showered the street with glass, wood, the fiery tatters of curtains and two clouds of flame so pale they appeared as only billowing heat in the binoculars.

The old woman had by then crawled to her husband, on whom she fell as though to protect him from the flames, but she was then obscured by the men, who proceeded forward to other "targets": a house here, a car there. About twenty men had gathered by a tall moving van, which, by rocking, they were trying to topple.

A young man now appeared beside Carty with an odd-shaped weapon in his hands. "What d'ya say, Joe."

"About what?" Carty asked, his good eye devolving on the curious shape—like a half-closed brolly, he thought—of the rocket. The man had raised the launcher to a shoulder, sighting in the van over the hood of a turned car.

"About dem. There must be fifty of 'em there."

Carty again raised the binoculars. It was no exaggeration, others having joined them as the van jounced back and forth, the fearful scuttling out from under it with each teeter.

The anger of outrage, Carty thought. When it subsided to the deep, abiding burn of a now enhanced hatred, many of the same men would return with real weapons and armored vehicles with firepower. "We might be needing that later," said Carty.

"But why?" somebody else roared. "When we got the fookers here. Gimme that t'ing—"

It was as if the rush of the rocket, leaving its tube, sucked the very air from Carty's ears, swaying his old body so that he staggered. In a swirling arc it shrieked the quarter mile down the street and struck the van in a phosphorescent fireball that left nothing but shards of twisted, smoking metal and an area littered for fifty yards with lumps of black, smoldering cloth. And it was suddenly so quiet that Carty thought for a moment he could hear the clock chiming across the Lagan at City Hall. Then the man that he could see trying to drag what was left of his body toward a blown-out door in a house began a pitiable wail.

"See if you can finish him off," said one of the men at the barricades to another, who had a rifle with a sniper's scope.

Carty turned and began walking away. If nothing else, what he had just witnessed would bring them: armed mobs, doubtless with their own rockets, seeking revenge. And, then, his wife had been feeling poorly of late. In his own way he had tried to stop it. He had failed, and now they all would be made to live with that failure. Or die.

22

With the weight, like that of a lover's hand, in her lap, she had kept the television on even after the picture had gone off from Finaghy Park, switching it with the remote monitor until she found that only ITN had re-established contact. It was presenting, in a kind of color that looked as if it had been filmed on a stage, more of the uproar following "the Paisley assassination"—an ITN voice that she thought she recognized was now stating flatly.

And she was sure of it, the "staging," when *her* Seamus Rhines appeared on the screen wearing a silver sash and a bowler hat, his arm cocked and his mouth tightened into an angry slit. "Look out there," another voice but strangely still Rhines's own—she was certain—said. And Rhines, wielding a blackthorn stick like a cudgel, began smashing at what Roisin assumed was the camera, all the while screaming, "*Bahs*-tuds! Yez rotten Romish *bahs*-tuds!" Until the screen went dark for a second time.

When the picture returned once again, it showed in a whirlwind montage fighting that the voice—still Rhines's, but now deep and sonorous—claimed was occurring throughout the North: nasty little scenes (the bombing of an RUC barracks, the attack on a Protestant school) in which he played some ugly part, interspersed with shots of crowds clustered in side streets and being driven, like cattle, by army patrols or men in ski masks brandishing weapons. In staccato stills—pictorial bursts that mimicked the firing that could be heard on the sound track—the dead and injured were shown close up, the focus on their wounds so sharp that even Roisin, whose mind so reeled with macabre images that she had not been to work in days, cried out and turned away.

It was then that the picture was stopped without an immediate explanation, and a graphic "PLEASE STAND BY" was shown. After a while, a voice—different, she had never heard it before—said, "The past thirteen minutes of programming did not—I repeat—*did not* picture the conditions that obtain presently in Belfast or Northern Ireland, but were, rather, a film clip which, in the confusion following the attempt upon Dr. Paisley's life, mistakenly was aired, and for which ITN accepts no responsibility.

"To rectify ITN transmission for the past thirteen minutes, I repeat—today at Finaghy Park, Belfast, an attempt was made on the life of the Reverend Ian Paisley. The Parliamentarian was wounded, it would appear, by the Donegal T.D., Mr. Neil Blaney, who was wielding a knife. Paisley has been taken to hospital, where he is described as seriously ill but not in imminent danger of death. At least two others were killed in the attack.

"Rioting broke out in the park and has quickly spread to other parts of the city. The fighting has already been described as the worst since 1969. A recent, unconfirmed report has it that as many as sixty-five may have since died. The RUC has announced a citywide curfew commencing at three o'clock this afternoon. Another unconfirmed report, from Londonderry, describes the sectarian fighting there as heavy. We

285

have received reports of other clashes in Armagh, Newry, and Strabane.

"The Dublin government has placed all elements of the Irish Army on alert. Taoiseach Charles Haughey has canceled all appointments and is watching the situation closely. Through a spokesman, he issued the statement, 'We cannot allow a repetition of the events of August 1969, with its life loss and the threat of pogrom to those whom some have called "the minority" in the Six Counties.'

"In London, Prime Minister Thatcher has condemned the attack as 'the dastardly act of one depraved man,' and has exhorted British commanders in Northern Ireland to do everything they can to keep hostile factions apart.

"In summary, and to rectify ITN transmission for the past thirteen minutes, I repeat—today at Finaghy Park in Belfast an attempt . . ."

Roisin switched off the set. *To rectify*, she thought, and it was then that a calm, which scarified the riot in her brain, spread over her, and, resting her head against the cushions of the wing-back chair that looked out on the kitchen, she even managed to sleep for a while.

At least, when she became aware of some slight sound at the back door and reached for the weight in her lap, it was pitch black in the house.

"Roisin?" she heard The Voice call to her. "Roisin? Are you there? Quick, now, there's no time. None at all."

He switched on the light in the kitchen, so that his body was silhouetted in the sitting-room doorway directly in front of her, and she fired. Once. Twice. Thrice. Dead on. Each blast bringing to her a blessed deafness from all VOICES, until, gagging from the gunsmoke, the hot barrel searing her palate and the back of her throat and tasting salty and rank, like oil on beach sand, she consigned herself to the rectification that she had sought.

After hearing the four shots, Ward hit the back door. Once. Twice. Thrice. His small body bouncing off the thick framing. His Walther was out, but he was too late, he realized. He had heard that sequence of reports before.

The old Humber behind him was ticking over reassuringly. Reassuring him of what? That life would continue? For some, he imagined. He wondered what had happened and why?

He reached for the radio on his belt.

Epilogue

Four days later, after a UN Emergency Force had begun to arrive in the Six Counties and a tripartite (British, Irish, and Northern Ireland Assembly) inquiry into what was being called the "Finaghy Park Incident" was being launched, McGarr found himself sitting behind the wheel of his own Mini-Cooper on the quays in Dublin.

"That's it," said O'Shaughnessy, catching sight of Ward, who appeared briefly around the corner on which a pub sat and signaled with his hand. "He's in there, if you still think you have to do it alone."

McGarr opened the door and climbed out. There had been too much trouble already.

He was sitting at a lounge table in the "Place of the Oaks Inn" or simply The Oaks, as it was known to quayside habitués, staring down at the grain of wood which a shaft of direct sunlight, angling in through a window, made seem golden. By day a toper's bar, by night a venue for amateur musicians, the "Derreigh" was spartan in its appointments, and at half-six of a summer evening—the supper hour; McGarr had selected the time—only a handful graced the bar.

Alone, the reek off him so putrid that McGarr had to pause

before taking the final few steps to the table, Geer was hunched over the dregs of a pint. Onto the shaft of sunlight McGarr dropped the box of complimentary matches he had removed from Carron's tobacco pouch.

"From George?" Geer asked after a while, raising his head. His sclerae were the color of old snot. He glanced back down at the matches. "Too many variables," he observed. "And too many—"

"Co-conspirators?" McGarr asked.

"—martyrs, I was thinking."

"A pity Des Suilly wasn't one," said McGarr, though he knew Suilly's exposure was a chimera that he could spend a lifetime pursuing. The complete story was one that would not be told. How could it? The charges, if provable, would bring down two governments and even further confound the problems of the North, if that was possible. Thus, the charges could not be provable, and would not be brought.

As if in delirium, his body swaying on the low stool, Geer muttered, "In the end—seven quiet men, please God. One martyr. Perhaps two. Another who deserved his fate. But, mind you, no more."

Legs appeared beside the table: O'Shaughnessy, who at the door stepped back so that Geer and McGarr could leave first.

"Paddy—look up!" somebody shouted out on the quay. A large group of journalists had gathered, the lights for their cameras harsh and achromatic in the encroaching shadows.

Their presence was something McGarr believed he might need, though he was to meet with Suilly that night.

DEC.   1984

F
Gill, Bartholomew
McGarr and the method of
descartes.